BILLIONAIRE GRUMP

JULIE CAPULET

It was supposed to be a fake date.
It turned out to be true love.

My assignment is simple. I'm the fake date of billionaire Alexander Maddox for the weekend. My job: to attend a Hamptons wedding with him and convince all the heiresses and socialites competing for his attention—including his ex, who happens to be the wedding planner—that he's very much taken.

Alexander Maddox is the oldest of the four Maddox brothers, Manhattan's most eligible bachelors. He's also the CEO of his family's legacy investment empire. Loaded beyond belief. And, according to rumors, sexy as sin. But this is strictly a business arrangement.

It's also an excuse for me to get out of town for a few days. I didn't exactly *mean* to break into my estranged father's house and accidentally discover his offshore bank account details. *Or* to leave those details lying around where my hacker of a little brother with a serious vendetta might find them. He covered his tracks, he said, but we both know it was never going to be that easy.

My plan: to lay low, spend the weekend by the pool, play my part like I'm an Oscar nominee and hope the little incident blows over by Monday morning.

But my weekend doesn't go according to plan. Alexander Maddox turns out to be the most infuriating man I've ever met. And also the hottest—*so* hot, in fact, that I end up giving him much, much more than I bargained for.

When the banking incident turns out to be a tiny bit more serious than I imagined, things get complicated. But by then I've already cashed in my V-card with the sexy billionaire and made a run for it—or at least tried to.

How do I get myself into these messes? And how did I let myself get knocked up by a possessive grump who suddenly seems to think I'm his one and only?

Against all odds, I think he might be right.

Billionaire Grump is a sexy standalone billionaire romance starring a grumpy CEO and the sassy fake date he never saw coming.

New York Billionaires

Julie Capulet LLC

BILLIONAIRE GRUMP

Copyright © 2024 by Julie Capulet

BILLIONAIRE GRUMP

1

"ARE you *sure* you want to do this, Ivy? I really think you're making a huge mistake."

I'm on the train, video chatting with my best friend Cleo, my hair tied back and my baseball cap pulled down low. I can always count on my level-headed bestie to be the voice of reason. "That's definitely possible."

I came straight from yoga, so I'm wearing leggings and a zipped-up hoodie, trying to look as inconspicuous as possible.

The train isn't overly busy. It's mid-morning on a Saturday and I'm on my way from Grand Central Station out to Stamford, Connecticut. I know I'm more likely to be recognized by the groups of college students and young couples who are filling the train than if I was on a Monday morning commuter train. Which is why I keep my cap low.

I don't mind if people want to say hi. That part of being sort-of famous is kind of cool. Most people are nice. They tell me they love my music or that they follow me on social media, they ask for a selfie, then they get on with their day. It's the silent, not-at-all-subtle filming and the stealth photography that freaks me out. I'd much rather people said something to me than try to stalk me when I'm sitting right next to them.

When I was sure no one was close enough to listen in, I called Cleo, who's trying to talk me out of what I'm about to do.

"Ive? Seriously. This is a bad idea."

I chew my lip, staring at Cleo's concerned face on the screen, framed by her honey-blond curls.

"You're probably right. But this isn't about me, Cleo. I'm doing it for Josh."

"Does Josh even *want* your father at his graduation?"

"I mean, he says he doesn't. But deep down I think maybe he actually does. Graduation is a big deal. It might be nice for him to have…you know, a family."

"*We* can be his family. Found family is just as good. And in this case probably better."

"I know." I *do* know. I've almost jumped off the train at each stop we've made. "But I figure there's really nothing to lose by extending the olive branch one last time."

Cleo sighs. "You're a better woman than I am, Ive. If my dad ditched me and my sisters when we were kids so he could lavish attention all over his new family, I wouldn't have spoken to the bastard ever again."

I shrug. "Like I said, it's about Josh."

"Even if your dad did come to the graduation—which we both know is unlikely—Josh might feel more anger over the whole AWOL father thing than joy over a family reunion that we all know is too little too late. It seems to me you're just inviting drama that no one wants."

"Maybe." I pinch the bridge of my nose. "Okay, yes. But maybe if our father sees what a great man Josh is growing into, he'll realize he screwed up by walking away. If he sees what he's been missing out on, it might make him want to be in Josh's life a little more. And it might give Josh some closure. He's just so pissed off at life in general. I was hoping maybe it would help."

Cleo shakes her head. "It's wishful thinking."

"It's hopeful thinking."

I know Cleo means well, but it's easy to judge when you come from the perfect family unit. Her parents are still madly in love after thirty years of marriage and support everything their children do—logistically, emotionally and financially. Cleo's parents never missed a single piano recital, softball game or school play. Not to mention a single payment for the upscale boarding schools or the college tuition. Mr. and Mrs. Ellis were and still are the kind of parents you'd find in a Disney movie about suburbia gone right, a successful advertising executive and his well-presented, loving domestic goddess of a wife who baked, sewed and was the PTA member everyone liked. "Your dad knows you're coming out to see him, right?"

"I sent him two emails."

"Did he reply?"

I pause as a group of teenagers walk past me onto the train, hiding under the rim of my hat. "Nope."

"But you think he'll be there?"

Part of the reason I'm making this trip on the weekend is because my dad is a lawyer and he works at a law firm in Stamford. I didn't want to visit him at work. A small part of me wonders if maybe his receptionists have been given strict instructions to turn me and Josh away, if we ever happened to turn up. At least if I visit him at home he has no buffer besides his trophy wife Anita.

But who knows, he might be a golfer or something, spending exorbitant amounts of money on country club fees and meanwhile disinheriting his two oldest children.

"If he's not there after he's seen my emails, then I guess that tells me everything I need to know. All I'm doing is taking him up on his offer to 'visit anytime.'"

I cringe when I think about the lame Christmas email he sent. In January. His half-assed once-a-year attempt to keep us from being completely estranged. It's almost more of an insult than if he totally pretended we didn't exist.

Merry Christmas! I hope the two of you are doing well. Visit anytime! Dad.

She says it gently. "I think he already told you every-thing you need to know when he didn't reach out when your mom died. I honestly don't know how he lives with himself."

"He did reach out." With another one-liner, but still. "It's just the way he is." I don't know why I'm defending him. Cleo's right. This is probably an epically bad idea.

"Exactly."

If it was just me, I wouldn't be here. Dad didn't come to my graduation or to our mother's funeral, but he did send me an email when my debut single hit the Billboard Top 100. *That*, he cared about, apparently. "Josh is just so angry, Cleo. It's not healthy. I worry about it."

"He's *seventeen*, Ivy. He's a mess of angst and hormones. He's also smart and successful and he's about to start college. He's going to be fine."

"I know he is. And that's the thing. I'm so proud of him. I want our father to see what a cool kid he is."

"No thanks to him," Cleo points out scathingly. "Basically the only thing he's ever done for Josh is to donate a DNA sample."

"Ew."

She laughs. "Sorry. But seriously, you've done a good job, Ive. You've worked like hell to make Josh's life easier, and you've done that. But he's a big boy now."

"I just don't want him hating me ten years from now when he's talking to his therapist and they're discussing why I didn't try to do more."

Cleo twirls a blond curl around her finger. "Maybe it's time for both of you to just let it go, honey, and get on with the rest of your lives."

"I know. I will let it go, I promise. After this."

Something in me is burning to tell my father face to face that we did it without him. We made it. We're successful people. Our mom and her sister did everything they could to make a life for us after he traded us in for a newer model. *They* lifted us up. And we lifted each other up. Even without him, we didn't just survive, we *thrived.*

Sort of.

"I want him to remember, even if it's for one miserable second of his carefree new life, that he left us behind. I also want to watch him squirm when he's forced to look me in the eye as he makes some excuse to miss his oldest son's high school graduation."

"Well, I wish you luck, babe. If you need some support after, come see us. We'll be back around three." She glances at her iWatch. "I better go. Sam will be back from the gym any minute and if I'm going to sell the idea of going downtown, I need to be on my A game. I might even have to resort to bribery. But call me later, okay? I want to hear how it goes."

"Of course. Good luck with the registry."

That's another thing about Cleo that puts us in different universes. Not only does she have the perfect family, she has the perfect fiancé. She and Sam met as juniors in high school and have been sweethearts ever since. They haven't set a date yet, but they're in the process of planning for their wedding, which will no doubt also be picture perfect.

It's icing on the cake that she also has a job she loves, as the assistant for Noah Maddox. He's the CFO of Invested Enterprises, one of the hottest companies in the city that literally everyone wishes they worked for.

I'm beyond happy for my best friend. She deserves all of her good fortune.

But I also know she doesn't entirely *get* some of the grittier details of my life, because she seems to have been born under a lucky star.

I've had to make my own luck, and I have, but it's taken 24/7 of grit and hard work, every single day of my life, to get here.

We end the call, and I pull my baseball cap even lower, sliding on my sunglasses as the train slows to a stop. Stamford station comes into view.

I get off the train and order an Uber.

It's a ten minute ride to my dad's house, through streets that get progressively leafier, more manicured and lined with bigger and more ostentatious houses.

I've never been to Stamford before, or at least not that I can remember. Josh and I were both born in Bridgeport, where my parents lived together when we were very young. I have a few hazy memories of a white house. And slamming doors.

Only a few months after Josh was born, my parents

went through a bitter, messy divorce. And then, after the three of us were cast out, we moved into my mom's sister's basement apartment in Bushwick, which is where we lived until around a year and a half ago, when I was able to buy the two of us our very own apartment.

Being both an asshole and a divorce lawyer, my dad was able to manipulate the child support payments into something that covered only our absolute basics, as he meanwhile married his pretty young secretary and continued to live a progressively more and more luxurious life. They have seven-year-old twin sons named Aaron and Adam who go to some elite private boarding school and who I've never actually met.

My father's neighborhood definitely has that safe, privileged family feel that the wealthy suburbs are known for.

Oh the irony.

It's not something I've ever dwelled on all that much —the kind of life we would have had if my parents hadn't split up—but this is like a cold slap in the face.

When the Uber pulls up in front of the house, it's clear that my father's house is one of the biggest and showiest on the street. It's a colonial style McMansion with columns and neatly-trimmed topiary bushes. It sits on a ridge and has a nice view. Not a single blade of grass on the freshly-mown lawn is out of place.

It's the kind of house where kids could run barefoot through the sprinkler having water fights. Where you'd have backyard barbecues on hot summer days with fresh-squeezed homemade lemonade. Snowy Christmases with a real Christmas tree you went out and chose from the farm on a crisp blue day filled with laughter. Snowmen with carrots for noses in the front yard. You just *know* that, every year, the mountain of artfully-wrapped presents piled under the tree on Christmas morning for the excited little boys is absolutely epic.

My stomach twists.

It's the perfect place to raise a family.

Just not *all* of his family. Only his favorite half of it.

There's a car parked in the driveway, a sleek, expensive black Range Rover. Anita's car, I'm guessing. No doubt my dad drives a midlife-crisis-style red convertible sports car.

Which means it's either parked in one of the three garages or he's not here.

He *could* have parked in the garage. He probably did.

But some sixth sense tells me he didn't. It's telling me he's not here.

My heart is beating fast.

I could turn back now and keep my pride intact. I could save myself a face-to-face encounter with the woman my dad left my mom for, who I've met only once, years ago now. I could avoid the reality that he doesn't care enough about me to be here, even when he knew I was coming to see him.

How hard is it to not be a total letdown for once in your goddamn life?

I almost get straight back into the Uber and request a ride back to the station.

But I'm here now. And maybe I've got it wrong. Maybe he's inside with a fresh pot of coffee waiting, ready to listen and apologize and, for once, do the right thing.

I take a deep breath and walk up to the front door before I can second-guess myself. I raise the heavy knocker and let it slam loudly, three times.

No one comes to the door.

I wait.

I knock again.

Still no signs of life.

So, I reach for the brass door handle.

I don't expect it to be unlocked.

The door swings open.

Shit.

"Dad?" I call into the hallway. The floor is tiled with white marble. High ceilings give the place a stark feel. There's a modern (hideous) white chandelier. The walls are white, with white art and white furniture. Peering in, I can't help but notice it looks like a very up-market dentist's office. "Dad? Anita? Hello? Anyone home?"

There's no response.

I bang the door knocker again.

There's still no sign that anyone is home.

I wait probably a full minute, wondering what to do next.

Almost against my will, I step inside.

I'm rooted to the spot, not daring to go further now that I've actually strolled into my estranged father's house.

What the hell do I do now?

I can't just turn around, order another Uber and disappear back to New York. That would be too convenient for him. I want him to know I came. That I took him up on his empty promise.

From where I'm standing, I can make out the room on my left. The door is open and it's filled with dark furniture—a nice change from the sterile front hallway. Bookcases, a heavy mahogany desk, one of those leather wing-backed chairs.

Dad's home office, I'm assuming.

"Dad?" I call out once more. I told him I was coming. I knocked. I did all I could do to announce my presence.

I'm not breaking and entering. I'm his own daughter. His flesh and blood. I just want to leave a note. This isn't illegal.

And now I'm standing in his office. There are built-in shelves with books and trinkets I don't recognize. This man is a stranger who's lived a life I have no connection to.

There's a framed picture of Anita and my dad, at a beach somewhere. She's in a bikini and looks every bit of her twelve years younger than he is.

There's another framed photo, of the twin boys. I go

over and pick it up, to take a closer look. As I do, of course I notice the glaring absence of *us*. I shouldn't be surprised. There's not a single shred of evidence in this office that Josh or I have ever existed. I'm so hardened to this by now, usually. But the in-your-face reminder hits me hard.

No picture of his other son, who's so smart and handsome and who's worked so hard to get into freaking Columbia. Why isn't that good enough? Why were we never, ever good enough?

You cold-hearted prick.

The boys are dark-haired with green eyes that are very similar in color to our father's. They're beautiful boys. They're identical twins and they look it. Neat haircuts and little ties. All dressed up for their photo shoot.

I place the photo back on its shelf. On a whim, I take out my phone and take a picture of it. They're my brothers, after all. I'm allowed to have one small keepsake of them.

Looking around, I have a very strong urge to leave.

If I leave a note, I will, of course, be incriminating myself. Announcing that I entered his house without being invited. Then again, the *Visit anytime!* comment is the reason I'm here. With an exclamation point and everything.

And this is the last time I'll ever try. It'll be a goodbye note. A fuck-you-and-have-a-nice-life final farewell.

I check the desk for some Post-Its or note paper.

There are piles of paperwork covering the desk. There's a *Finlay & Hobbs Law* mug filled with pens. I take a pen and carefully rummage to find a blank piece of paper. As I do this, a small stack of papers slide off their pile, fluttering to the floor.

Shit.

I pick them up, carefully trying to return them to the way I found them.

I can't miss the fact that the page on the top of the pile is a bank statement.

Of course I shouldn't look. It's none of my business. But the numbers printed onto the page seem to take on an almost 3D quality, jumping out at me and insisting I read them.

It's the number at the bottom of the page that catches my attention. A lot of zeroes tend to do that.

Six zeroes, to be precise, with two ones in front of them. The high-interest savings account is based in the Bahamas and holds…holy shit…*eleven million dollars.*

I read it again, as if there might be some explanation on the page.

The account is in his name. There's no other conclusion to jump to. This is Roy Laine's bank account and it contains Roy Laine's money.

Eleven million dollars of it.

My chest aches with sadness. I shouldn't be here and I definitely shouldn't be snooping, but seeing this just about breaks my jaded heart.

I have to stop myself from ripping the statement to shreds, from pushing everything off his mahogany desk and letting it crash to the floor in a pile of chaos.

How long has he had this money? Where did it come from? I'm sure he's making bank as a lawyer but this is some serious cash.

My dad is a moderately successful divorce lawyer, so he intimately knew the loopholes that would get him out of paying real child support. He went out of his way to not only abandon his family but to twist the truth and use his inside knowledge to corrupt the system—just so he could get out of doing the right thing by the people he was supposed to love the most.

The numbers are blurry now and I impatiently brush away tears.

Why did I come here? Cleo was right. This was a huge mistake.

Does he have no heart whatsoever? Did he really care so little for us that he would hide this from us to deliberately make our lives harder?

Does Anita even know about this? Is he planning a second getaway, leaving those little boys in the lurch like he did to us?

Fucker.

My emotions are raw.

I take out my phone and I snap a few more photos. Of the bank statement. The top page and several more. I make sure I'm thorough.

What are you trying to do right now?

I don't know. Nothing. I just want to make sure I didn't dream this.

Then I cover the pile back up with some other paperwork. And I scrawl a note.

> Dad,
> I showed up like I said I would. I came to tell you that Josh is graduating in June. He's been accepted at Columbia and he'll be starting there in the fall. It would mean something to him to know that you cared about any of the above. If you can make the effort to call me back, I could give you the details about maybe coming along to his graduation to support all his hard work and amazing achievements.
> Your daughter,
> Ivy

I leave the note on the white marble table in the white marble foyer of the gigantic house. Then I slam the door behind me.

As I RIDE on the train back into New York, I take a deep breath, doing my best to push the entire experience out of my brain. To forgive and forget—again. To not let the twisted rage eat me up. I'm usually good at seeing the bright side of things. I've worked a lot on my mindset. Gratitude is always the best way to be positive about life in general, and I have a lot to be grateful for.

But letting my father off the hook again for shutting us out of every part of his life is hard. It hurts. Today it hurts more than it has in a long time.

I guess that's what I get for trying to force something that he's made it very clear he doesn't want to do.

He won't call, obviously. It's best to rise above it and put it out of my mind, especially the part where my dad is a deceitful asshole of a multi-millionaire.

There's no point mentioning any of this to Josh.

In fact, that would be an exceptionally bad idea. It'll only hurt him if I tell him why I went out there and that, once again, our father hasn't chosen us. So I do what I've done so many times before: I shove the morning's revelations back into their little cage in my mind, securely lock it and mentally throw away the key. Done and dusted. Time to make peace with it and move on.

When I get back to our apartment, it's quiet. Josh will have finished his early shift at the café where he works on Saturday mornings. He's probably holed up in his room by now, working on the three-giant-screen computer set-up he's got going on in there.

It's part of the reason I insisted he get a part-time job, just to make sure he gets out of the house on weekends and doesn't spend *all* his time coding or whatever it is he does.

I used to worry about how much time he spent staring at screens, like every parent (or close enough) does.

But Josh is savvy enough to know how to handle his time. He has a group of good friends he hangs out with (often gaming with them, but whatever). As long as he's getting good grades, I don't bug him about the rest of it.

It was easy to see from an early age that my brother was going places. He almost got expelled from school when he was twelve for hacking into the school's database and changing all his grades to A's. But I somehow convinced the principal to give him one get-out-of-jail-free card. Which she did, as long as he promised to use his powers for good instead of evil from now on. She punished him by giving him an after-school job building an online check-out system for the library, which was so good they ended up franchising it and selling it to a few other school libraries. Josh got a cut of the money, which he spent on high-tech computer equipment. He was written up in Young Entrepreneur magazine and put on their "young coders to watch" list.

I encouraged him endlessly to try as hard as he could, to aim high and try to get into a top school that would propel him into the kind of shit-hot job he's capable of. Maybe I was a little *too* overzealous at times, but he knew why.

Somehow, it must have sunk in. He ended up getting accepted at Dartmouth, Cornell, Yale and Columbia. I don't think either of us could believe it at first. He'd really done it.

He decided on Columbia because he can live at home. I told him I don't care how much room and board costs and that I'll figure out a way for him to have the full college experience if he wants it.

Josh said there's no way in hell he'll let me pay for his entire degree. Tuition is one thing but room and board is an extra cost that Josh said we don't actually need to spend. We argued about it.

The thing is, I *have* enough money. At least enough to get started. I can take out a loan if I need to, to get him through all four years. The price tag for Columbia is insane, of course, but it's worth it.

And since I'm not going to college, at least not for now, I can focus on what's best for Josh.

I thought about college. My grades were good enough and I was interested in studying music or graphic design. But it felt frivolous to spend that kind of money on something I wasn't sure I needed. I felt like I was getting my life experience through different channels, and that those channels were working for me enough to justify sticking with them.

I make money through downloads of my music and from the small-venue shows I do around New York, which almost always sell out. But most of my money comes from advertising products through my social media platforms.

I'm a musician and an "influencer" and I have a huge following. As much as I hate that term, I have to admit it's a pretty sweet gig. I post around ten times a day, basically just showing how I live my life and play my music.

Because I have a combined total of almost ten million followers through TikTok, Instagram and Spotify, companies send me their products and pay me to promote them. This is usually as easy as staging a few photos and recording a few videos.

It's taken me a lot of time and effort to get my platform to the level it's now at, but it still sometimes feels like a weird way to make money.

I don't *love* selling myself 24/7, but I also don't mind

it. I'm good at it. I mostly enjoy creating the content. And I have a very good reason for doing it: my brother. I *need* to earn money, so I can help him realize his full potential.

Just because I've been Josh's legal guardian for the past four years doesn't mean we don't act like siblings most of the time. He's still a pain in the ass who leaves his shit everywhere and argues with me like a typical teenager.

Josh doesn't take for granted the sudden change in our fortunes. When my first song blew up online and our lifestyle began to turn around, he appreciated it—more than a lot of kids would have. Because we knew what it was like to struggle.

Two years ago I bought us a two-bedroom loft in Soho. It's small but was still a ridiculously huge improvement from the Bushwick basement we lived in until we could afford to move.

"Josh?" I step into the sun-drenched hallway. His sneakers are inside the front door, so I know he's home.

"Hey," he calls out from his room before sticking his head round the door. He leans a shoulder against the doorjamb. "How was yoga? Did you take an extra class?"

"Oh. No, I had some stuff to do for work. How was your shift?"

"Busy."

"I need your mad photography skills when you have a minute."

Josh is used to being my photographer. He used to

complain about it, but when I told him how much I can make from a single post, he stopped complaining. I pay for our lifestyle (and college) and he helps me with my content. He knows he's getting a pretty sweet deal.

He walks over to the fridge where I know he'll drink the orange juice from the carton just to piss me off. I've tried my hardest to train him to behave like he's *not* a Neanderthal but by now I know it's better to choose my battles.

"What are you selling this time?"

Yep, here it goes, orange juice carton in hand…

I force myself not to react. "Organic Nation Yoga sent me their latest line so I'm going to set up my yoga mat on the balcony. It's nice enough to shoot out there today."

"Maybe I should skip college and become a pro photographer. You could employ me."

"You couldn't handle me as your boss. I'd stick to being a tech genius if I were you. It'll be much easier."

"True. And much less annoying." He grins and I'm struck by how grown up he is now. He's 6'1" and he's filled out a lot over the past year. My brother has grown into a good-looking almost-man. But I can still see the little boy in him when he smiles.

I want so much for him to get everything he deserves out of life. "I'll meet you outside."

Within a few minutes, I've changed into the buttery-soft shorts and sports top with the built-in bra the sponsors sent me and have rolled out my yoga mat onto the tiny but fabulous balcony of our apartment. Now that the weather's warmer, I've moved all my plants outside again. We have a table and chairs and a seating area with a south-facing view. I've strung strings of pendant lights, so at night it looks like a magical little outdoor room.

Josh moans something about how I'm interrupting his flow, but once my phone is in his hand he slips into his usual bossy art director role with ease.

I work through some poses, looking over my shoulder and down at my fingertips but never directly at the camera, posing so it looks like a photographer has just stumbled across me mid-practice. Josh has a knack too. He knows what it takes to get the shot.

"I've got about a dozen." He hands my phone to me and waits as I scroll through them.

"Just take a few more." I get into the lotus position. "Make sure you get the plants in the background. And the water bottle on the table. They want me to promote that too."

Josh takes my phone again and takes a few more. As he scrolls through the pictures he's taken, I realize half a second too late that I don't want him scrolling too far. But I can see by the look on his face that he has. And he's riveted—and shocked—by what he's looking at.

Why the hell didn't you think of that, you idiot!? You should have deleted them! You shouldn't have taken them in the first place.

I'm so used to Josh helping me with my content, I

completely forgot I have a ticking time bomb sitting only a few swipes back.

"Josh—"

"What is this?"

I get up—which takes me a few seconds because I'm still in the lotus position—and by then he's already zooming in. "*Josh.*"

Josh's eyes are dark and his glare is full of questions. "Why do I get the feeling you skipped yoga class this morning, Ivy?"

Damn it.

"I didn't skip it. I just took a detour after." I reach for the phone but Josh is so much taller than I am he easily holds it out of reach. "Give me my phone."

"You went to his *house*? When? Today?"

I'm trying to snatch my phone back out of my brother's hands, but he just holds it higher. He's got a good five inches on me plus he's strong as hell now.

"Did you *see* him?" His question is more hurt than angry. Both emotions are twisted up and awful-sounding.

"No. I didn't see him. I went to tell him…that you're graduating and that you got into Columbia. Because I'm proud of you. And I was hoping—"

Josh holds up a hand in a *stop* gesture. "If you continue that sentence I'm going to smash this phone to smithereens, Ivy. You were hoping what? That *he* might be proud of me too? Well, let me guess. He isn't. There, mystery solved. I could have saved you a trip."

"Please don't smash my phone. We need it. Can I please have it back?"

"Sure. Right after I email these photos of our asshole father's Bahamas bank account to myself. What do you know, the snake is even more loaded than we thought." He continues swiping. And then he goes quiet.

"Josh?"

He's staring at the photo of our twin brothers. "And here are the little apples of his eye. Getting their own framed photograph on a shelf and everything, how touching."

Josh turns away from me and strides across the balcony. For a second I think he's going to throw my phone over the edge out of anger, but then he sits in one of the chairs sort of heavily.

"Josh, it doesn't matter," I say gently. "We know why. He wasn't in a good place when we were young. He and our mother ended up hating each other and he just wants to forget about it and move on. Just like we're doing."

"If you're over it then why did you go to his house?"

"To try for the very last time and now I'm done. We don't need him. We're okay and we're only going to get *more* okay. Now, please, give me my phone."

After Josh finishes sending the photos to himself, he gets up. He walks over to me and he hands me my phone.

"Thank you," I tell him, searching his eyes for some kind of sign that he's okay. "Josh?"

"What." It's not a question. It's a deep, emotional scar.

"I love you."

He stares down at me, his golden eyes stormy. They aren't really words we throw around that often but I want him to hear them. And now feels like a good time.

"I love you too. And if that prick shows up at my graduation I'll fucking throttle him."

With that, he walks back to his room and slams the door.

I look up as the sun disappears behind a bank of dark clouds, forming in gigantic looming puffs at the edges of the blue sky.

A storm is coming. I wish the metaphor didn't feel so damn ominous.

I sigh without meaning to.

Parents.

They really fuck you up.

3

ALEXANDER

I AM NOT MY FATHER.

I am not my father.

I am not my father.

I repeat the mantra every time I step into my office at Maddox Enterprises and take a seat in what used to be my father's chair.

The look of the place is very old school, like I've just time-warped into a 1960s New York gentleman's club. The office is huge and the expansive windows showcase views of both the Empire State Building and the Chrysler Building. Symbols, my father used to say, of the kind of power we strive for.

My assistant Esther encourages me on a daily basis to have the place redecorated, but I want the reminder of the legacy this company was built on. I need it. Because if it's not in my face every fucking day, I might just walk out on a whim and go live a completely different life.

Inheriting a company from your tyrannical mogul of a father is one thing. Inheriting an entire empire that was founded by your great grandfather and then being expected to continue to make the family name proud every day of your life—according to their terms and *only* their terms—is another thing altogether.

All those voices in my head are dead and gone. But still I'm anchored here. Or chained. Some days it's hard to tell.

There have always been heavy expectations on me, as the oldest son and heir to the throne as CEO. My father started training me on how to run the company on my seventh birthday. I remember it clearly. He brought me to this very office to sit in this very chair. He told me that, one day, all this would be mine. I was expected to act like the Maddox I was "and not fuck anything up."

My brothers and I agreed a long time ago that we aren't and never will be clones of our father. We would have all gone mad by now if we were.

The three of them have managed to remove themselves from under the heaviest of his burdens. For me, it was never going to be that easy.

Our father was a very successful man, but it came at a cost. He was more interested in making money than he was in nurturing any of the relationships in his life, even with his own children.

I respected my father. I still respect him. I recognize his genius. I look like him and I have his name. But I can't honestly say that I loved him.

And I've never aspired to his style of doing business. I prefer not to raze everyone's self-esteem to the ground in the process of making a buck.

But as much as I might hope that I'm not like my father, I sometimes feel like assholery is baked into my DNA.

Trying like hell not to turn into him while still growing the company at a respectable rate takes a lot of effort. Some days the legacy I'm mired in feels like a pressure cooker. I often think about throwing in the towel, leaving it for someone else to manage and skipping the country to go live anonymously on some secluded beach in the South Pacific.

Sure, this life has its rewards. I have more money than I could ever spend and so will my children. If there are children. I'm about to turn thirty and I can genuinely say I've never met anyone I would even consider having children with. Which makes me wonder if it'll ever happen for me.

Maybe the whole assholery angle means I'm not made for the kind of relationships that would give me a family. Maybe I'm too much like him. Maybe I hate that part of myself so much that I end up self-sabotaging my love life. Who knows.

It's a very depressing thought.

Which isn't going to get any less depressing this weekend, I'm reminded by the pink note attached to a certain envelope that's staring up at me from my great grandfather's gigantic mahogany desk.

Esther put it there. The wedding invitation from Blake.

It came in the mail over a week ago. I've been avoiding it.

Esther has reshuffled my desk so the invitation is front and center. She's scrawled on the pink note, *READ AND REPLY TO THIS REGARDING YOUR PLUS ONE AND YOUR MENU OPTION ASAP!! Leah has called twice!* So I can't pretend I haven't seen it.

Damn my very capable assistant and her determination to not let me go AWOL.

I tried to get out of the wedding when Blake first called me. Not because he's not a good friend. He is. We met back at Harvard Business School and we've stayed in touch ever since.

He called me a while back and asked if I'd be his best man. I told him I was busy but he railroaded me into it and I finally relented.

As a general rule, I try to avoid obligatory formal social occasions. I live my life in a suit. Wearing a tux on the weekend is hardly my idea of a good time.

I also found out—*after* I'd already agreed to be in the wedding—that Margot Russo is the wedding planner.

I hate weddings on the best of days. I hate weddings planned by Margot with a feral passion.

Margot happens to be one of the most sought-after wedding planners in New York. She's also my ex. She's also batshit crazy.

I have no idea why I "dated" her for almost six weeks. I'm usually more of a one-night stand kind of guy. It was almost more of a case of trying to placate a lunatic than it was about wanting to spend time with her.

I *tried* to feel something. I tried to make an effort, because it's what people do. They date. They have relationships. They think about settling down when they're staring down the barrel of turning thirty.

We met at one of Leah's dinners, around nine or ten months ago. She asked for my number and I gave it to her. We had things in common. We understood each other's grueling schedules.

The problem was, I never *felt* anything. No attachment. No excitement. No passion.

Nada. Zero. Zilch.

For me, the whole thing was tedious as fuck.

For her, it was a dream come true.

I waited for something—anyfuckingthing—to kick in. I expected my feelings would grow over time, if I just stuck with it for a while and gave it a chance to evolve. In the end I got tired of forcing something that just couldn't be forced.

Her life revolves around making people believe that the only way to guarantee a happily ever after is by spending obscene amounts of money on floral arrangements and coordinated table linens. And of course, diamonds.

Everything about her is wired to show off. The restaurants she wanted me to take her to had to be trending. The jewelry she wanted me to buy her was worn by celebrities on their social media.

If we could have approached our relationship from a place of let's-talk-about-how-we-*both*-feel instead of you've-wronged-me-on-a-million-levels-you-unfeeling-asshole, maybe we would have had a chance. As it was, everything I did offended her.

She started dropping hints about marriage. She half-joked she'd booked us into some ultra-exclusive hotel for our wedding, claiming there'd been a last-minute cancellation. I dodged the topic until I got an email from the event coordinator congratulating us on our engagement and asking when we were free to come in to discuss details.

I broke it off the next day.

Margot did not take the break-up well. To put it mildly. She cried for five minutes and she's been screaming ever since, about how heartless I am, how I'm cold and indifferent and completely incapable of love.

Which, unfortunately, is all true.

She obsessively begged me to take her back, showing up at places she'd heard through the grapevine I might be. Calling. Generally acting unhinged and borderline psycho. Until I blocked her number and gave strict instructions to the doormen both in my apartment building and at work that she's no longer welcome.

She knows I'm still single, which is part of her problem. She insisted in one of her notes, *I'm better than nothing!!*

Actually, no.

I suggested to Blake that he consider hiring a different wedding planner, but apparently his fiancée Leah's mind was made up.

This wedding will be a test of my patience, at the very least. More likely it'll be two days of pure hell. I'm expected not only to attend the wedding on Saturday, but also be at both the rehearsal dinner on Friday night and the send-off on Sunday morning.

It's going to be a very long weekend.

As if confronting Margot wasn't bad enough, she isn't the only woman from my past who will be at this wedding.

Blake is a hedge fund manager and Leah is an interior designer who's constantly trying to set me up with her very large circle of friends. They throw a lot of parties and events, inviting select members of the cream of the Manhattan glitterati crop, which they insist I'm part of.

Leah happens to thrive on match-making and she puts a lot of thought into her guest lists, hoping to entice me. She loves to joke about the Forbes article that named me and my brothers as "Manhattan's hottest and most eligible bachelors."

Occasionally I've gone with it.

Very rarely, I let my workaholic guard down and I surrender to my animal urges. I'm only human, after all. I'm not a fucking monk. But I have very strict rules. *I* provide the condoms to make sure they haven't been tampered with. I tell the girls I'm unlikely to call them again and I always leave before morning.

See? Assholery is baked in. I know I'm an asshole and I've accepted that.

Blake's wedding will be a minefield of women I've briefly hooked up with then never called again, eyeballing me coldly and/or trying their luck a second time, and new ones lining up. Women with visions of houses by the water in Connecticut and two point five kids who are probably already on the waiting lists of every exclusive daycare/prep school/college, even though they haven't even been conceived yet.

It is what it is. Despite the asshole detail, women *love* me.

In me they see their wildest dreams.

I have blue eyes and black hair. I'm six three and I work out a lot to relieve the sexual frustration that goes along with never really clicking with a single person I meet. So there's that.

But most of all, they're already practically in love with

me for my name and—you guessed it—my money. Because of this, I have to be careful. I'm not joking when I say they try to get their hooks into me any way they can. If I give them an inch, they'll take a country mile. Especially the heiresses and socialites, whose daddies expect them to marry up. Most of these girls have been around the block a few times and are starting to get desperate.

They all have dollar signs in their eyes and plastic pumped into their faces.

Maybe I should be grateful I'm in demand. But all I can think about is how shallow it all feels.

And how fucking lonely I am.

I've never, not even once, felt that magical *spark* you read about. The one where you just *know*. Like the connection is meant to be.

It's hard to imagine.

I pull the card out of the unsealed envelope and read it. There's a menu to choose from. And a space for a "Plus One." Leah's written, *I can provide one if you want!!*

It would make things a hell of a lot easier if I had a plus one, come to think of it. The problem is, I don't. And I definitely don't want Leah choosing one for me.

As I sit at my desk, thinking once again about that secluded beach on the other side of the planet, my phone rings.

"Hey, Noah."

"Dude, don't tell me you forgot we have a meeting here at IE. You've got fifteen minutes."

"I had to come by my office first to deal with some paperwork." I glance at my Rolex.

"Colton and I need big brotherly advice about something. Cash took the week off."

"The whole week?" I've never known Cash to take even a day off in his life. Until he met Dusty, that is. I never thought I'd see the day that Cash the Cynic would fall in love, but the boy is whipped like nothing I've ever seen.

"Now that IE is free and clear of the SEC's watchdogs, he decided to take Dusty back to Hawaii," Noah tells me.

I shake my head. "I always thought *you* were the romantic in the family."

Things have finally quieted down for my brothers at their company, Invested Enterprises. One of their employees was suspected of insider trading and it caused some major headaches for them, but the problem has blown over. I'm a shareholder in the company, so I sit in on the occasional meeting with them.

Noah's a genius at what he does, but he also has a few blind spots. Of all of us, he's the one who managed to dodge the asshole gene almost entirely. It's because of this that he occasionally lets his empathy get the better of him, which is never ideal in business. So he calls on me now and then.

"Turns out I'm just as cynical as the rest of you." There's a note of gloom in his reply. Noah is—or was, until Cash fell—the only one of us who actually believes in the concept of true love. But he's having trouble finding it.

"I doubt that. I'll see you in fifteen."

We end the call and I get up to grab my jacket as I leave.

"Did you see my note?" Esther asks as I walk past her desk.

"It was pink, in the middle of my desk and written in underlined capital letters, Esther. Yes, I saw it. I filled it out and you may now call Leah with the information."

"Would you like me to book a commuter flight for next Friday? Or will you be taking the Gulfstream? Or the helicopter?"

"I'll take the helicopter. Tell Marco to have it ready to leave at five p.m. on Friday."

"And the plus one? If you're bringing someone and they've got dietary restrictions—"

"No plus one, Esther," I say gruffly.

"Understood."

"Thank you," I add and she smiles, which helps me feel like less of a prick for snapping at her.

I'm not a total monster. I don't make any unreasonable demands on her time and I make sure she gets a ludicrously generous bonus every year for putting up with my moods.

She's obviously made of tough stuff. I inherited her

when I took over as CEO, and she's told me on at least two separate occasions that working for me is a cakewalk compared to working for my father.

At least I'm not *that* much of an asshole.

I can only hope.

4

ALEXANDER

By the time I get to Invested Enterprises, it's a little after ten.

Noah's assistant Cleo announces my arrival. Noah's already waiting for me in one of their meeting rooms. He looks up when I walk in.

"Hey. You made it." Noah's tie is loosened, his hair slightly longer than it was last time I saw him. If I had to describe Noah's style, it might be biker romantic meets hot-shot CFO. He's hard to categorize.

He's also the best person I know.

Noah manages to weave all of his broad, 6'3" frame around New York City on a Ducati and takes any opportunity he can to mock me for being driven around in a limo.

"Help yourself to brunch, if you're hungry." Noah gestures to the side table, which is overflowing with fruit, donuts and deli sandwiches. "Cleo got a little carried away."

Colton walks in, grabbing a donut. "Hey, bro." He slaps me on the back. Colton is the youngest of the four of us and acts like it. He's the COO here at IE and, as the most social of all of us, is good at managing people. I think by now he's slept with half of New York City—and has had the time of his life doing it. Unlike the rest of us, he never takes anything very seriously. "How's it hanging?"

"It's hanging just fine, thanks for asking. It looks like you guys have recovered from the almost-meltdown of IE."

Noah takes a seat. "Yeah, it turns out the publicity actually did us some good in the end. We've grown more in the past month than in the six months before the incident."

"That's what happens when the three of you pose for the press like you're in a goddamn boyband."

Colton laughs. "It's not our fault the camera loves us. Especially me."

This almost makes me smile. Which is a mean feat these days. "As long as it translates into good business, go for it."

"It does," Noah says. "Share prices have sky-rocketed. Things are going well."

I pull out a chair and sit. "So, what do you need my help with?"

If I know my brothers—and I do—they almost look guilty. "We may have called you here for a slightly different reason than I mentioned," Noah admits.

"What reason?"

Colton takes a bite of his donut, grinning at me.

Noah pours me a cup of coffee, placing it on the table. "It's been too long since you emerged out of Dad's office into broad daylight, bro. You're working too hard."

At first I assume this is some kind of joke. "Sure."

"We thought you'd turned into a vampire," Colton says. "We've hardly seen you in months."

I glare at them both. "Wait. You called me over here to…check on me?"

Colton nods, stuffing the rest of his donut into his mouth.

My brothers are good at many things, but talking openly about their feelings is not one of them. Noah is more perceptive than the other two, but even he struggles sometimes to lay it all out on the table. A hangover, maybe, from our father's influence. A.J. Benjamin Maddox II thought therapy of any kind or talking about feelings was for idiots and weaklings.

"You need to get out more," Noah tells me. "Working this much and hiding from life in general isn't healthy."

I lean back in my chair, almost amused. "Jesus, Noah, just send me a text like a normal person."

"I have, but you're always in the gym or still at the office."

"Because I have to be. And I'm not 'hiding from life.' I'm working."

"You need a distraction. A day off. A night out. Something. If you keep working yourself into the ground like this, you'll end up like—"

"Wait. Let me guess. Dad?"

Noah pins me with a look. His eyes are the exact same color green as our mother's were. "You just seem…dark."

"Dark?" I shrug, exasperated. Problem is, he's right. I'm in a tunnel because I'm about to vacate my twenties and I have nothing emotionally satisfying to show for any of it.

I guess it's affecting me more than I realized.

I level a glare at Colton, then Noah. "Working out keeps me sane. At least I don't spend my days smoking cigars and drinking my way through copious amounts of top shelf whiskey." Which is what our father did. He was a heart attack waiting to happen for at least a decade before one finally caught up with him. "Working a lot comes with the territory of being CEO. Next question."

"You haven't dated anyone since Margot."

I rub a hand roughly across my jaw. "Seriously? *That's* what this is about? Margot? *I* broke it off, remember? Not only did I not love her, I didn't even like her. It was over before it even started."

"Then find someone else," Colton suggests lightly, like it's that easy.

"Trust me, I wish I could."

"Do we need to call Esther and get her to book you a trip to, I don't know, the singles resort at Club Med?" Noah asks.

"Club Med," I scoff, like it's a ridiculous idea. But I can almost admit the idea sounds tempting.

"It's not a terrible idea," Colton insists. "Maybe *I'll* go."

I'm going to regret telling them this, I can feel it. "I'm going out of town this weekend, actually."

Noah raises an eyebrow. "You are?"

"Blake and Leah's wedding, in the Hamptons. I'm the best man." I run a hand through my hair, dreading the thought so much it feels heavier than usual. My brothers are right. I'm strung out as fuck. "Margot is the wedding planner," I admit grumpily.

Noah laughs sympathetically. "Oh, shit."

"So I'm going to spend the weekend on the receiving end of her gleeful little power trip, wishing I was dead."

"Take a date," Colton suggests. "Get all hot and heavy with some debutante on the dance floor. That would keep Margot at arm's length."

"Unfortunately, every 'date' I've had lately is just as grasping as Margot. Or even worse."

"I could call someone." Colton blinks at me.

I exhale something that's not quite laughter. "Absolutely not. I'd rather pay someone than help myself to your leftovers, little brother."

Noah's watching me. I can practically see the cogs

whirring inside his brain. "That's actually not a bad idea. You could hire someone."

"*Hire* someone? Please." I shake my head, pushing my chair back from the table. "Now that you've finished the Spanish Inquisition, am I free to go?"

But Noah's on a roll. "That could actually work. Pay someone to go with you for the weekend as a front. It'll keep Margot off your back. And, who knows, with the stress taken out of the Margot equation, you might even enjoy a weekend out of the city, poolside, among friends. People *do* occasionally enjoy weddings, you know."

"Sure they do," I grumble. Other people, maybe.

"You definitely need a buffer," Colton agrees.

"I don't need to *hire* someone to spend time with me. I'm not Dad."

We all frown at the memories.

But Colton is just warming up. "Dude, you're not paying her to have *sex* with you. You're paying her to let Margot know that you're no longer available."

I sigh heavily. I hadn't let myself think too much about the actual logistics of being at a wedding with Margot.

Knowing my luck, we'll be sharing a goddamn room due to some mix up with the bookings—something that's actually possible because she's in charge. Everything with her is deliberate and calculated. And relentless. She's like a fucking event planner terminator with one mission.

"The wedding's this weekend?" Noah pulls out his

phone and punches the call button. "Cleo, come in here for a minute, would you?"

I've had enough. I stand up, getting ready to leave. "I'm not taking *Cleo* as my fake fucking date."

"I'm not setting you up with *Cleo*," Noah laughs at the thought. "She's engaged. But she does know literally half of New York City. She'll know of someone who'd just love a weekend away in the Hamptons with a hot billionaire."

Noah's still smiling as Cleo opens the door, ten seconds later, her eyes bright with the kind of enthusiasm that's going to spin this project into a nightmare I can't escape from, I can just tell.

Cleo is probably 23 or 24 and is a hundred percent attitude. I don't know how Noah puts up with her.

"Hi, Alexander," she smiles. It's annoying, how she calls me by my first name even though I never asked her to. Noah's style is much more informal than mine.

"Cleo."

Colton is enjoying this immensely. "Cleo, we have a little problem we were wondering if you could help us with."

"Sure." She glances at me, reading that the problem is mine. "What's the problem?"

"Alexander has a wedding to go to in the Hamptons this weekend," Colton explains. "But his crazy ex who won't take no for an answer will be there and he needs a date to act as a...well, a shield. A front. To keep her off his back and to convince her it's time to move on. Do you know anyone who'd agree to be his plus one at such short notice if he paid them extremely generously?"

"Two nights," I add, hating that I'm suddenly considering going along with this. "And this is completely confidential."

Cleo looks me up and down, like she's trying to figure out if she knows anyone nuts enough to do this. "You're that desperate, huh?"

"He is," Noah confirms.

Cleo flashes white teeth. "Oh, I can definitely help you. I've got a hundred friends who would kill to get close to a Maddox brother. People ask me all the time if I can get them one of your numbers."

"And now's their chance." Noah's grin as he watches my face is making me want to strangle him.

"I just want to make sure I'm clear on all the details." Cleo starts taking notes on a fucking notepad. "The payment you're offering includes…staying in the same room with you?" She glances up at me.

Fuck. I hadn't thought of that.

"Definitely," Colton says. "The staging has to be convincing."

"Maybe it could be a two-room suite or something," I mumble. "I can—"

"No, that would be too obvious," Noah insists. "Especially since Margot is the event planner. She'll zero in on that detail like a circling shark."

"You mean the evil ex is the *event planner*? Oh, this is too good." Cleo is enjoying my pain as much as Noah. "Okay, so definitely in the same room. Do you want your fake date to, like…lay it on? Like, sit on your lap, play with your hair, kiss you, that kind of thing? To really show the ex you've completely moved on?"

"Absolutely," Colton answers before I get a chance to tell Cleo there's no need for any of that. "It's the only way to keep Margot at bay. The woman's a nightmare. She thinks she still has a chance of winning him back."

True enough, unfortunately.

Cleo scribbles a few more notes. "So, are you going to want your fake date to…you know…"

"To what?" I ask grouchily.

"To have sex with you?"

"What? No. Jesus," I splutter. "Of course not."

Noah is biting his lip, trying not to laugh.

I'm about to pull the plug on the entire idea. "It would be an act, only. She can have the bed. I'll sleep on the floor."

Cleo considers this. "If Margot is as savvy as she sounds, she'll detect that something is off if you do that. I just think you should both sleep in the same bed. It needs to be as believable as possible."

I eye her, considering this. "All right, then. But no sex," I say again.

Colton muffles his laughter.

Cleo's mouth quirks. "Right. Got it."

I can't tell what she's thinking. I don't know why I feel compelled to explain. "I mean, I like sex, a lot…not too much, like…the appropriate amount. But I don't need to pay someone for it."

Kill me now.

Not only am I going to be forced to share a bed with some air-headed barely-legal friend of Cleo's, I also have to admit that I'm as desperate as I sound. To make matters worse, I haven't been laid in months.

After the Margot disaster, then a few nightmarish "rebound" dates organized by Leah, I lost my urge to deal with women's demands altogether, leading me into a dry spell of epic proportions.

What if I…when I'm sharing a bed with the girl…when I'm so pent up…what if I crack a…

Fuck.

Cleo looks at me, the arch of her eyebrow disappearing underneath her blond bangs like she's reading my mind. "For a billionaire, you're not exactly smooth."

"Come on, Cleo," Noah jokes. "If he was actually charming or decent company, do you think he'd be single?"

I glare at the brother who used to be one of my favorites, but his grin only widens. "You're supposed to be helping me here."

Cleo looks unfazed. "Don't worry, Alexander. I know exactly what you're like. Surly, serious, aloof. The brooding oldest brother with the weight of the world on his shoulders. I get it. But your company and your money…well, that makes you a catch, no matter how awful your personality is. So you're still going to need someone pretty impressive to make this whole thing believable. She'll need to be someone special. Someone who can make Margot wildly jealous."

Noah and Colton are both nodding.

"Hey, I don't have an awful personality—"

Colton waves off my protest. "It's irrelevant, Alexander. You're *paying*. It's not a real date. Who cares how uptight you are? So, Cleo, do you think you could find someone?"

"There are a few people that come to mind, yeah. One in particular."

"Could you…uh," I grab a fistful of my hair because it sounds like this might actually be happening. "Could you make sure she's—"

"Hot?" Cleo smiles sweetly. "Of course. I have lots of hot friends."

"I, uh…and could you make sure she doesn't have like a nut allergy or is a psychopath or anything like that." I'm gun-shy at this point. "It's just…"

Noah laughs. "Wow, we're getting very specific here. A hot non-psychopath with no food allergies. You got any of those on your roster, Cleo?"

"Actually, I might."

"And she can't be afraid of a little PDA," Noah adds.

"PDA?" I'm confused.

"Public displays of affection," Cleo clarifies. "Oh, don't worry about that. I have someone in mind and she's a born performer. And seriously gorgeous. But I'm not sure she'll agree to it. She isn't exactly desperate for the money. And she has very high standards."

"Alexander's willing to pay her *extremely* well." More grinning from my brothers, who are enjoying this far too much.

"*If* she does a good job," I say churlishly. "And no drama." I've dealt with enough meltdowns from women to last me a lifetime. "She acts the part when we're in public, she's willing to sleep in the same bed—strictly platonically—and she agrees to sign an NDA. I don't want any of this going public."

"Of course," Cleo says. "And she'll do everything she can to convincingly pretend to be interested in you. Which will take some talent, and she has that in spades."

Damn these overconfident Gen Z types. They're tactless ball-breakers. "Thanks for your insights, Cleo. I knew there was a reason I don't come by here more often."

Cleo makes a sympathetic face, but I'm pretty sure it's staged. "I'll do my best to find you a date, but she won't come cheap, especially considering the parameters you're describing."

"Money isn't an issue," Noah takes the liberty of adding. "If she does a good job and keeps Margot out of his hair, she'll be worth every penny."

"What kind of numbers are we talking here?" Cleo blinks.

"I don't know," I say. "I've never had to make this kind of proposal before. What do you think?"

We all look at Cleo. She thinks for a few seconds. "A hundred?"

"That's very…" I'm about to say it's very reasonable when it occurs to me she means a hundred grand. "A hundred *thousand?*"

"At least. You could double that if she does an exceptionally convincing job. Let's say one-fifty and you can always tip her if things go swimmingly."

I can't believe I'm considering this.

"Actually," says Cleo, "I think you should offer two hundred up front. She's more likely to agree to it if it's an impressive, no-nonsense offer."

Noah's sympathetic but undeterred. "It's worth it, bro. Margot will stop calling you, your fake date will finish her performance on Sunday afternoon and leave you in peace, and you can take a much-needed vacation on the tropical island of your choice knowing you stepped up for your best friend on the most important weekend of his life."

He's got a point. Fuck it. "Fine. I'll do it. But she better be good."

"*And* hot," Colton clarifies.

"And you'll be getting *me* coffee for the rest of the year if I can actually make this happen," Cleo smiles at Noah, standing up and heading toward the door. "I'll let you know once she confirms. *If* she confirms."

I've never heard an assistant talk to their boss—or his brothers—the way Cleo sasses Noah, but he seems to actually enjoy her no-nonsense attitude.

Lord knows if Esther ever leaves me, I will *not* be poaching Cleo from Noah. I'm not sure I'd survive the week.

"If this goes wrong, you'll be lucky to still be in one piece in order to *get* Cleo her coffee," I growl as the door closes behind Cleo.

Both my brothers are laughing.

Colton pats me on the back. "Lighten up, bro. Who knows, maybe she'll be the girl of your dreams."

5
____

ALEXANDER

I DECIDE to take the rest of the day off.

I tell my driver to take me home. On the way, I text Esther. Twenty minutes with Cleo has made me pretty fucking grateful for her.

> I'll be taking a plus one to the wedding. No dietary restrictions

> She'll have the steak too

But what if she's a vegetarian?

> And the vegetarian option. Tell Leah I'll pay the extra for both

My phone buzzes instantly. I expect it to be Esther giddy with excitement that Oscar the Grouch finally has a date, but it's just a notification saying I've received a call from a blocked number.

Margot.

It's like her bitch radar has detected the latest possible development through the airwaves.

I ignore it.

After I ended it with Margot, I threw myself into work more than ever before. I guess that's why Noah is worried.

In a way, he's right. As much as Margot and I weren't compatible, I do miss occasionally spending time with people who aren't employees. I *have* been feeling that part of the break-up, no matter what I tell my brothers. I've felt more existentially *alone* than I ever have in my life. I'm not sure why.

It might be partly because my brothers are now working so closely together at Invested Enterprises. They all have each other. Not that I wanted to join their start-up; I don't have time. And I never wanted to break free of Maddox Enterprises like they did—or maybe it's more of a case of not having that luxury. Either way, now, I'm steering the ship alone, with a handful of Dad's old cronies.

Every night I go home to my five-bedroom penthouse, which should feel like a haven, or at least a success story. For a while, it did. But lately, it feels more empty than it ever has before. Just another reminder that I seem destined to be a grumpy lone wolf for the rest of time.

My driver drops me off outside my building, ready to park the limo in the basement garage.

I should head straight to my home office, but I'm too distracted. The conversation with Noah and Cleo is playing on a loop in my brain.

I was stupid to tell Esther I'd be taking a plus one. What are the chances of Cleo finding someone who would agree to such a ridiculous plan, and at such short notice? And even if she does, do I really want to go ahead with it? A fake date for the weekend suddenly seems more terrifying than a real one.

Knowing my luck, the kind of woman who would agree to such a thing will probably be a total nutcase.

The one thing that stops me from calling the whole thing off is the thought of pissing off Margot. It's too damn appealing.

If I do end up bringing some air-headed (hot) twenty-three year old, Margot will be absolutely livid.

The thought makes me feel a fraction less surly.

I pour myself a whiskey and take it out onto the roof terrace, leaning against the balcony railing to take in the city.

I bought this apartment six years ago. The helipad and pool are nice to have, but being this high up, with these panoramic views over the city, that's what really sold me on this place. The sunsets are something else.

Not that I make it back from the office in time to

enjoy them most nights, but that's just part of the Fortune 500 lifestyle. I know this. This is how I've lived my life.

Tonight it doesn't stop me from wondering what it might be like to experience what everyone else seems to find so easily in life. Fun. Enjoyment.

Love.

I've never even detected an inkling of that feeling. Of caring. Of wanting more. Every single time, inevitably, the women want more and I want less. They get clingy and greedy and I pull back. They get mad because I'm too distant and I retreat even further. They cry and I get more jaded and more pissed off. It's always the same.

Sometimes—like right now—I feel like I'm missing out on something huge.

According to my brothers, my love life wouldn't be such a disaster if I could just loosen up a little, and they're probably right.

It occurs to me that I'm turning into the exact thing I've spent my life trying to avoid. I watched my father work his guts out, spending far more time in the board-room than he ever did enjoying his money.

So what am I doing, then? Why am I repeating the same pattern?

What's it all for?

Maybe I *do* need a vacation.

And suddenly, the thought of hiring a tween to act as a buffer between me and my bitch of an ex feels like too much work. I feel exhausted just imagining how it might play out.

My phone dings with an incoming message. I take it out of my pocket, preparing to ignore yet another blocked call from Margot.

But it's Noah.

I just heard from Cleo. It's a go

The deal's off. It was a ridiculous idea. I'm going solo

Three dots appear immediately to tell me he's typing back.

Nice try. Cleo's having a drink with the lead candidate as we speak and she's willing to do it. Two hundred up front

I said the deal's off

Did we actually agree on those numbers?
More dots.

Apparently she's hot AF

Damn it. Something in me twitches.

Cleo says you're the "luckiest grump on the planet" to get this girl to agree to it

Who is she?

She wants to start out with first
names only

Why? Is she on the FBI's Most Wanted
list? She knows my last name, I'm
assuming

Cleo tried to convince her you're cool but
she's cautious

I guess that's fair enough.

It's too late to back out, bro. She said
she'll be ready on Friday afternoon. Just
name the time and place

I can't believe I'm considering this

Cleo says to tell you this girl is (direct
quote) "waaaaaaaay out of your league."
She's ordering me to tell you that you
have to promise to be nice to her. Where
do you want her to meet you?

Now I'm curious. Out of my league? I'm a billionaire. I'm ripped as fuck since I have nothing else to do when I'm not in the office besides work out like a maniac and swim laps in the Olympic-sized pool on the roof garden of my penthouse. I'm also hung like a fucking Trojan. I won the lottery on a lot of levels but especially that one.

I want to meet the girl who's "out of my league."

Dude, you owe me big time

There's a photo attached to his text.

Is this her?

Duh. Yes. Her name is Ivy

Ivy.

I zoom in on the photo.

Hell.

She's young. She looks younger than twenty-three, in fact, and it makes me wonder where her parents are. Do they know she's accepting fake dates with men for money? Is she desperate? Is she okay?

I zoom in closer.

To say she's beautiful would be a wild understatement. She's so cute and stunning, it's weirdly…painful. It makes my chest feel strangely tight.

She has dark hair that's pulled back from her face, which is so beautiful I'm wondering if she's used one of those filters. No one can be *this* flawless. Her eyes are amber-colored, framed by long, dark lashes. A few curls have escaped to frame her face delicately. She's staring directly at the camera but she looks almost bored. Sultry. Her lips are full and pink. She's wearing what looks like a tight, skimpy yoga outfit. She has a tattoo of a musical note on her wrist.

I'll admit I'm intrigued.

Not bad, right?

What if she's a psycho like all the rest of them?

It's a joke, almost.

Dude, when did you get so cynical?

Somewhere between crash and burn 800 and Margot The Lunatic

A little "ha ha" attaches to the text.

Seriously tho, Cleo has assured me she's a "sweetheart with grit" and an "insane talent"

Talented at what?

I guess you'll find out

I sigh heavily, taking another look at the photo of the girl. She really is stunning.

Fine. I'll have my driver pick her up at 4:30 pm sharp. We'll take the helicopter

Lol. Sure thing bro. Have a good night. I'll call you tomorrow

The night goes quiet and I zoom in on the photo again.

Ivy.

It's dark in my apartment except for the city lights and the blue reflection of the pool outside. And my phone, which glows with the girl's perfect face.

Today's Tuesday.

I'm surprised by the turn of my own thoughts. Because what I'm thinking is: *only three more days to go.*

6

———

IVY

I wake from a deep sleep, my eyes blinking open to almost-darkness. It takes me a few seconds to get my bearings.

I live in Soho now. In the loft I bought for Josh. And for me.

A deep sense of relief settles.

It's so nice here and I don't need to panic because our mother's sick and Josh is acting out again and Aunt Sarah is leaving for California.

When you grow up with a sense of fear that's almost paralyzing some days, it takes a while for your subconscious mind to shift.

We're okay now.

I had a sold out show at a new, tiny but perfect little venue in the East Village last night called Starstruck and I didn't get home until after midnight.

I reach to check my phone. It's 9:51 a.m. I must have been really tired.

Closing my eyes again, I start the little gratitude practice I started doing soon after we moved into this apartment. Because I *am* grateful. I also read a book that says thoughts have an actual frequency. You're creating cosmic waves with your thoughts. You attract or deflect things by thinking about them either positively or negatively. According to the book, you're creating your own reality with whatever thoughts you spend the most time thinking.

I found this wildly intriguing. What if it's true?

So I figured it couldn't hurt to spend a few minutes a day being grateful for the things I already have and also for the things I want to achieve, sort of preemptively. Maybe if I'm grateful enough, I'll attract good things and all my dreams will come true.

Sure.

But I push the little kernel of cynicism out of my head. It's useless to me.

I concentrate instead on five things I'm grateful for. I do this every morning before I get out of bed.

The strange thing is: it *works.* I end up talking myself into a frame of mind and it begins to act like a self-fulfilling prophecy after a while, which feels almost magical. So I've kept it up.

So I start with the obvious. These things sometimes take on their own momentum.

I'm grateful we live in this awesome, fabulous apartment. Josh and I finally have our own rooms—that was way overdue—and there's a balcony. I love being able to grow my own plants. And I love that we're not living in a dingy basement apartment with our dying mother and our aunt who helped us but never really fully enjoyed having us live with her. I can't blame her. We were a mess and it was hard. And then having her sister get sick and Josh was a handful sometimes—okay, most of the time—it can't have been easy. I'm glad she's happy in California now, even if we hardly ever hear from her. I guess she had enough of us and was glad to move on.

I hear the front door slam and a banging noise. Josh must be home.

I'm so, so grateful Josh got into Columbia. That's huge. Mom, you'd be so proud. I know you can see him. I know you'd love the person he's becoming. Even if he's still a surly seventeen-year-old most days, you can see the good man in him starting to peel back its layers. I love that he's on track to achieve everything he's capable of.

More banging. The fridge door slams.

I'm grateful I get to play my music for people who appreciate it. The show last night was one of the best I've ever played. I'm grateful that it was sold out and that I made money from doing what I love.

What else?

I'm grateful that people came up to me after the show and told me how much they enjoyed it. Seven different guys asked me for my number. Even if I didn't give it to any of them, I guess it's nice to get noticed in that way. Not that any of them really stood out as someone I wanted to talk to again. And of course I'd never bring a guy back here when Josh was here. I mean, how awkward would that be? Plus he's six-feet or something now and sort of protective of me, so the thought of something going wrong or them not getting along makes me cringe. But it would be nice to meet someone…someday. I've been too busy lately but I hope it'll happen. Once Josh starts college, I'll have more time and a little more space.

How many is that? Four. I need one more.

I guess I'm grateful—no, I am grateful—I went out to Connecticut last weekend. Even if the whole thing sucks and was a total disaster. I'm glad I got a final answer from him. His no-show spoke volumes and I'm grateful it's now over. No more wondering. We can have some closure now and move on. I'm grateful he at least donated his DNA (ew) and stuck around long enough to give me Josh. Goodbye, Dad. And good riddance. Have a nice life.

I take a deep, restorative breath. Then I open my eyes and climb out of bed, doing a few quick yoga stretches on the mat in my room by the windows. I can see my plants out there and I *am* grateful. This shit works.

Then I put on a short silk kimono over the bralette and boy shorts I slept in, tying it. I grab my phone and head out to the kitchen.

Josh is sitting at the table, scrolling on his phone and drinking directly out of the orange juice carton again.

"Morning, Josh. You can finish that because no one else will be drinking out of it."

"Hey, Ive." He's in a good mood. "How'd last night go?"

"Really well. That venue is amazing. It's small but has great acoustics. And it's a cool atmosphere."

"Awesome."

I study him for a few seconds, trying to get a read on why he's in such a good mood this morning. Usually he'd grunt at me or give me some kind of non-answer.

Then I notice he's wearing a new hoodie. A nice one. And there's a bag sitting on the chair with the end of a white box sticking out of it.

With an Apple logo on it.

"Josh?"

"Yeah?" He takes a bite of the bagel he's eating.

"You got a new laptop?"

"Yeah."

"That's…great. How?"

"Well, I walked into the store and I bought it."

"With what money?"

He's still chewing.

I pay for Josh's expenses and give him money to spend, and he earns money from the café and from a minor YouTube channel, which has been useful for getting late night burgers with friends. But neither would give him enough to splurge on a new MacBook Pro on a whim.

"I do work, you know," he tells me.

"In a minimum wage job for a few hours a week. Try again." I fold my arms across my chest. "How'd you afford it?"

"I've been saving."

"Keep bullshitting me and I'll go into full ballistic

mode." I don't do it often, but he knows I'll pull out the big guns if I have to. Which involves turning off the Wi-Fi and hiding the modem. I know he doesn't have enough data on his plan to hotspot all the things he has going on online. It's all I have. He's much bigger than me now. Not that there's ever been anything physical about my so-called authority, but now that he outweighs me by almost two to one, he's a lot less likely to toe the line just because I tell him to.

"I just took what was ours."

I blink at him as this information absorbs. "What?" I stare at him, but he glares right back, eyes flashing like he's getting ready for a fight. "What do you mean?"

He shrugs. "Nothing a thousand other people couldn't do with that sort of information."

"What information?" No. Surely not. "Wait. Please tell me you didn't..."

I noticed after Josh gave my phone back to me that he'd deleted the photos of the bank statements from my camera. I was almost relieved when I saw that. It made me think he wanted us both to move on from it and forget it ever happened. I hadn't really given the whole thing a second thought since. But he obviously sent himself the pictures and then has gone full criminal mastermind all over our dad's unsuspecting fortune.

"Holy shit, Josh. You didn't. Please say you didn't."

"He's never given us a dime, Ivy, and he never will. I just took what he owes us."

I shake my head a little, hoping I'm not hearing him correctly. "Josh. Are you serious right now? What did you *do?*"

He looks me in the eye. "I transferred it into a different Bahamas account."

"What?"

"I didn't take all of it. I left him a mil. I figured that was fair."

I can't quite compute what he's telling me. "Please tell me you're joking. Please tell me you didn't just steal ten million dollars from someone else's bank account."

"He can afford to share."

"Josh," I whisper. My hand covers my mouth.

"I just took what he owed us for fifteen years of neglect, with interest. It just about adds up."

"*You stole ten million dollars?*"

"I redirected ten million dollars."

"Are you *crazy?* Do you want to go to *jail* instead of Columbia?"

"How do you think I'm affording Columbia, Ivy?"

"*I'm* paying for Columbia! I *told* you that! You can't just *steal* ten million dollars and not get caught for that! What's wrong with you?"

"Don't worry about it. I've covered my tracks. No one will be able to trace it."

"*Josh.* Jesus. Of course they'll be able to trace it! You have to give it back. Now. Immediately."

"No."

I stare at him, dumbfounded and irate. "Yes!"

"I'm not giving it back, Ivy. He owes us. He owes me."

"Josh, you'll go to jail if they find out, don't you get that? *Jail!*"

He's infuriatingly unrepentant. "As I said, I was very thorough. And discreet."

"Josh, be reasonable! You have to put it back right this second. *Please.* I promise you, we can afford Columbia. You know that. I make enough money. We'll be fine. We don't need his money."

He's quiet for a few long seconds, contemplating me gently. "You know I love you, right, Ive?"

This shocks me a little. I say the words to him all the time. Sometimes he says them back, offhandedly, if he's in the right mood. But I'm not sure he's ever said them first, just out of the blue like that. "I love you too, Josh."

"And I appreciate the hell out of everything you've done for me. I know how hard it's been. I know how hard you work. And I'm going to pay you back one day. But for now, I think it's okay if we quietly allow our father to help us, when it's so little to him. It's not his only offshore account. He has two others. I did some research. And it looks like his money-making schemes aren't always a hundred percent legal. So it's safe to say he's not going to be destitute. He'll also think twice about getting the authorities involved. He might not even notice."

"Josh, of course he'll notice! It's ten million dollars!"

"I don't want you to pay when he can pay. It's too much for you to do that. You've done enough already."

Josh knows that Columbia, by the time he graduates, will have cost us close to half a million dollars—if he lives on campus, which he still hasn't decided, but I'd like him to do that if he wants to. Josh also knows that, when I did my research about how much he might be able to get in financial aid, the answer is zero. Because I'm his legal guardian and I make enough to keep the option of assistance out of reach.

I have money, but it's not regenerating at the rate it was when I first burst onto the TikTok scene. I know I could ramp up my platform if I toured more. Social media loves travel, exotic locations, keeping it fresh and exciting.

I haven't traveled because I'm here, taking care of my brother. I do local gigs and record new music but my plate is very full and it's sometimes hard to keep up the staged illusion of fun and perfection when my life isn't always those things.

I don't regret spending all my money on buying us a beautiful home where we can feel safe, or for sending Josh to a private high school his last two years to help his chances of getting into a good college, but it's all added up.

"Ivy, you've literally paid for everything for *years*. It shouldn't be up to you to do all that for me. Not when he can."

"Josh. Come on. I get how angry you are. I do. But it doesn't mean you can *steal* from him. It's not worth risking everything and it's definitely not worth going to *jail* for. You *have* to put it back before this spirals into something uncontrollable. You have to do the right thing. Please."

"I am doing the right thing."

He seems so calm, so unfazed, it's freaking me out. "You must be able to put it back though, right? If you do it quickly enough, he might not even notice it was gone. If it's an account he doesn't check every day, then he might not have contacted the bank." *Or the police.*

"I'll take care of it, Ive."

Most parents don't have to deal with this kind of shit, right? Underage drinking, smoking weed, cheating on a test…I can handle all that. What I can't handle is my brother throwing his entire life away. And I definitely can't handle him getting locked up.

Josh stands up to his full height, which seems taller every time I look at him. He grabs his stuffed-full duffel bag from under the table. I hadn't seen it there.

"It's Spring Break, Ive," he informs me. "Cameron's dad has a condo in Fort Lauderdale. We're flying out this afternoon for the weekend and I have to go now."

"Fort Lauderdale?" I still feel stunned. "That's in Florida."

He grins down at me. "You nailed it, Einstein. Maybe you should be the one going to Columbia."

"You're not going to *Florida*." I'm about to ask him

how he can afford the plane ticket, but of course I already know. "Not until we've solved this problem."

"The problem has already been solved. And guess how old I'm turning on Sunday, Ive? Eighteen. Which means you can't stop me from doing any damn thing I want."

"It also means you'll be tried as a fully-fledged adult," I can't help pointing out.

"Never going to happen." He blinks at me and goddamn it, I want to cry.

"*Please*, Josh. Please put it back. Promise me you'll put it back. I'll pay for the plane ticket. I'll put some money in your account for Fort Lauderdale. I'll pay for the laptop."

He leans down to kiss my cheek, saying nothing. "Later, Ive."

"Okay? Josh?"

"I said it before and I'll say it again. I'll do the right thing."

"Do it now. Get the screen up and show me."

"I'm afraid I'll miss my flight if I do that now." He's infuriatingly blasé about this. He seems…happy.

"I want to see the restored statement of the bank account by the time you get back."

"Sure thing, Ive."

"You will?"

"If that's what you want, I will show you the restored bank statement by the time I get back."

"Okay. Good. Good. Thank you."

He grabs what looks like a shiny new phone and shoves it into the pocket of his baggy new jeans. He heads for the door. "Have a good weekend, Ive. See you on Monday night. I think I get in at around three."

"Make sure you—" He slams the door and I feel the vibration in the pit of my stomach.

Shit.

Shit.

Shit.

I spend the rest of the afternoon mired in the zone of the powerless, pissed-off parent. I send Josh a bunch of texts, but I keep it light and vague, so nothing incriminating can be found on either of our phones. In case they get seized or something.

He ignores every message. I get one text that confirms he made it to Florida, he's alive, and he's going to be busy partying, so he might not be able to reply to my messages right away. He tells me to "chill."

The little punk.

I should be enjoying my alone time. God knows I don't get much of it.

I open a few of the mountain of boxes that have been sent to me by companies wanting me to advertise their products. We keep them stacked along the wall by the door and they've become part of the furniture.

There's a forest green sports bra and matching bike shorts, wrapped with tissue paper. A note reads:

> *Ivy, we love your Insta! We hope you enjoy this breathable fully-organic yoga outfit, made with 100% sustainable fabrics. We'd love to work with you!*

And a sweater.

> *Hi Ivy! We're so excited to present you with this luxurious and one-of-a-kind cashmere crew-neck, weaved from the wool of free-range, hand-reared Kashmir goats here in the gorgeous Catskills region of Upstate New York! We hope you might consider working with us on some product advertising. We're in awe of your platform! We'd love to meet with you via Zoom. Please get in touch xx*

I've got a reputation as working mainly with ethical companies who do their best not to destroy the planet.

My phone rings.

I pick it up, thinking it might be my walking cyber-crime of a brother. But when I see the name on the screen, I do a double-take.

Roy.

There's only one Roy on my contacts list. I changed his title from Dad to Roy in a fit of rage years ago.

I answer the call before I can second-guess it. "Dad?"

"Ivy?"

Who else does he think it would be? "Yeah, it's me."

"Hi, honey. How are you?"

Hi, honey? How am I? How *dare* he? "I'm…fine." My voice sounds cold, and it is. "I was sorry I missed you last weekend. Did you get my note?"

"Yes. Yes, I did. That's…part of the reason I'm calling."

"Oh. What's the other reason?" I want to make him squirm. Because I know what his other reason is, and it's not to chitchat about the weather.

"There's something I need to discuss with you."

"Josh's graduation?" Just to twist the knife a little.

"Uh, no. I don't think Josh would want me there."

"True. He doesn't. Which is too bad, considering it wouldn't have been hard to reach out to him once or twice during his lifetime. What did you want to discuss?"

"You were…in my house. In my office." He sounds very unhappy about this discovery and his unhappiness has the effect of a very red flag waving in front of an extremely ornery bull.

My reply is sassy and unremorseful. "I knocked. The door was unlocked and no one was home. I called out to you. I wanted to let you know I showed up, even if you didn't. I wrote the note to you, then I left."

"You don't have the right to let yourself into our home, Ivy."

Okay, I'll admit it: this makes my blood boil. *Our home. But not your home. No, never that.* "I told you I was coming. I thought maybe you'd left your door unlocked on purpose." Not true, but it might sound reasonable in a court of law. I am, after all, his daughter. Even if he's forgotten that detail.

"Ivy, there's…" He's not sure how to explain it to me. It's a tricky one, I'll give him that much. "Something has gone missing."

"What's gone missing?" I realize I'm already considering my words, in case the police come after us. Maybe this phone call is being recorded. I wouldn't put it past my neglectful excuse for a father. And I've already lumped myself into this crime with Josh because I'm hardly going to let him take the fall alone. It was me who provided him with his own red flag, even if I never meant to. "Something in your house?"

"No. Not exactly. What…what did you see when you were here?"

"What did I *see*?" *Besides a Bahamas bank account statement?* "Well, I saw a lot of sterile white walls and ugly decorating choices. I saw a pen and a piece of paper. I saw a table to set the note on. And then I saw a pristinely manicured front lawn as I was leaving." *Asshole.* "What's gone missing?" I ask again. *Ten million dollars, by any chance?*

Does my father remember the hacking incident when Josh was twelve? Probably. "Something very valuable."

"Well, I didn't take anything, if that's what you're implying. But let me know if you find it."

I'm about to hang up when he says, "I'm going to have to contact the police, Ivy. Unless you'd prefer to return what you stole without involving the authorities."

"*Stole?* I have no idea what you're talking about." My heart seizes with the kind of terror you can only experience when you and your little brother are about to get arrested and thrown into Rikers Island for the rest of your natural born lives. But I keep my cool, even though my fury is burning me. "As I said, I didn't remove anything from your house, *Dad.*" I say the word ironically. "I didn't even lift your pen."

"Ivy. I mean it." So *now* he chooses to be a disciplinarian.

"And so do I." I'm not sure I've ever experienced this kind of cortisol spike before, but it's intense in the worst kind of way. "I didn't take anything."

"Then I guess you'll be hearing from my lawyer and the detective assigned to this case."

"I'll look forward to it. And you're welcome, for raising your son, into the best version of himself, without any help from you whatsoever. Have a nice day, Dad." *You deserve to have your money stolen, you unfeeling prick.*

I end the call, walking into my bedroom and putting

my phone down on my bed. My hands are shaking. My eyes fill with tears but I impatiently wipe them away.

Damn it.

Deep breaths. Stay calm. Josh said he would put the money back. He said he covered his tracks. He can do it with both transactions.

Can't he?

Glancing through the windows to the balcony, I try to center myself. *I'm grateful for the twilit sky and for the air I get to breathe, even if it is heavily scented with exhaust fumes. I'm grateful for all my goddamn plants because they sure as hell won't have balcony herb gardens at Rikers Island.*

8

When my phone rings again, I half expect it to be the cops telling me they're about to bang down my door and drag me away in handcuffs.

But Cleo's name lights up the screen.

I answer it, relieved. "Hey, Clee."

"I'm around the corner, heading toward JJ's, and I demand you come down and have a drink with me. I haven't seen you in two weeks and we've hardly talked."

The familiarity of her bossiness is comforting. "Sure. I'd love that. What time is it?"

"It's almost six. I have a proposition for you and I think you're going to want to hear this."

"A proposition? What kind of proposition?"

"I need to talk to you about it in person or you'll never agree to it. Plus I haven't seen you since you went

79

out to your dad's last weekend. I want to hear about how it went."

"There's nothing to talk about."

"Let me guess. He wasn't there."

"Good guess."

"I'm sorry, honey. The man is and always will be a shithead. Meet you at JJ's in twenty?"

"Sounds perfect."

I throw on a cute dress that one of my clients sent me. Pulling my hair up into a messy bun, I put on some mascara and lip gloss. I pull on some tall boots and wrap a pink silk scarf around my neck. Most of my clients know by now that I only wear natural fabrics and that I have a sort of bohemian-meets-Ralph-Lauren style with a wild-child-musician twist. I take a photo of myself in my full-length mirror and post it to Instagram, tagging the designer and adding a link to the dress on her website. *How cute is this organic cotton mini dress?? Shop my outfit!*

Another three grand into the Josh Goes to Columbia fund (if he doesn't get thrown into jail first).

I force that last thought out of my head. I absolutely can*not* mention this to anyone, and most of all Cleo. So I lock it into its own little compartment in my brain, next to the Move On From Asshole Father one, labeled Worry About Later.

Spring is definitely in the air and the streets are busy with people enjoying the city.

JJ's is one of our favorite places to meet. It's right around the corner from my building and it's a funky little rooftop bar and restaurant with some of the best food in the neighborhood, which is saying something, since Soho is full of good restaurants and bars designed specifically to be Instagram-worthy and to generate the best reviews possible.

By the time I get to JJ's, Cleo is already at our usual table. I can see that she's ordered us a bottle of champagne that's sitting in an ice bucket. Two glasses have already been poured.

"A whole bottle?" I lean in to give her a kiss on each cheek before sliding into the booth seat across from her. She knows I'm not much of a drinker.

"The occasion calls for it."

"What occasion would that be?"

"Sam and I set a date." She's absolutely beaming.

"You *did*? When?"

"We're going to have a fall wedding. September in Vermont."

"Cleo, that's amazing! That will be *so* beautiful. Congrats!"

If I didn't know better, I'd say my bestie has a tear in her eye. "I haven't officially asked you this yet, but will you be my maid of honor? I need you right next to me the whole time."

I lean across the table to give her a hug. "Of course I will. I'm so excited for you."

She picks up her glass and clinks it against mine. "To true love. For both of us."

I take a sip. "For you, at least. I'll bask in your glow. I haven't been on a single date for over a year, can you believe that? It's depressing."

"That's what happens when you feel compelled to babysit your brother 24/7. You tend to miss out on a lot of action."

She's right, of course. "As soon as Josh is all set for Columbia, I'll be able to start thinking about my love life, which at this point has tumbleweeds rolling through it. I just want so badly for him to be okay."

"Ivy, he's fine. He *is* all set for Columbia. I thought you said he's enrolled now and he's chosen his classes for the fall."

"He is. And he has. And right now he's in Florida for Spring Break, partying it up in Fort Lauderdale."

She makes a face, like she can't think of anything worse. "Good for him. So that means you're free this weekend. No gigs?"

"No gigs. I had one last night. My next one's not for a few weeks."

"Good." The look on Cleo's face is mischievous and borderline guilty, if I'm not mistaken. "Because I sort of set you up with someone."

I stare at her. "You what?"

"Hear me out. Please, just listen to the details. This is way too good."

"What details? What are you talking about?"

"It's more of a business proposition than a date. I just talked to Noah again and they're willing to pay two hundred thousand for the weekend."

"Wait, what?"

"They'll pay you two hundred thousand for two days."

"Who will?

"Noah and his brothers."

"Two hundred thousand *dollars*?"

"All you have to do is pretend to be Alexander Maddox's date at some swanky wedding in the Hamptons —purely for show. He's the best man and his ex is the wedding planner. He needs a front so she'll keep her distance. Apparently she's, like, crazy and won't take no for an answer."

"What?" My brain can't keep up.

"They're willing to pay so much because they want you to…you know, lay it on."

"Lay what on?"

"You know, make it convincing."

I blink at her. "Alexander Maddox?" Of course I've heard of him. "Isn't he, like, a billionaire?"

"Many times over," Cleo confirms. "He's also hot, even if he is an absolute grump. I don't know if I've ever seen the guy in a good mood. But I do think there's a diamond under all that rough if he were to have a little fun for a change. He's what you'd call…uptight. He's under a lot of pressure with the company he's in charge of. But the way I see it, what's the point of having so much money if you can't enjoy it once in a while? Alexander doesn't seem familiar with that concept."

I shake my head. "There's no way I'm going on a fake date with Alexander Maddox."

Cleo has worked for Noah Maddox for a couple of years now and loves her job. She fills me in on the office gossip and has mentioned Alexander every now and then. According to her, he runs the old money family empire but is also a shareholder at Invested Enterprises, the company set up by his three brothers.

She holds up her phone, completely ignoring what I said. "This is him. See? Admit it. Extremely hot."

I glance warily at the photo. He's tall with thick dark hair, wearing an obviously-expensive suit. He could be a rugged male model, complete with the aloof frown. "As I said, I'm not going on a fake date with Alexander Maddox."

"Did you forget about the tiny detail of the two hundred thousand dollars I just mentioned?"

"As if he'd pay that much for one weekend."

"He would. Trust me, it's nothing to him."

"Well, you're going to have to find someone else. I'm busy."

"Doing what?"

"Working."

"Your work would benefit from a weekend in a very lively, scenic environment in which to show off your clothes and bikinis and whatnot."

"Paying someone to go on a date is just…weird."

"He's desperate to keep his distance from the insane wedding planner, according to Noah."

"Can't he just get a regular date?"

"He doesn't want complications. Which many women seem to give billionaires, who knows. And, as I mentioned, he's grumpy so he couldn't get one."

"Which is another reason to not do this. Forget it. Count me out. Who's next on your list of people crazy enough to consider doing something like this?"

Cleo sets her phone down, waiting for the waitress to top up our glasses and walk away.

She takes my hands across the table. "Ivy. I love you like a sister. I admire you, respect the hell out of you and I'm in awe of your beauty, talent and the way you've managed to hoist yourself from a difficult situation into a to-die-for Soho apartment and an amazing lifestyle. I've also supported you through your near obsession with getting your little brother into an Ivy League school. Which you've now done. Achievement unlocked. But I'm going to be honest with you. It's time for you to stop fixating on Josh and start thinking about yourself. Okay? You've put in the time and you've gotten the results you wanted. Now it's time for you to live a little."

I give her a look. "And you think fake dating Noah's grumpy brother is going to help me do that?"

She tilts her head, like she's studying me. "I think it would help you get a little bit of perspective. You'd wow the entire Hamptons. I want you to get out of the little cocoon you reside in for one weekend, to witness first-hand the effect you have on people. Plus, it'll be crazily luxurious. It might be fun."

"Fun?"

"Yes, that thing you don't get enough of? It's called fun, and even though Alexander is a grouch of epic proportions, he's seriously gorgeous, fabulously loaded and, if he does prove to be completely awful, at least there will be other hot, eligible bachelors galore at the wedding. You might meet someone else."

"Cleo—"

"You'll also make two hundred grand in two days. *More* than enough to make sure that Josh can live on campus or in his own apartment near campus and get the full university experience." Sometimes I regret telling her every tiny detail of my life. "In a single weekend, you can take all the worry about that part of his expenses completely out of the equation. It's totally worth it."

Damn it.

"I think it would be good for Alexander too," Cleo continues. "I've gotten to know him through Noah over the past two years and somewhere under all that moodiness—deeply buried, but I've detected it from time to time—is the inkling of a sense of humor. I almost feel like the two of you might actually hit it off."

"Are you saying I'm moody?"

"No. I'm saying you're so beautiful and smart and cool that you could thaw out even the most frozen, uptight billionaire into something that might resemble a decent human being."

"It's a ridiculous idea."

She takes a sip of her champagne. "Let me say it again. Two. Hundred. Thousand. Dollars. For *two* days, girlfriend. All you have to do is show up at his building on Park Avenue at five o'clock sharp on Friday afternoon. You'll be taking the helicopter. He's got one that takes off from his rooftop helipad."

"Holy shit."

"Yeah, we're talking serious money. He's the wealthiest of all the Maddox brothers because he took over Maddox Enterprises while the other three basically jumped ship to start their own company."

"I've never been to the Hamptons." *Am I actually considering doing this?*

"See? You're not living your best life, Ive. You've been too mired in self-preservation and parenting that precocious little nerd. Who, by the way, is now fully realized and ready to go off and live his own life."

"Hanging out with a total stranger and pretending to be his fake date sounds like it would be awkward as hell."

Cleo smiles at me, sensing that I'm starting to cave.

"You're a born performer, darling. Just think of the money. You'll be able to play the part like a freaking Oscar nominee. Enjoy the pool, drink your body weight in Moët and rub shoulders with the Hamptons elite for a weekend. It'll be interesting at the very least. Oh, and you'll be sleeping in the same bed."

"What?" I huff a laugh. "Absolutely not."

"No sex, of course. It'll probably be a ridiculously big king-sized bed. Just keep to your side and it'll be fine."

"Cleo, I'm not—"

"As I said, your performance needs to be *really* convincing, down to the tiniest detail. The ex is cunning. If she gets a whiff that this is anything but true love, I'll have to get Noah his coffee every morning for a whole year. Which would be a nightmare. He'd milk it for all it was worth."

"Ah," I say, leaning back in my chair, fully resolved to definitely refuse to do this. "So this is a bet."

"Not a *bet*, Ive. A *plan*. To stop Alexander's night-marish ex from hounding him all weekend. Noah and Colton have actually been really worried about him. He hasn't been himself lately because he hates the thought of spending the weekend with her. He's been miserable and even more grouchy than usual. Noah said he's just… really sad."

I fold my arms. She knows how to get to me, I'll give her that much. I'm much more likely to agree to this now that she's told me Alexander is in emotional turmoil. She's appealing to my empathic side. But something occurs to me. "You're Noah's assistant. Don't you get him coffee every morning anyway?"

Cleo rolls her eyes. "I'm an administrative and organizational genius, not a *coffee girl*." Like I've insulted her.

I smile, despite myself. "And if the evil ex *is* convinced, then what?"

"Noah has to get *me* coffee for a year. Please, for the sake of my self-respect, you have to really lay it on, Ive."

I ask her warily, "And how would I do that?"

"You know, sit on his lap, play with his hair, kiss him, that kind of thing."

I laugh, biting my lip. "Would you listen to yourself? You can't really expect me to do this, Clee."

"Why not? It's better than slouching around worrying about Josh all weekend. Which is exactly what you'll end up doing."

She doesn't know the half of it.

At least a weekend away would distract me. If the cops show up, pounding on my door and wanting to question me, I won't be there. I'll be at a weekend-long party. Which actually sounds like more fun than sitting around, waiting to get busted.

"Just think about those cool two hundred big ones," she reminds me.

I let it sink in. Josh could get the full college experience. He could live on campus and make a bunch of new friends and I could finally have some time to myself. I could start to relax after all these years of worrying about him. I could concentrate more on my music, without distractions. I could start dating. I might actually get a life.

For Josh, it's worth it. And for me.

I inwardly cringe. I know I'm going to wildly regret this, but two hundred grand is two hundred grand. I'm sure I can put up with 48 hours of living hell for the rewards this windfall will offer me. "Okay."

"Okay?"

"I'll do it."

Cleo's eyes light up. "You will?"

"It's only two days. I'm sure I can handle that. I hope. But I want the money in my bank account before four-thirty on Friday. I'll put on a good act—*if* you make it crystal clear that I'm not doing anything…real. No sex or anything like that."

Cleo nods earnestly. "Absolutely no sex. He said the same thing."

"He did?"

"Yes."

"Okay. Good. This is a fake date and nothing more."

Cleo clasps her hands with glee. "God, I wish I could be a fly on the wall and watch how this all plays out. It's going to be absolutely delicious."

"Either that or a disaster in slow motion."

Cleo takes my hand. "Don't worry about anything,

okay? Alexander's a reclusive CEO who gets out even less than you do, but he's not a bad person. Noah's always saying that he's a grump with a heart of gold. He just doesn't get an opportunity to express that side of his personality very often. And you'll be putting his brothers' minds at ease about his well-being."

"If you say so."

"Let's talk outfits," Cleo says. "The skimpier the better. What bikinis do you have?"

"One of my clients just sent me a white one that's not a thong but might as well be, and an animal print one that's basically a tiny few shreds of strategically placed fabric."

"Perfect. What dresses? The more skin, the better. Your body is insane, you might as well show it off."

I give her an exasperated look.

"What?" She asks innocently. "If we're doing this, we might as well do it correctly."

"We?"

"Okay, you. But I'm going to be cheering you on from Hell's Kitchen like a banshee. You'll be able to feel my supportive energy all the way out there in Southampton. What've you got for the wedding day?"

I think about it. "I've got a cute gold sleeveless dress I haven't worn yet. It might be perfect for a wedding."

"That sounds fabulous. What about Friday night? There's the rehearsal dinner. You know that little pink dress you tried on when I was visiting you a few weeks ago?"

"The short one with the lace?"

"Yes! That dress is stunning."

"I guess I could wear that one on Friday."

"I can come over and help you pack if you want."

"Okay."

She contemplates me for a few seconds. "Ive?"

"Yeah?"

"I just thought the money might come in handy, and he's a Maddox. I've preemptively made him promise to be nice to you. But I don't want you to do it if you feel unsure."

"It *would* be nice to have the money. For Josh. Just don't tell Noah my last name. Maybe I can fly under the radar and blend in for the weekend."

She tilts her head, smiling. "That's extremely unlikely, but okay, I won't tell them your last name. I'm sure Alexander will figure it out though. People will probably recognize you."

"They don't always. Maybe the Hamptons crowd doesn't know me."

"Please," Cleo says. "You have, like, a billion followers. But I won't tell. They might want to see a photo of you though. Is that okay? I've got this cute one on my phone I took the last time you came to dinner. Can I send Noah this one?"

She pulls up a random photo. "I guess it's not bad."

"Are you kidding?" Cleo squeals. "You're a freaking supermodel, girlfriend."

"Why do I get the feeling I'm totally going to regret this?" I mutter, as our waitress appears with our food.

Cleo's grinning at me. "Why do I get the feeling you're not?"

9

By Friday morning, I'm convinced this whole "fake date" is an extremely bad idea.

Cleo came over last night and packed my weekend bag for me, with bikinis, a few barely-there dresses and several minuscule silk shreds of lingerie. I've been instructed to "pull out *all* the stops" to make entirely sure that Alexander's ex believes beyond a shadow of a doubt that he and I are madly in love.

I keep checking my phone, expecting the text message from Cleo to tell me Alexander has called the whole thing off. I'm sure he'll come to his senses. Two hundred thousand dollars for one weekend seems very over the top. Can't he just tell his ex he's no longer interested in her and be done with it?

The message doesn't come.

Nothing from Josh either.

I also haven't heard from any detectives or lawyers, so at least there's that.

I go through my yoga routine. Then I do my ten minutes of meditation.

Then I grab my guitar, go out to my sunny little balcony and make the most of my brief window of quiet. I start strumming the new song I'm working on.

From where it's sitting on the table, my phone vibrates with an incoming text.

Checking my phone, I see the text is from Cleo and I'm relieved. I can spend the weekend working on my music instead of awkwardly pretending to be some random billionaire's true love.

> Thank me later. I managed to talk them into adding an extra fifty grand. Work it, girl!

Shit. So this is really happening.

> Also, a limo will pick you up in front of your building at four thirty. So you don't have to schlep your way over to Park Avenue. Alexander suggested it

Oh, and according to Noah, he's been staring at your photo "raptly" since Wednesday. But they have no idea about your identity beyond your first name and that one photograph. Your girl has your back!! Call me at 3. I need to give you another pep talk before your limo pick-up [heart emoji] [kiss emoji] [painting nails emoji]

A flurry of butterflies flutters through my stomach at the thought of getting picked up by Alexander Maddox's limo.

Like Cleo pointed out, I *am* a born performer—on stage. I love playing music and I don't really get stage fright. I genuinely enjoy having an audience.

But this is different.

Sit on his lap, Cleo insisted. *Play with his hair. Kiss him when the ex is watching.*

I don't even know *how* to kiss.

Even Cleo doesn't know I'm still a virgin. I don't know why I'm secretive about it. I guess I'm a little self-conscious about the fact that I'm 23 and incredibly inexperienced.

I've hardly ever dated, mostly because I've always been so preoccupied with doing my best to improve our situation. It's taken a lot of work and a lot of time.

I also shared a bedroom with my little brother until two years ago. And since then, well, guilty as charged: I've been focused on making sure Josh is on track.

It's true that I get a lot of offers from men. Online and at my gigs. But my schedule is full and it always feels like too much to take on. I can admit I'm overly protective of Josh, or maybe it's just that I don't want to introduce someone into his life until I'm sure it's someone who will stick around—and who I *want* to stick around. And I can never be sure about that.

I have trust issues when it comes to men, for obvious reasons. I don't overanalyze it. It is what it is. My father is the most unreliable person I've ever known and it's caused Josh and me a lot of pain and angst over the years. But we're okay now. So the last thing I want to do is rock our boat by inviting some fly-by-night stranger into our home and our lives. It's taken me too long to feel safe to risk that.

I know I'm overly cautious but I've forgiven myself for that. It's always been my plan to wait. To make sure Josh is good, and once he is, then I'll eventually focus on my own needs and wants.

Which, according to Cleo—and I guess I have to agree—it's now time to do.

After this weekend, I decide I'm going to do exactly that. I'll have enough money in the bank to not have to panic, knowing the finances are at least on track to give Josh whatever he needs.

Then I'll begin to test the waters in the dating scene.

Maybe the fake date with the billionaire will be good

for me. A trial run. A nice warm-up round for the real thing.

Sure, it's out of my comfort zone, but it can't be *that* hard. It's not like I have to do anything beyond possibly sitting on his lap and giving him the occasional kiss, very lightly. It's not going to be a *real* kiss, so it hardly matters.

If he's as aloof and uptight as Cleo described, he might not even want me to. It might just be a case of sitting next to him at the wedding, making polite, stilted conversation and pretending to find him appealing.

Easy.

Out of curiosity, I check my banking app.

Holy shit.

He's already deposited the two hundred and fifty thousand dollars.

I immediately transfer it into Josh's Columbia account. There's already a hundred grand in there from my savings, for his tuition, books and anything else he might need. But this will give us a buffer for next year, and the next, while I continue to save for the full amount.

We could have applied for a loan. A lot of people do. We still might. But I loved the idea of him being free and clear. I just want so badly for him to soar.

And maybe he actually will.

Wow. He's really going to Columbia. It still seems surreal. *He's going to college. I'm sure he's already transferred the money back into our father's bank account. He's having fun with his friends and the detectives haven't called.*

For the first time in a long time, I allow myself to relax a little.

Hell, maybe I *will* have fun in the Hamptons. Drinking obscenely overpriced champagne, being wined and dined, dancing. It doesn't sound so bad. I can't even remember a time when I had a whole weekend to just go with the flow and be pampered. In fact, I've never been pampered.

I've been very fortunate to have the success I've had, but growing up poor, you never take these things for granted. I spent shitloads on this apartment (and I'm still paying it off, which I will be for life), but other than that, I've never been frivolous.

Maybe frivolous feels good, who knows.

Checking the time, I notice it's already 2:54. I still need to shower and get ready. At least I'm already packed, with my outfit laid out by Cleo.

More butterflies take flight in my stomach when I think about the limo picking me up in just over an hour and a half. I'm not sure why I'm nervous. I don't need to be.

I do a quick Google search. For now, I have the upper hand. Alexander Maddox won't be able to search for me since he doesn't know who I am.

Alexander J.B. Maddox IV, 29, is the oldest son of A.J. Benjamin Maddox III. Alexander inherited the CEO position of Maddox Enterprises from his late father, who in turn inherited it from his father, who inherited it from his father. Maddox Enterprises was established in 1894 by Alexander's great grandfather Alexander J.B. Maddox, and, since its inception, has consistently been among the top ten highest-grossing investment groups in the country. It is rated as the ninth most profitable investment firm in New York State history.

Okay, so when Cleo described him as a multi-billionaire she wasn't joking.

Additionally, Alexander Maddox is on the Board of several prominent Fortune 500 companies, including Invested Enterprises, which is owned and run by Alexander's three brothers, Cash (CEO), Noah (CFO) and Colton (COO).

Alexander Maddox is famously reclusive. Little is known about his dating history, which he keeps fiercely private. Most recently, he's been photographed with Margot Russo, one of New York's most sought-after wedding planners, but whether or not they dated was not officially confirmed and they haven't been seen together in at least six months. According to socialite Sydney Valentine, who claims to have "shared time" with Mr. Maddox, he's a "commitment-phobe" and "has a personality that's as cold as ice…but in the sack he's a f#&?!ng inferno."*

Yikes.

I scroll through the few images of Alexander online. There's one of him at a charity event last year, but he's in the distance. One of him in his office, standing with his arms folded, photographed for an article in Forbes. And one of him on a red carpet with a woman. She's clinging to his arm, dressed in a puffy beige gown that looks like a slightly burnt meringue. She's smiling widely but Alexander looks pissed off.

Is this the ex?

I zoom in a little.

There's no denying he's handsome. Okay, like, insanely so. His hair is black. His eyes are strikingly blue. He's tall and fills out his tux like…well, like he's got serious muscles hidden under all those buttoned-up layers.

With his looks and all that money, it would be easy to be intimidated by him. But I make a decision here and now…*not* to be intimidated by him.

It's not a real date. I've already been paid. I promised to put on a good show and I will.

For a split second I think about darting over to Saks Fifth Ave and buying something linen and conservative. The clothes Cleo insisted on packing are the opposite of demure.

I check the time again and it's 2:59. I call her.

"Hey, Ive."

"Are these outfits actually appropriate for a Hamptons wedding?"

"Of course they are. Especially if it's *you* who's wearing them. Girl, you could wear a paper bag and still outshine all the socialites. Trust me. You want to make an impression."

"What kind of impression are we talking about?"

"A rock 'n roll impression. A gorgeous bohemian

genius goddess impression. Don't you dare second guess a single thing. I want you to promise me something, Ive."

"What?"

"Promise me you'll live in the moment, enjoy the stunning person you are and make the most of it. Your assignment—and I won't take no for an answer—is to let loose and have some fun. That's an order."

"Yes, drill sergeant."

She laughs. "I'm sorry. It's just that it's overdue."

"Okay. You're right."

"Are you wearing my favorite little pink number?"

"I'm just about to jump in the shower."

"Girl, it's three o'clock! Your limo will be there in an hour."

"You said 4:30."

"It'll probably be waiting by 4:15. Alexander is very punctual."

"It doesn't take that long to get ready."

"For you, maybe. I'm hanging up now or this will stress me out."

"Okay, I'm getting ready now."

"Good. Ive?"

"Yeah?"

"Love you. Thanks for doing this. Have fun. Call me the second you need any kind of moral support whatsoever. He *promised* to be nice. He's a little bit scared of me so I know he'll be true to his word."

I can't help laughing. "I'm sure he is. Love you too, Clee. I'll keep in touch."

"Embrace your stunning gorgeousness and go wild."

"I'll do my best. Talk soon."

We end the call and—shit—it's ten after three.

I jump in the shower, washing my long hair with the Extra Shine Luxe shampoo one of my clients sent me. Then I dry myself with a fluffy Infinite Puff towel I was gifted, and I put on the Tropical Bronze With A Hint of Glitter body butter I promote for another client. Being an "influencer" definitely has its perks. I have naturally olive skin but I love the light extra tan this body butter gives me, and it makes my skin look almost shimmery.

I have a few tiny tattoos on my arms, one on my hand and one on my right shoulder blade, all of which are fully on display. I wonder how many other guests at the wedding will have tattoos, almost smiling to myself. I bet Alexander Maddox doesn't have any tattoos.

I guess I'll find out, since we're sleeping in the same bed.

I've never slept in the same bed as a man before.

Deep breaths.

I dry my hair, leaving it down, flowing silkily over my shoulders.

I shimmy into the dress Cleo raved about. It's got a fitted lacy halter top with satin straps. It definitely shows off my boobs, which I know is part of the reason Cleo chose it. The skirt is pink and lightly fitted—and very short—with a slightly flouncy hem. I put a few gold cuffs around my wrists, put on some gold hoop earrings and drape a gold chain necklace around my neck.

My eyelashes are naturally long, but I put on some Magic Length mascara, Barely There Flawless foundation and Candy Pink Lusciousness lip gloss.

Finally, I find my gold heeled sandals to complete the look.

I take a few photos in my mirror, tagging my clients.

Cleo was right though. I love this outfit.

Ready or not, Mr. Hot MegaBucks, here I come.

I quickly text Josh.

> Going to a wedding in the Hamptons this weekend, believe it or not! Hope you're having fun (but not too much fun haha)

Checking the time again—oh, shit—it's 4:37. Oops, I'm seven minutes late.

I grab my bag, my small wheeled weekend suitcase, my keys, my charger, and I let myself out.

10

By the time I get to the street—*whoa*—the limo is waiting there, the driver leaning casually against the car checking his phone.

He looks up when I struggle to get my bag through the door with one hand. He steps onto the sidewalk to help me. "Miss Ivy?"

"Yes. Sorry I'm late."

"It's not a problem, Miss Ivy. May I?" He reaches for my small suitcase. I nod and he takes it and puts it into the trunk of the limo. Then he opens the passenger door for me. "Can I pour you a glass of Moët?"

"Um…no, thank you." But Cleo's command echoes through my brain. *Let loose and have fun. That's an order.* "Actually, maybe just one."

"Of course, Miss Ivy."

He pops the bottle that's on ice and as I slide into the back seat of the limo, he hands me the glass.

"Thank you."

"My pleasure, Miss Ivy. My sister's a big fan."

"Oh. Tell her thank you."

He bows a little, then closes the passenger door and soon we're on our way through Friday afternoon rush hour traffic.

I use the time to answer a few emails but we don't have far to go and before I know it we're pulling up in front of a large, intricate iron gate.

Who has a gate in New York City?

On Park Avenue, no less.

The gate is part of a walled courtyard that leads to the entrance of a tall, very stately-looking building. The driver retrieves my bag and uses a key card to unlock the gate. A doorman is waiting for us. The driver gives him my bag, bows again and leaves me with the doorman. From there we enter the building and take an elevator up.

"Are we meeting Mr. Maddox at his apartment?" I ask the doorman.

"No. At the helicopter. It's ready to depart. He's waiting for you."

I steal a glance at my phone. It's 5:17. Something gives me the feeling Alexander Maddox isn't used to waiting for people.

We get to the top floor and the doorman opens a door for me that leads out onto the roof.

Holy hell.

It's a roof garden, but much more than that. It has several levels and takes up the entire roof of the building. On a lower tier, there are trees planted in giant pots. There's a covered seating area and closed-in outdoor kitchen. There's a huge pool and hot tub. And a large greenhouse-type structure with wooden beams, chandeliers, couches and tropical plants inside. It's all very groomed, swish, wildly expensive-looking and so, so beautiful.

The entire city is sprawled around us. We're literally on top of the world.

I feel a twinge of nervousness at the sheer grandeur of it all. This kind of luxury would have cost millions and *millions* of dollars. But I guess it's not surprising that a man like Alexander Maddox would live in a sprawling penthouse with an accompanying roof garden in what looks like the most exclusive building in the city. He probably owns the whole building.

My gaze returns to the nearer, upper tier of the roof, where a giant helicopter sits on its circular helipad, its blade barely beginning to turn. The pilot is already in place. And a man is standing next to the helicopter, checking his watch.

Who could only be Alexander Maddox.

He's tall. Big, but lean. He's wearing a suit that's obviously been cut by the best tailors in the world to showcase every detail of his masculine perfection. I don't know if

I've ever really considered what a "good" suit might look like, but this is far beyond that. It's suit porn on freaking steroids.

When he looks up from his watch—a real watch, like a Rolex—and sees us approaching, his scowl barely softens.

Okay, wow.

Alexander Maddox is seriously gorgeous.

I walk closer. His eyes are pinned on me and they're an unusual shade of dark, smoldering blue that's almost violet. The glint in them is…electrifying, causing those little butterflies to flutter again.

He's watching me, his expression both stern and cocky, and it's a cockiness that's baked in. This is obviously a man who rules the world and always has. He was born as what you might call an alpha male and lives his life as one, in every conceivable category, and this detail sort of radiates off him.

But there's also an edge to him—of fascination, maybe. I get the feeling I've somehow caught him off-guard.

His hair is thick and black, smoothed into place, but a fraction longer and less tamed than you might expect from a billionaire mogul. Little flicks curl around his ears almost romantically.

He's rugged-looking, even in his bespoke Armani or whatever and he reminds me of a hero from another time. Like a Roman gladiator or some conquering general. I don't know why I say that. He seems larger than life. He's more good-looking and impressive than any man I've ever seen.

I'm standing in front of him now and he towers over me. I feel small and feminine next to his outrageously confident masculinity.

His gaze hasn't left me once and his fascination holds. The sternness has faded out. He looks almost beguiled.

He holds out a tanned, strong-looking hand. "You must be Ivy." His voice is deep, almost dark, with a husky edge to it that makes the tiny hairs on my arms stand up.

Whoa.

I hesitate for a split second, only because I'm not used to dealing with men, or at least not ones that look like *this*. His presence is intense. Even outside and with the breeze now being created by the helicopter blade, ruffling his hair, his energy feels…commanding.

I finally return the handshake and his big, warm hand completely envelopes my own. His grip is careful but hints at a ridiculously powerful strength. "Alexander Maddox."

"Nice to meet you, Alexander. I'm sorry I'm late."

Something behind his expression flickers at my use of his first name. He must be used to formality. He doesn't reply with the usual, *it's fine,* or *don't worry about it*. His gaze slides over me slowly, taking in my face, my hair. My outfit. My bare legs and my painted toes.

I can't help doing the same, sort of enthralled by all the details of him. The shape of him is somehow…

magnificent. His brawny shoulders and the muscles of his burly arms are defined even under the layers of his beautiful clothing. And it's fitting, I can't help thinking. This man *needs* gorgeous, obviously-expensive clothes. Nothing else would be good enough for him.

He's incredibly handsome, with strong, masculine features. *He's got nice eyes,* is what I'm thinking. His irises are vividly blue, framed by thick, dark lashes. The strong stripes of his eyebrows are barely furrowed. There's a detectable five o'clock shadow against his square, manly jaw.

Wow.

"I'll forgive you," he finally says. It almost sounds like a barely-playful warning. "Once."

Some deep instinct flickers. For a second I wonder if he might be dangerous.

He reads this in me and it amuses him. And maybe even pleases him. A challenge simmers in those smoky eyes.

I can feel my heartbeat in strange places as his smug, layered arrogance settles into me. I'm aware of a deep warmth low in my belly that's surprisingly...erotic.

Yikes.

But I hold his gaze, clinging desperately to my inner calmness and self-control. I think of the money. I think of Josh. And I can admit that this assignment doesn't feel nearly as awful as it did yesterday.

Fine. I'll see your challenge and raise you two hundred and fifty thousand dollars. This is a fake date and nothing more. I can handle you.

At least I hope I can.

He almost smiles and it occurs to me that Cleo's descriptions of this man don't match the first impression he's giving me at all. I'm not getting aloof or uptight. I'm getting self-assured animal power and purely *male* physicality.

"Are you ready?" he asks in that low, smooth voice, stoking the small rush of…whatever's going on in the low pit of my stomach…and lower.

God. Am I getting…wet?

"Yes," I say, sounding almost breathless.

My bag has already been loaded into the helicopter. Alexander opens the door and holds my arm as I climb in. He leans over me to fasten my seatbelt and his huge, looming presence gives me a not-entirely-unpleasant feeling of being dominated.

Cleo, I don't know whether to kill you or kiss you because damn, those Google images did not do this man justice.

Soon the helicopter blades are a blur and we're lifting off.

The view of Manhattan in the late afternoon light is stunning.

But I find myself more riveted by the hot, buff billionaire who hasn't taken his eyes off me once.

And we're on our way.

11

ALEXANDER

Twenty minutes earlier...

Fucking wonderful.

I should have known this would happen. The girl who won't give her last name—if Ivy is even her real first name—and who's already pocketed my quarter of a mil is now a no-show.

I'm not worried about the money. As annoying as Cleo may be, she does happen to be one of the most reliable people Noah has ever hired, according to him. Which means she can reliably make sure the money is returned.

Of course it's better this way.

It would never have worked. *Staging* being in love with someone would be impossible, now that I think about it. It was a monumentally terrible idea.

It's 5:12.

I don't wait for people. Ever. Especially Gen Z airheads who don't know how to stick to a goddamn timetable.

Taking my phone out of my pocket, I bring up her photo once more, getting ready to delete it.

I'll admit I've spent some time looking at it. Because it's a good photo. She looks sort of…dreamy. Her eyes are inky, her expression calm and somehow wise beyond her years.

Would you listen to yourself?

Something about the photo makes me feel a fraction less cynical about life in general. Which is unusual for me. The girl is stunningly, painfully beautiful.

It's probably just one of those filters people use. No doubt that's some app-developer's *intention*: to make you practically fall in love with people, just because they look so fucking perfect.

Not people. Just her.

Whatever.

I knock on the window, signaling to the pilot. I'm not waiting any longer.

I'll just have to cowboy the fuck up and tell Margot she can fuck off. Again.

What the hell was I even thinking? Noah and Cleo of all people somehow managed to talk me into something I would never usually consider.

All because of this photograph. Which is probably A.I.-generated anyway.

Still, I still can't quite bring myself to delete it.

Damn it.

I shove my phone back into my pocket and take one more look at my watch.

5:16.

The helicopter blades start to slowly spin and I'm about to open the door and climb in when I notice movement out of the corner of my eye.

The doorman has opened the door that leads to the main elevator. He's wheeling a small bag and he holds the door open.

The girl steps through it.

Well, look who finally decided to show up.

But my annoyance fades out almost immediately as I watch her walk toward me.

Holy hell.

I might have expected cute…but not *this*.

Okay, so it wasn't an A.I.-generated photograph.

In fact the photo doesn't even come close to capturing how stunning the girl actually is.

She's cute as fuck but also sexy in a way she doesn't even seem to be aware of.

She's wearing a little pink dress that barely covers the tops of her thighs. It's low-cut but not scandalously so. The lacy top part of it looks like it has one of those built-in wonder bras because her breasts—*holy fuck*—are just…

unreal. Very faintly, I can see the outline of her nipples, which are high and so fucking sweet, my cock, which is not at all happy about my extended dry spell, thickens hotly.

Her long hair is dark but has highlights of reddish-blond at the ends. It lifts gently in the breeze that's being kicked up by the helicopter, like she's a supermodel on the catwalk. Her bare legs are lightly tanned, like the rest of her. Her skin is golden, glittery and so flawless it makes my chest weirdly ache. She's wearing high-heeled sandals and her toenails are painted pink.

Jesus.

And her face.

Holy hell, her face.

She's devastatingly, jaw-droppingly beautiful. And there's more to it than that. Like the photograph, she has this sassy but at the same time soulful look on her face. Her expression is somehow both kind and determined. It's hard to describe, but something about the directness of her gaze slays me.

Okay, so she's not an airhead.

She's an absolute knock-out is what she is.

She stands in front of me and it takes me a second to snap out of the trance I seem to be mired in. Against all odds, I'm momentarily starstruck by her blinding, over-the-top beauty.

Get it together, Maddox. What the fuck.

I hold out my hand. "You must be Ivy."

It's a few seconds before she offers me her hand, like she still isn't entirely sure she'll go through with this. When she finally does, I take it carefully. She's so small, her skin cool and as soft as silk.

"Alexander Maddox."

"Nice to meet you, Alexander. I'm sorry I'm late." Her voice is angelic. It's sweet and soft, with the lightest smoky husk to it. I can't help but notice there's an innocence to her, but one that's seen the harder edges of life. I might be losing my mind, but her voice is the most alluring sound I've ever heard in my life. It makes me want to protect her—savagely, like a knuckle-dragging caveman—and it also makes me wonder if she's got a good singing voice. I bet she does.

Are you losing your marbles, asshole?

It's the sassy little attitude that's getting me hotter than anything else. She's not intimidated by me in the slightest—or she's masking it very well.

Most people I meet *are* intimidated by me. I'm big, I'm powerful, I'm bad-tempered and I'm rich as fuck. More often than not, people are daunted by the combination.

But not this one. She's feisty. Self-assured. Not remorseful in the least about keeping me waiting.

Her insolence is politely delivered, even if she chooses to call me by my first name, which hardly anyone I see on a daily basis does. Because I'm the boss. Her attitude makes me suddenly feel downright depraved. I have the raging urge to bring it down a notch in the most primal way imaginable. *By stuffing my big cock between those ridiculously luscious lips. By making her moan until she begs.*

Okay, I really am losing it.

"I'll forgive you." But I want to rile her. To get a reaction. To ruffle that calm facade. "Once," I add.

Her gaze lingers on mine. She bites her bottom lip gently and I watch her girlish white teeth barely sink into it. My cock hardens even more. *Damn it.*

She's so damn *beautiful.*

Her eyes are amber-colored, framed by long, sweeping lashes. Warmth colors her cheeks but she doesn't look away.

Good girl.

The wind is starting to pick up. I don't want her to get too windblown. She's too perfect for that. "Are you ready?" I open the door of the helicopter.

"Yes," she says, and we both hold each other's gaze, locked in a mutual fascination.

I help her climb in, fastening her seatbelt before taking my own seat.

Cleo deserves a goddamn promotion.

The pilot gets out to check that the doors are securely locked before climbing back in. Immediately the noise level drops. The Maddox helicopter was one of the last things my father bought before he died and it's a no-expenses-spared piece of machinery. There are eight roomy seats and two tables in what looks like a swanky, upmarket lounge. A bottle of champagne has already been popped and sits in a refrigerated, see-through chiller.

I pour two glasses and hand her one. She takes it, and her fingers graze mine, causing those light flags of pink to warm her cheeks again.

"This wedding might be easier to deal with when inebriated rather than stone cold sober," I warn her. Although—and the thought is an unfamiliar one—I suddenly find myself almost looking forward to the weekend.

"Whose wedding is it?" She takes a sip.

It's impossible not to notice the contours of her body in that dress. The way the silk glides against her sweet, lush curves. I make a point of not staring but it takes effort. Her beauty is clean-looking, like she's glowing from within with freshness and health. She's absolutely gorgeous. "A friend from Harvard Business School. His name is Blake Anderson. His fiancee's name is Leah Preston. I've known both of them for years. Blake asked me to be his best man."

"Cleo said your ex is the wedding planner." Her amber eyes are earnest. There's no awkwardness in the mention of my "ex," but it annoys me—not that Ivy has asked, but that she's going to have to put up with Margot Russo for two entire days. I have the sudden urge to protect this exquisite girl from the hurricane of melo-drama that always surrounds Margot.

"Yes. I'd hardly even call her my ex though." I'm not sure why I feel the need to clarify this, but I do. "We dated for a short time and it was…well, it was a living hell, if you really want to know."

She's watching me, like she's not sure if she believes me or not, and she's not sure why I would be telling her that.

"I'm not sure how I let Noah and Cleo talk me into this," I admit. "But thank you for being here. I'm going to apologize in advance for the scrutiny you'll be under. People are going to be curious about the date I'm bringing."

"It's fine. I'll put on a good show. That's what you're paying me for, right? And thank you, by the way. It's very generous. I promise I'll be worth the money."

She's already worth the money. And there's an unrecognizable corner of me that wishes this wasn't about money.

Ivy tucks a strand of her hair behind one ear and I notice the sprinkling of tiny tattoos on her arms. There's the musical note on her wrist, the one I noticed in the photo. One of a feather on the delicate skin of her inner arm. A dragonfly. And, further up, a tiny dove.

She'll definitely get attention in the Hamptons, for many reasons, including her Bohemian, artistic style. Most of the people who will be attending this wedding all have the same personal shoppers, or might as well, who source their clothing from some overpriced store that only stocks linen.

And she's young. Really fucking young. Cleo mentioned she's 23 but she looks younger. Cleo also mentioned she's "talented" and I'm curious. "What's the significance of the musical note? Are you a musician?"

She blinks those long lashes at me, clearly hesitant about giving me too much information. "Good guess."

I don't want to find out more about her just because I'm paying her to be my fake date. I genuinely want to know. "What kind of musician?"

"I'm a singer and a songwriter."

"Anything I would have heard?"

"I guess it depends on what kind of stuff you listen to. We should probably get our stories straight, if we're going to be convincing." Her abrupt change of the subject almost makes me smile. Not a lot of people surprise me. She's not at all what I was expecting. "People might ask us how we met. How long we've been dating. What would you like me to say?"

It's a good point. "How about we say we met at a party at Invested Enterprises. At the Sky Bar, on their top floor. Have you been to their offices with Cleo?"

"Yes, once."

"Let's say…two months ago."

"Okay." There's a shyness to her, but one she's practiced at overcoming. Something gives me the feeling she's used to performing and I find myself not just wanting to know more about this detail of her, but *every* detail of her. I know for a fact I've never been more beguiled by a woman in my life.

"You should probably tell me your last name," I suggest, "so I can introduce you to people. Or you can make one up if you prefer."

She fixes me with those eyes the color of cognac that's been warmed to the perfect temperature. "Jones," she finally says.

"Jones?"

"Yes."

I almost laugh and it's an unfamiliar feeling. "You can't do any better than *Jones*? Really?"

She laughs lightly, against her will. And if I thought she was pretty with the sassy pout and the *I-can-do-this* determination to make light of what's bound to be an awkward situation—us—her smile and her angelic little burst of laughter literally tilts my world off its fucking axis. I don't know why. Okay, I do know why. Because she's the most enchanting, beautiful creature I have ever, ever seen.

"Okay," she admits. "It's not Jones but I'd prefer to keep a degree of separation, if you don't mind."

"Up to you." I adjust my jacket to—hopefully—disguise the fact that my cock is really fucking hard at this point. And I *do* mind. "I'd rather you found me to be trustworthy with information like that, but I like a challenge. I'll just have to try to convince you I'm not a stalker or the devil by Sunday afternoon."

Another coy smile and it hits me somewhere in the middle of my chest. Her mouth is so damn perfect. Her lips are pink and plump and lightly shiny. The whole effect is doing things to me that are new. I can feel my fascination digging deeper in a way I can't control. Which is fucked up. I control *everything* in my life.

She twirls a coiled strand of her long hair around a finger. The sassy attitude is back.

Which makes my cock throb. "It might make the act more believable if I can answer questions when people ask. And they will."

She relents, but barely. "What do you want to know?"

"Anything you want to tell me."

"I just turned twenty-three. I live in Soho. I have one brother who's almost eighteen. I'm a musician and an influencer."

"An influencer?"

"Yes."

"I know what it means, but I've never really thought about what someone who 'influences' actually does."

"I create content. And advertise products on my clients' behalf through my platform, mainly on Instagram and TikTok."

"And they pay you to do that."

"Yes."

"To be honest, I've never actually looked at Instagram or TikTok," I admit.

She smiles and shakes her head a little, like she finds this unbelievable, and maybe it is. I read somewhere that American teenagers spend an average of five hours a day looking at social media. "I figured that. I googled you. I know you don't do social media. But it can be very lucrative. So I try to make the most of it."

I top up her glass, then my own. "It's hardly fair that you googled me but I can't google Ivy Jones."

She giggles and takes another sip of her drink but dismisses my complaint. "What else do you want to know?"

"What's your favorite movie of all time?"

She thinks about this for a few seconds. "That's way too hard."

"Name one."

She gets that dreamy look again and this downright fucking charms me—and I can't ever remember being *charmed*—because it's a look I recognize, from the photo, and it makes me feel like I know her, even though we've only just met. "I like the classic rom-coms. You know, the ones you can watch over and over and they never get old because by the end, you always feel good that they got their happy ever after that was meant to be all along."

I'm not sure I've ever seen a movie like that. "Like what?"

"You know, like Sweet Home Alabama, Sleepless in

Seattle, The Holiday. They're fantasies, but they make me feel…I don't know…hopeful."

"Hopeful?" My question almost makes it sound like the word is foreign to me. Come to think of it, it basically is.

"Yes."

"I'll have to watch them sometime."

"You've never seen them?"

"No."

"*Any* of them?"

"No."

She's shocked by this. "What kind of movies do you watch?"

"I don't know. Mainly war movies. Occasionally the movies of premiers I get invited to or the ones made by the studios I own a share of. I don't really have a lot of time to watch movies."

Her mouth quirks empathetically. "Well, that's too bad. Escapism can be good for the soul."

"Really?"

My question is funny to her. "Yes. Sometimes unplugging from the harshness of reality for a few hours and just having a little bit of mindless fun can be healthy."

"As I said, I don't really have time."

She bites her lip again and—*goddamn it, her mouth.* "You don't have time to be happy?"

I consider the question. "No. Not usually."

A little huff of laughter escapes her. "No wonder

you're grumpy," she teases, but she follows it up quickly. "That's what they told me, that you're grumpy. But I get it. I didn't used to have time either. But it helps. I'll show you if we have time. Maybe we could watch a movie together, since we've got the whole weekend. You can tell me what you think."

"Okay," I'm surprised to hear myself saying. I can hardly get offended that Cleo thinks I'm grumpy. I *am* grumpy, especially around Cleo. And I want nothing more in this moment than to be given lessons in escapism by this gorgeous, fresh-faced little nymphette.

It feels connective, that we've made this plan together. That we have this thing we're going to do together that no one else knows about.

The helicopter starts to descend and the estates of Southampton are dotted around the landscape below us.

I watch Ivy's face, reflected in the glass and illuminated by the low sun, which hovers at the horizon line, painting the water with an orange glow. She's taking in the view of the green of the trees and the manicured lawns, the stripe of the beach and the blue water of the Sound.

I'm relieved to have a minute to just stare at her beauty. Her full, pink lips barely parted, her eyes that are light gold in the sunlight.

For the first time in a long time, I allow myself to savor the moment.

The girl is a unicorn. I've smiled more in the past forty-five minutes than I have in the past ten years.

She's here, she's gorgeous and she's mine for the entire weekend.

It takes me a few seconds to identify the emotion I'm feeling.

It's been a long time since I've felt it.

Too long, is what I'm realizing.

I feel hot and spellbound and fully alive, but most of all what I fucking feel is *happiness*.

12

WE START to descend into Southampton, giving us a better view of the grand houses surrounded by lawns so manicured, checkerboard patterns have been mowed into the neon-green grass. The wide strip of sugar-sand beach and the blue water just adds to the perfection. Who *lives* like this?

The scene is surreal and hyper-fantastic, like something out of a fairytale instead of real life.

Alexander doesn't seem interested in the view. I guess he's used to it. He's watching me, as he's been doing the entire trip, and a smile almost touches his lips, like he's amused by my wide-eyed awe.

"It's been way too long since I left the city." I try not to stare at the little dimple that appears then disappears on his cheek. The man even has a *dimple*. Billionaires shouldn't have dimples. Especially not sexy, built ones with wide shoulders and muscular arms that look like they're testing the limits of Armani's stitching capabilities.

It's unfair that every single detail of him is somehow ideal. It's easier to take in one thing at a time. The combination of all of it—the handsome face, the thick hair, the big, outrageous body—is dazzling me. It's like staring at the sun.

"Have you traveled much?" His low, husky drawl makes me aware of a warm, light pulse in…an incredibly intimate place. *Yikes.*

"I've been to New Jersey a few times. Philadelphia. And once to Virginia." To perform, but I don't mention that part. "Other than that, I've lived most of my life within a two mile radius."

I've had plenty of invitations, from all over the country. Austin. L.A. Seattle. Even London. But of course I've always been worried about leaving Josh for too long. I figured I'd get a chance to travel later.

Now, it feels both exciting and daunting that my life is about to change so dramatically.

In fact, it already *has* changed. It's changing right now. I'm on the arm of a hot billionaire, ready to take the Hamptons by storm. Okay, maybe not by *storm*, but a small corner of me is excited by the newness of this weekend's adventure.

And my personal fake-date-for-the-weekend matches the fairytale. He's ridiculously beautiful and not at all what I was expecting.

He's definitely grumpy, as Cleo promised, but it's more of a hardened cynicism than actual *mean*ness. Like he's lived his entire life being thrown into the deep end of corporate hell and has no time to be anything but laser-focused. Which I guess comes with the territory of running your family's four-generation multi-billion dollar empire.

"If you could go anywhere in the world, where would you go?" His question catches me off-guard. It's genuine. It feels weirdly personal.

And it's easy to answer. "Tahiti or Bora Bora or one of those places where they have those little huts that sit above the water and it's so blue and clear it doesn't look real. The hut has a glass floor so you can see the colorful tropical fish swimming around underneath. There's a deck off the front of the hut and you can dive straight into the turquoise ocean that's as warm as the air. I have a picture of one of those huts on my screensaver. I think about it all the time."

He smiles at my description. A real smile—and *wow*. He reminds me of one of those mythical gods that flies down from Mount Olympus every now and then to mix with us mere mortals. "I'll see if I can get us a couple of tickets."

"Maybe for our next fake date," I joke.

His five o'clock shadow seems to have darkened. His mouth is full and masculine and lightly sneering. His dark hair has that barely-there wave to it and makes me wonder what it might feel like to run my fingers through it.

He might let me, is what I'm thinking—as part of the show we're putting on. The man is practically dripping with sex appeal.

But this is purely a business arrangement, of course. I try to ignore the fact that his closeness is having a physical effect on me. My body feels warm and flushed and *reckless* in a way that's new to me.

We land on a huge stretch of immaculate lawn that's a short distance away from a cluster of large saltbox buildings. Clearly the wedding venue.

It's just beginning to get dark now.

The pilot jumps out and comes around to open the door for us.

"Are you ready?" Alexander asks me.

This is it. Show time. "How do you want to do this?" I ask him. "Should I…hold your hand?"

Those little crinkles around the edges of his eyes as he smiles are unfairly…endearing. "How about I hold yours. Don't worry about anything. I'll take care of you."

It's a heavier offer than I was expecting and it touches some deeply-rooted emotion in me that I can't name. No one's ever said those words to me before. Not once.

He unfastens my seat belt and helps me climb down from the helicopter. Alexander's hand, as he takes mine, is warm, his grip sure and strong.

I'm a little nervous, but I'm used to being stared at.

I've spent a lot of time on stages and I live my life in the public eye.

Still, this is different. This role is new. I'm fending off Alexander Maddox's rabid admirers, and one in particular. I'm the enemy in this situation. Or at the very least, the rival.

I psyche myself up for the performance I'm about to give. Whenever I'm about to go on stage, I visualize a glowing orb of power inside my chest that radiates warm stars of energy that charm everyone they touch. It sounds crazy when I describe it, but it works. An old jazz pianist who I happened to meet the night I had my debut solo performance at a little venue in the West Village called Eva's gave me that advice. His name was Rocky and he told me it's what he always does when he plays; he pictures every musical note he's playing as "a firefly of magical resonance that charms everyone who hears it." I loved that. The words stuck with me and I've used Rocky's method ever since.

So I do it now.

Alexander squeezes my hand, glancing down at me from his six-foot-whatever, and his expression is sort of beguiled, like he can *feel* my little fireflies. "I've got you," he says.

And there he goes again with these intense little promises that are basically the nicest things anyone has ever said to me.

I've got you?

No one's ever *had* me. Not really. Not my mother, who handled her imploding marriage, her bitter divorce, her sudden and very solo parenting gig and her illness as well as it could all be handled. But she was understandably overwhelmed. Distracted. Heart-broken. And because of all of that, profoundly disengaged from having my back. It became too much to ask and so I never expected it.

Not my father, of course.

Not my brother, who always saw me as a guide, a provider but also as an annoyance, at least some of the time, cramping his style, like a typical teenager does.

So the words hit me harder than maybe they should. Tiny pieces of my soul react to them like parched earth that's just received its first drop of rain. I want to drink them in.

I'll take care of you. I've got you.

Not only is my soul reacting to Alexander Maddox in a way I can't quite control, so is my body. It's an intimate thing, holding hands. His grip is firm and sure. The contact causes my heart to beat faster. I'm aware, again, of a pulsing warmth between my legs. A light, tingling ache and a low excitement that's needy and slippery and restless.

Wow.

Fairy lights and lanterns are everywhere, and carefully-placed spotlights illuminate statues and trees around the expansive lawn area. Under a grapevine-laden pergola, tables have been set, decorated with flowers and dozens of candles. There's a stage, where instruments and a sound system have already been set up and a lone harp player is playing Mozart.

There's a dance floor. A stonework path leads toward an arch, covered in roses, looking out over the beach. Rows of chairs have been set up for tomorrow's ceremony.

The hotel is stately and picturesque, Cape Cod-style but with white columns and a modern, luxury flair.

Clearly no expense has been spared. Every single detail screams *this cost a boatload of money!*

We walk toward the small crowd of people who are all watching us approach.

A gorgeous blonde woman in a light green dress comes running over to us on sky-high heels. She's followed closely by a good-looking man dressed in an outfit that could be straight out of a Tommy Hilfiger catalogue.

"You made it!" the woman exclaims. "And you're only half an hour late! Just joking."

"My fault," I confess. "I'm so sorry."

"Leah," says Alexander, "meet Ivy. Ivy, this is Leah, the blushing bride. And Blake, her lucky groom."

Blake shakes Alexander's hand and pats him on the back. "Ivy, it's a pleasure."

"Nice to meet you both."

Leah glances at our hands, noticing how Alexander's is still tightly clasped around mine. "Blake and I have been *dying* to know who this mystery date is! Anyone who can make Alexander late for *anything* must mean it's serious," she laughs. "We're so glad you're here."

She seems nice, and I internally breathe a sigh of relief. But then she gasps. "Wait a minute. You're Ivy Laine!"

Shit. "Um…yes."

Alexander catches my eye.

Damn it, my cover is already blown.

"What? Oh my god! Alexander, you never told me you're dating *Ivy Laine!*"

"So it would seem," Alexander murmurs.

Leah is overcome. "I am *such* a huge fan. I've been listening to your newest album on repeat for *months*."

"Can confirm," says Blake.

"I absolutely *love* your music," Leah gushes. "That song called Dreaming of You, oh my god, it just hits me where I live every single time. You're *so* talented."

"Thank you so much." It's always nice to hear.

Alexander is watching me slyly. I should have known this would happen. It's getting harder for me to go out in public without someone recognizing me.

Leah chides him. "Alexander, I can't believe you didn't tell us you're dating Ivy Laine! How did you two *meet?* How long have you been dating?"

I answer without missing a beat. "We met at a party in the Sky Bar at Invested Enterprises. My best friend Cleo works there and Alexander's brothers, of course, own the company. We started talking and we just sort of clicked. I guess it was around two months ago, wasn't it, honey?"

His eyes are blue with intensity. "Yes, sweetie, it's been exactly two months."

"Alexander, you sly dog, keeping this from me for *two whole months*!"

"I knew you'd demand to come over and meet her," Alexander replies smoothly. "And we've been busy."

"Doing what?" asks another woman sharply, who's just joined our circle.

I guess immediately that she's the infamous ex. She has a dark brown bob and she's wearing statement tortoise-shell glasses. She's slim, with impeccable posture. She's carrying an iPad and is dressed in a beige linen jumpsuit with a beige belt and beige shoes. Her look is very…beige. She's beautiful, in a severe, in-control, one-too-many-fillers, Hamptons kind of way, but my first impression is that she's just…completely wrong for him.

Alexander immediately tenses. His expression changes, to the grouchy glower I recognize from the photo I saw online of the two of them. He's suddenly morphed into the grumpy workaholic Cleo described, and I find myself missing…*him*. The softer, playful version of his personality that shone through when we were alone together.

"This must be the highly-anticipated plus one," the woman says, her voice full of authority and self-importance, but with an edge. There's a longing behind her expression that's hard to miss. It's easy to see she's still pining for Alexander.

"Margot, this is Ivy J—Laine," Alexander quickly corrects himself. "Ivy, meet Margot Russo, the wedding planner."

Margot scowls at the job title, like she would have preferred being introduced as The One That Got Away.

All the humor in him is suddenly, completely gone and I remember what Cleo told me, about how Alexander's brothers were discussing how miserable he's been lately. It was one of the reasons I agreed to do this fake date in the first place.

Margot's checking out my outfit, my hair, the fit of my dress. My tattoos. I'm here to play a role and this is my moment. But I also want to ease the obvious tension that's now radiating off Alexander. I slide my arm around his waist under his jacket, like it's second nature. His body is unbelievably hard and so warm I instinctively lean in. "Alexander was telling me how in-demand you are. And how you're the most sought-after wedding planner in New York."

"Oh." She wasn't expecting me to compliment her. She watches as Alexander wraps his arm around me, pulling me closer, playing his role perfectly.

God, he smells good. That woodsmoke and whiskey spice. So incredibly masculine.

Leah is still beaming. "Margot, are you familiar with

Ivy's music? She's *amazing*. She writes all her own songs and has literally *millions* of followers." Leah pauses. "I mean, only if you'd agree to it of course, Ivy, but maybe you'd consider…singing a song at our wedding? Can you imagine, Blake?" She places a hand on my arm. "But no pressure. You're here to enjoy a weekend away. I would only want you to do it if you wanted to. But we would be *so* honored."

Margot looks highly pissed off by the suggestion. "The wedding is already planned, down to the minute. I'm afraid it would be too difficult to try to squeeze that in, especially since it's so last minute."

Leah's persistent. "How about tonight then? At our rehearsal dinner?"

Blake smiles at his fiancée. "Honey, I'm sure Ivy would prefer to just enjoy the evening as our guest."

"Of course she would," Margot agrees.

Leah bites her lip, blinking expensively-enhanced eyelashes. "Maybe…one song?"

I glance at their faces, all of which have very different expressions. "I mean…I wouldn't mind at all, but only if you're sure it wouldn't disrupt the schedule."

"Really?" Leah clasps her hands together gleefully. "Oh my god, are you kidding? You definitely would *not* be disrupting the schedule. When do you want to do it? Like…now? Can you sing Dreaming of You?"

Blake chuckles. "Leah, honey, Ivy just got here. Let's give her and Alexander a chance to get a drink and find their table. Are you sure you don't mind, Ivy? Don't let my almost-wife bulldoze you into it."

"I'd be happy to do it for such a special occasion."

"I can't believe *Ivy Laine* is at my *wedding!*" Leah exclaims. "And she's going to *sing!* This is unreal. It's *such* a good omen, I can feel it."

Even Margot can't argue with that. Staging as many good omens as possible is part of a wedding planner's job description. She begrudgingly types something into her iPad as she watches Alexander's thumb gently grazing my neck, almost absent-mindedly but in a way that's surprisingly intimate.

I wasn't expecting his warmth to be so…comforting. "Come on, sweetheart," he says. "My girl needs more champagne."

My girl.

Margot scowls at his endearment, a flicker of real heartbreak behind her eyes. But then she's temporarily distracted by the caterer, who approaches her with some issue from the kitchen.

More people are arriving, diverting the attention of our hosts, which gives us a chance to escape. A passing waiter offers a tray of champagne flutes and Alexander takes two, handing me one. He leads me over to the area where the tables are set up and we find our seats.

Decorative place cards have our names stenciled into them, and I notice that Leah has seated Alexander next to her. Someone named Ethan has been allocated the seat on my left.

Alexander pulls my chair out for me and we both sit. "Ivy Laine, huh."

"Guilty as charged," I admit.

"Cleo didn't mention the part where you're a famous musician."

"I'm not that famous."

As we take our seats, Alexander takes his phone out of his pocket. "L-A-N-E?"

"L-A-I-N-E. Please don't google me."

"Oh I'm googling you, sweetheart."

But I gently take his phone from his hands and he lets me do this. I put it face-down on the table. "Just ask me. I'll tell you whatever you want to know."

"I already tried that. In the helicopter."

"I'm sorry. I just didn't want it to get in the way."

"In the way of what?"

"I thought maybe I could fly under the radar for the weekend."

"No such luck." He's doing that thing again where he studies my face sort of raptly. His eyes linger on my mouth. "It would be impossible for you to fly under any radar, Jones."

I smile at the nickname. "If I didn't know better, Maddox, I might have mistaken that for a compliment."

He pulls my chair closer so my knees are in between his. The pendant lights cast a halo over his dark hair and his strong features. His blue eyes burn with that ever-present challenge that seems to have the power to plant a tiny pulse inside me. I can feel my heartbeat between my legs and my panties feel…*wet*.

Help.

The harp player bows to some light applause as she leaves the stage.

"I hope you don't mind that they want me to sing," I say. "It wasn't really part of our…deal."

He's relaxed now, still holding my hand. His thumb lightly caresses my palm. "Clearly it would break Leah's heart if you refused. Are you sure *you* don't mind?"

"It's fine."

Margot is hovering near three members of a band, who are preparing to take the stage. She points in the general direction of where Alexander and I are sitting, her eagle-eyed gaze lingering. On how close we're sitting. On the way Alexander is holding my hand.

So I do what I'm being paid to do. And I find myself…*not* hating the thought of it. I mean, this isn't difficult. The grumpy billionaire is turning out to be more than a little irresistible. I've been quietly wondering what that thick black hair would feel like between my fingers since the minute I saw him.

"Cleo told me to…play with your hair," I murmur, almost breathless with the heady cocktail of his man-scent, his warmth and the anticipation of what I'm about to do.

"She did, did she?"

"Do you want me to?" I'm pretty sure he's okay with it. Not only because he paid me two hundred and fifty thousand dollars to do exactly that, but also because his eyes are glowing like blue embers, with a danger-edged challenge behind them.

"As a matter of fact, I do."

Watching his eyes, I lean closer and I slowly, carefully smooth back an unruly lock of it.

He smells like warm sun and late nights. Like whiskey and smoke on a fall afternoon, Upstate. Not that I know what an Upstate fall afternoon actually smells like, but I can imagine it. Laughter on a crisp sunny day with low golden sun and the reds and oranges of the falling leaves. I crave him with a deeply romantic side of myself I'm just beginning to discover. It's a part of myself I've never really had a chance to indulge. I let my fingers weave into the course silk. "She's watching," I whisper.

"I don't care what she's doing. I only care about what you're doing."

He doesn't like the mention of *her*, I can see this. And I suddenly feel the desire to free him from whatever grasp she feels she has on him. "Do you want me to…"

"To…?"

"To kiss you?"

His dark amusement makes him look even more handsome, if that's possible. I can feel the heat rise to my face. He pulls me onto his lap, his burly arms supporting me. "Make it good, Jones."

God. The huge ridge of him underneath me is rock-hard. *He's…holy shit…is that his….?*

I can practically hear Cleo's voice through the airwaves. *Of course it is, girl! What else would it be?*

He's…freaking…*huge.* I mean, I've never sat on a man's lap before. Not once. I didn't have a father or uncles and both my mother and my aunt had been so badly burned by men, they completely gave up on trying to find someone who wouldn't smash their hearts once again into smithereens. Of course I have friends and acquaintances and fans, but I've been distracted by work and by Josh. I've also been wary, because of my trust issues. I really haven't had a lot of time for…exploration. Right now I'm learning more about the anatomy of a fully adult and very virile male body in the prime of its life than I ever have.

I'm also learning what a fully adult and very virile male body in the prime of its life *does* when it's pressed up against an *incredibly* intimate part of me in all its gigantic, rock-hard glory.

It cranks a mild curiosity and a half-baked craving into something else altogether. A wild need courses through my veins in hot pulses. The silk of my dress is very fine and my panties are nothing more than a shred of barely-there lace. *I can feel every ridge of him as the throbbing heat of his massive hard-on presses against my pussy, which feels soft and slippery, cradling the huge, rigid shape of him invitingly.*

Holy shit.

Not only that, but a warm, sweet ache centers in my clit, making me squirm against him.

Oh my god.

If I kept doing that, if I kept squirming just like that, I think I could...I *know* I could...*come*. Something I've never, ever done before. The elusive orgasm, which all of humanity is having thousands of, if the internet has any truth to it, every chance they get. Except for little old me, who's been my brother's caretaker for as long as I can remember—and if you want to know if sharing a bedroom with your baby brother when you're going through puberty, or how living in the same apartment with him as *he's* going through puberty might dampen your sex drive, I can tell you it really does. Because I know all about it.

And right now, I'm much, much more turned on than I've ever been. I so badly want to...*get there*. I want to *feel*, so desperately.

"How many times has Ivy Laine been kissed?" comes the low growl, like he can guess that I'm inexperienced.

I don't know why I feel compelled to be honest with him. "Twice," I admit. "Once in middle school and once at a party in high school. I can't remember either of their names."

"Seriously?" A half-incredulous, half-sincere smile

touches his lips. "*Middle* school counts for half of your kisses?"

"I know. It's a little sad but it is what it is. I've been busy."

"Doing what?"

"You really want my life story right now? I'm supposed to be kissing you."

The humor in him is back, inked with heat. "You can tell me all about it when we're watching the movie."

"Movie?"

"The rom-com."

"Oh. Yeah. Okay."

"I guess it's going to be a serious case of third time lucky for Ivy Laine, then."

I stare into his midnight-dark eyes as his head barely tilts. "You think so?"

"I know so." His voice is dark. Commanding. His CEO's voice. "Do it."

A newly-discovered piece of me—the one I discovered as soon as I sat down onto his massive erection—*wants* to obey him. It wants to please him and turn him on. It wants to drive him crazy with lust.

Girl, who are you?

Most of all it wants to taste his sneering, perfect mouth.

So I place my hand gently on his square jaw, letting my fingers explore. It's rough with his stubble. The scratchy, swarthy textures of a man are so foreign to me, it's almost daunting. But my new craving has a restless edge. I lean closer and I slowly, slowly brush my lips against his.

Alexander goes very still, letting me softly kiss his mouth. But the ridge underneath me rears up, hardening even more, pressing more strongly against my clit.

Oh my god, that feels good.

He makes a low, savage sound and it's basically the sexiest sound I've ever heard in my life. I go shamelessly wet, my practically nonexistent panties clinging to my pussy, making the writhing squirm of my body feel so good I think I'm…*god, I'm so close.*

Alexander grips my hip in one hand and my jaw in the other, holding me in place. And he kisses me back.

He tastes like champagne and mint and something darker—something almost unbearably appealing. His hand moves, wrapping around my hair, pulling me closer until my breasts are pressed against his broad chest and I'm pliant against him.

His mouth opens mine, and as soon as he gains entry, his tongue slides into my mouth, tangling with mine, sending warm currents of warmth directly to my softening pussy. *He tastes so freaking good.* Wanting more, I gently suck on his tongue, which makes him groan.

Oh my god.

This is supposed to be a performance. It's not even close to that. The *need* in me to get closer to him feels greedy and primal. He tastes like lust. He tastes like dreams coming true.

Both my hands are in his hair now and I hold soft fistfuls of it as his tongue thrusts and his kiss deepens.

"Ladies and gentlemen, we have a surprise for you this evening," a strident voice comes through the microphone, jarring me a little. Margot, of course. "Turns out we have a superstar amongst us who has generously agreed to perform a song for us this evening. Please find your seats. Ivy Laine, please come to the stage now."

We break the kiss slowly, like we're drugged from each other's effect. His eyes are an unholy blue, his black hair ruffled now from my hands. I gently smooth it a little.

The timing isn't ideal. I'm flushed. *I'm wet.* I'm crazily turned on.

There's the low commotion of people murmuring. They all turn to look at me.

Alexander reluctantly lets me go. I climb off of his lap, doing my best to inconspicuously smooth my dress. "I-I'll be right back."

"I'll be waiting." Gruffly. Like he's pissed off now that I agreed to Leah's request.

I make my way up to the stage. One of the guys in the band hands me an acoustic guitar. "I'm a fan," he grins.

"Thank you."

I sling the guitar across my body, grateful for the small shield it provides, and I make a point of visualizing my inner glow. Rocky's rock-solid advice that never fails me.

It's easy to do tonight, like it's tuning into *another* glow. The new one, that's hot and wet and just discovered what it feels like to *almost* come from a single kiss.

I send a few imaginary fireflies into the crowd. I send the brightest one to Alexander, who's watching from his seat.

The other people at our table are taking their seats now and he shakes someone's hand but doesn't get up.

I strum a few chords. And I start to sing.

13

ALEXANDER

As soon as Ivy starts to sing, my new obsession revs up around a thousand goddamn gears, landing somewhere around overdrive. I vaguely remember wondering if she had a good singing voice the first time I heard her speak.

Her voice is more than "good." It's the kind of voice that stops people in their tracks. Not a single person at this party is talking. Everyone is completely riveted by her. Not just by the way she sounds, but also by the way she looks under the spotlights, like a gorgeous little tattooed angel who just fell from heaven and decided to sing us a song.

She has a stage presence that I might not have expected when I first met her. She's practically glowing with endearing charisma and pure artistic radiance.

She's so fucking *beautiful*, her soft presence somehow

buffering all the harder edges of reality as she gives off a magical, otherworldly vibe.

The song is smooth and melodic. Perfectly in tune. There's a bell-toned clarity to some of the notes and a smoky edge to others.

Like everyone else here tonight, I'm starstruck. Ivy Laine is very, very talented.

And I'm in very, very deep trouble. Not to mention so hard it hurts.

If I'm meant to love, then give me the greatest love
    there ever was.
Ask me for a match and I'll give you wildfire.
Ask me for a light and I'll give you the sun.
I don't know how to feel except in tidal waves of
    roughed-up, star-studded emotion.
I don't know how to love except with the glow of a
    thousand stars.

And *I* don't know how to deal with this vision of her, with her pink lips still wet from our kiss and her face still flushed with her innocence. Her third kiss.

Bring it on, baby girl. I'll see your glow of a thousand stars and raise you the whole goddamn universe.

I don't know how she does it, but my hardened cynicism has lifted at the edges—and this part of me is so ingrained, the absence of it is wildly noticeable, like a dark cloud has moved away from the sun and the world is suddenly much brighter. I don't quite know what to do with my new sense of…calmness. Of something that almost feels eerily like hope.

"We were about to tell you two to get a room." Someone laughs and pats me on the back.

I look up to see Ethan Jackson pulling out the chair next to Ivy's. He shakes my hand but I'm in no state to stand up right now. I'm hard as a fucking rock from…*that kiss.*

Holy hell.

From the feel of her warm little squirming body on my lap, I could tell she was wet for me.

Fuck.

The girl is like something out of my wildest fantasies. And I don't *have* fantasies. Until the minute that cute-hot little goddess stepped through that door and into my world, I only did reality. 24/7. Every minute of my goddamn life.

Fuck reality.

I'm sick to death of reality.

My soul feels parched and needy for some of that escapism she was talking about. With *her.* I want to feast on her and bask in her glow like I've never wanted anything.

I murmur some expected reply to Ethan. He's a guy I've met a few times at Leah and Blake's dinner parties in the city. He's a broker who works for Blake's company, probably four or five years younger than me. Leah once described him as a "manwhore." I didn't give it much thought at the time, but I sure don't like the fucking sound of it now. He sips his champagne, watching Ivy, like everyone else at this party is doing. Not appearing to have his own date.

"Ivy Laine, huh?" he says. "How the hell did you score *her*?"

I glare at him, furious that he's distracting me from the little goddess on stage. I don't even know how to reply to that. What I feel like doing is strangling the little punk with his own tie. I can hardly tell him the truth. *I scored her by paying her a quarter of a million dollars to pretend to like me. And now I'm drowning in a brand new obsession that's digging into me with razor-sharp, lust-spiked claws because she's addictive in every sense of the word and I'm already dreading Sunday afternoon, when I potentially have to watch her walk away and disappear from my life only to be preyed on by douchebags like you. Which feels strangely, insanely unbearable.*

I have two days to convince her.

Convince her of what, you asshole? You've known the girl for a total of two hours. What the fuck are you planning to do?

I don't know.

I have no idea.

But something. Definitely something.

Ivy finishes her song, strumming her last chord to enthusiastic applause. Leah is close to the stage, clapping happily with Blake by her side. Ethan whistles loudly and it takes every ounce of willpower I possess not to punch the little fucker in the face.

I have no idea where this caveman tendency is coming from but I'm feeling it *hard*.

Ivy takes a bow. "Thank you so much." She picks up her half-full glass of champagne from where it's sitting on a nearby amp and she raises it. "To love. To Leah and Blake and a lifetime of wedded bliss and beautiful happiness."

Everyone raises their glasses and I tip back the rest of my Moët.

The band takes the stage as Ivy steps off. She's accosted by an excited Leah and stops to get hugged before making her way back toward our table.

Ethan watches her approach. "*Damn*," he comments. "You lucky bastard. How long have you two been together? Are you exclusive?"

I seriously can't handle this.

At least my fury is calming my lust by a single degree.

I stand, buttoning my jacket. I pluck his named place card from the table, crumpling it and tucking it into the pocket of his lapel. "In the interest of not making a scene by rearranging your face at Blake and Leah's rehearsal dinner, I'm going to ask this politely once and once only. Do not even *think* of going anywhere near her. Don't talk to her. Don't even fucking *look* at her. She's *mine*. I'm therefore not responsible for how fucking ballistic I go if you don't fuck off immediately. We both know I can get you fired with a single conversation. I can also make sure you never get hired in the state of New York again. Third, I can easily pummel you into next week if I choose to. The only way I want to see you for the rest of the evening is from a long fucking distance. And to answer your question, yes, we are exclusive. Very. Fucking. Exclusive. Am I making myself clear enough?"

What are you even doing right now?

But my common sense is no match for the enraged yeti who's taken up residence in my subconscious. All he wants to do is *claim* Ivy Laine and keep her entirely to himself.

I don't understand it but I'm going with it tonight because it's the only thing I'm capable of.

He stares at me. "*Jesus*, dude." But he gets the message loud and clear. Maybe it's because my fists are clenched and the rage is practically beaming itself out of my eyes. "Fine. Fine." He stands up from his chair, noticing that I'm a good six inches taller than he is and outweigh him by a significant margin.

He holds his palms up and wanders into the now-lively crowd to try his luck elsewhere.

"Thank you to Ivy Laine," Margot says, into the microphone. The shrillness of her voice mostly takes care of my hard-on. "I'd now like to welcome to the stage The

Sailors, the Hamptons very own local and much-loved band! Please help yourself to more drinks at the bar and the delectable hors d'oeuvres, which our wonderful wait-staff has just begun to pass around. Dinner will be served at eight o'clock."

Ivy stops to sign an autograph. The candlelight catches the red and gold hues of her dark hair. Her olive skin is so flawless and smooth-looking, she doesn't look real. She laughs at something the woman says to her and she looks so gorgeous, not only does my cock spring back to instant rock-hard life, but my chest aches with an acute kind of longing that's new to me.

Damn, she's pretty.

I shove my fists into my pockets and watch her walk back to me. She sees me and smiles, at my intensity maybe. I offer her my arm. "Come for a walk with me."

"Where are we going?"

"Over to the water. It's a nice view." I'll use any excuse but the truth is, I want to be alone with her, without the curious gaze of a hundred or so people watching her every move.

She slides her arm through mine. The light scent of her citrus-spice perfume makes me practically fucking dizzy.

How can I be so hopelessly addicted to this edgy little stranger?

I feel like I just tasted a brand new drug that I'll burn my entire world to the ground to get more of.

I need to calm the fuck down.

We walk in silence for a minute, past the fountain, to the covered pergola that looks out over the water. Pendant lights hang from the rafters and the moon is low, painting the ocean water with its shimmering white trail. Most importantly, there's no one else over here.

I've spent enough time in the Hamptons to be familiar with its scenery. The view of the hotel, the expansive garden, lawns and the ocean, with sailboats and yachts anchored offshore, could be enough to make even a die-hard skeptic like me appreciate the view. But I'm not looking at the view. I'm too captivated by my gorgeous little date—so much that I'm really starting to hate that it's technically a fake one.

"This place is something else," she comments, still holding my arm. "I have to hand it to Blake and Leah. And Margot. They really know how to throw a party. The whole thing is beautiful. I'm sure tomorrow will be even more over the top."

"I'm sure."

"I'm sorry again for making you late. They acted like that was way out of character for you."

It's true. Punctuality is just another one of those things that was drilled into me as I was being groomed for my role by my father, who absolutely would not tolerate waiting for people. Especially his sons. And *especially* his oldest son. "Diligent oldest child here."

"I'm the oldest too." She already mentioned she has a

younger brother. She doesn't elaborate and I don't ask her to. I don't want her to withdraw from me.

"For you, I didn't mind waiting," I hear myself saying, trying like hell to ignore my raging urge to kiss her again and to distract myself from *how hard and hot my cock is*.

And how addicted to my fake date I already am.

14

I'M NOT sure I entirely believe that he didn't mind waiting for me, but now that we're alone together, the hardness of his personality has once again shifted, revealing the playfulness he seems to save just for me.

Which is sort of crazy, considering we only just met.

"Cleo said you were talented, but that description doesn't come close to doing you justice," he says. "You're crazy good."

"Thanks." It's a nice thing to say. And not quite articulated in a way I might have expected from such a high-powered CEO. It makes him sound...like someone I could almost relate to.

"I mean that," he says with sincerity. "Do you have a record deal? A recording contract?"

I slide my arm from his and lean my hip up against the railing of the gazebo, looking out over the spectacular view. "No. I've had a few offers, but the thought of someone else controlling me and my music doesn't really appeal to me. Plus the timing wasn't right. And the offers weren't what I was looking for."

"I might be able to help you, if you wanted to pursue something like that."

I suppose he'd have all the connections in the world. But it's hardly the time and place to talk about recording contracts, especially since I don't expect our "relationship" to last longer than around two o'clock on Sunday afternoon. "I'm good. But thanks."

"Really, Ivy. You're something special."

Now he's just telling me what I want to hear. I elbow him lightly. "Thanks, Maddox."

"You're welcome, Jones."

How about that, me and the hot billionaire have our own little inside joke. "What do your friends call you? Al? Alex? Xander?" I give him a slow once-over. "I think Alfonse kind of suits you."

His laughter is low and sexy as hell as he leans against the railing next to me. Close to me. He's so much bigger than I am, I get the vague sense of being dominated, and it's surprisingly…not unpleasant. That tiny pulse that got *way* out of control when I sat on his lap starts its warm, secret rhythm again. "My brothers call me Alex. Everyone else calls me Alexander."

"Even your friends?"

His smile lingers—and wow, he really is dazzling

when he smiles. "Yeah. My father called me Alexander. And everyone I work with, which is most of the people I see most days, call me either Alexander or Mr. Maddox."

"Well, since you're paying me a lot of money to be your friend for the weekend, I'm going to call you Alex. Whether you like it or not."

His amusement is layered with something darker and I regret mentioning that he's paying me to be here. It puts up an invisible barrier between us.

"So how do you sell your music if you don't have a recording deal?" he asks.

"Through streaming platforms, mainly."

"Show me."

"Show you what?"

"Show me one of your platforms."

I look out at the reflection of the moon on the water. "I don't think it'll be all that interesting for you."

Little crinkles lightly frame the edges of his eyes as he watches me. "Well, *I* think it'll be *very* interesting for me. Let me see your Instagram."

I'd say no, but it's not like he won't search for it the minute he's out of my sight anyway. And I'd rather see his reaction first-hand.

I pull my phone out of the clutch that's looped over my shoulder on a delicate leather and chain strap. Pulling up my Instagram, I hand him my phone.

He takes it, riveted as he scrolls. "Ten million followers," he drawls. It feels strange to watch him analyze my posts as though he's studying them under a microscope. "You really thought you could fly under the radar this weekend?"

"It's getting harder to do," I admit.

He's frowning now, turning slightly to shield the screen from me as he zooms in on something. "Some of these are…"

"Are what?" I reach for my phone but he turns further, keeping it out of reach.

"…very revealing." There's mild shock in his statement.

"What are you looking at?" I grab his arm and manage to see the photo he's looking at. It's the recent one of me doing yoga on the balcony, taken by Josh. "Oh. That's just a campaign I was doing for a company that sells yoga wear. I've been working with them for a few years. I love their products."

He keeps scrolling. "Yoga, huh?"

"I practice yoga every day."

He stops scrolling to glance at me, my legs, my body, my arms, letting his gaze clock that information almost dreamily, before returning to my phone, where he zooms in again. This time it's a photo of me at a party that was thrown by one of my clients to showcase their swimwear. I'm on a boat out on the East River and my back is to the camera but I'm looking over my shoulder so my face is still visible. Manhattan is in the background behind me. "You have to get practically naked to make money off this stuff?" He seems pissed off by this.

I grab my phone, sliding it back into my bag. "I'm not naked. I'm selling *swimwear*."

Okay, I'll admit that one was one of the more risqué photos I've ever posted. It's a minuscule thong bikini with very little coverage. But they paid me a lot for that shoot. "They're marketing to women," I point out.

"My guess is that most of the people who spend time staring at that photo are men. Let me see the comments."

"No." I'm annoyed now. It's easy for *him* to judge. He doesn't have to put his little brother through Columbia.

"I'm going to look later anyway."

I roll my eyes. "Go right ahead. It's a free country." *Damn it.* I sound like I'm arguing with a seventeen-year-old. Which, to be fair, I spend a lot of my time doing. "I don't read the comments anyway."

"Because they're all lewd and suggestive come-ons from men?"

I glare at him. Of course I look at the comments every now and then. And he happens to be partly right. There are plenty of kind comments from fans and followers. But I also get a lot of propositions, more X-rated offers than I can bear to read, and at least a few marriage proposals every time I post. "The comments are irrelevant. The income, however, is very relevant. And that's what I'm focused on."

His expression is hard to read. It's…protective, if I'm

reading him correctly. Concerned. Maybe even empathetic. And very determined. Which is the detail I like the least.

The band has finished playing and someone else steps up to the microphone on stage, tapping it three times. Margot. I'm almost grateful for her interruption. "Ladies and gentlemen, please make your way to your seats. The band will resume for another short set after dinner. You'll find your name on a place card at your allocated table. Dinner will be served shortly."

I take that as our cue, stepping away from the railing. "We should go."

But Alexander doesn't follow me. His muscular arms are folded, like he hasn't finished disciplining me. "How many listens or whatever do you get each day for your music? Is it not enough to pay the bills?"

God. He's so direct and so damn *bossy*. "I don't know how that's any of your business. I do just fine. And I'll wear whatever I want to wear and post whatever I want to post, without your input. But thanks for asking." I realize my fists are resting on my hips. I make a point of toning down my attitude. I'm not being paid to argue with my fake date over my own life. He has no say in it whatsoever, so it hardly matters if he's curious.

He's quiet and it's contemplative, but his pause also has a power to it, like he's used to people hanging on his every word. This is a man who knows how to wield silence like a holstered weapon. "Where are your parents? Are they local?"

I'm not expecting the question. And I'm not sure why I'm honest with him. "My mother is dead and my father is…estranged, I guess you could call it. We don't really talk anymore."

I almost expect him to demand to know why. Instead he says, "I'm sorry."

"Thank you. Now can we please go back to our table?"

"You said you had a brother. How old is he?"

The topic of Josh always feels personal. I hesitate, but I can't figure out how to dodge the question. "Seventeen."

"Does he live with you or your father?"

I don't know how this is any of his business. But he's waiting for his answer. And I think of all that money that's now padding Josh's bank account, thanks to the bossy billionaire who's now grilling me. "Me."

"So you're responsible for him."

"I have been, yes. Completely. In every way."

"For how long?"

"A few years."

"I see."

He *sees*? Sees what? From where I'm standing, he sees nothing and knows even less. I didn't come here to get interrogated by some ego-inflated jerk who now thinks he understands me from two morsels of half-true information. And I can't stand the heat of his knowing intensity. "I'm going back to our table. Are you coming?"

Two hundred and fifty grand hardly seems worth the Spanish Inquisition from a guy who got handed his damn fortune by great grandpa.

Before I can start making my way back toward the now-rowdy party, I see the silhouette of a woman approaching us. Even her silhouette is beige.

"It's Margot," I say.

"Yes, it is," Alexander mutters. "Brace yourself."

As pissed off and flustered as I am, I've come too far to have him demand his money back. What's about to happen here and how I handle it is the exact reason I'm being paid so generously.

So I walk back over to him and stand in front of him. Slowly, because his eyes are still dark, I reach up to carefully touch his face, brushing my thumb softly along his bottom lip. "Put your arm around me."

He does and Margot stops a few paces from where we're presenting our united front. "Alexander?" Her voice sounds almost little-girl-ish, like she's purposely dialed back the army commander/wedding planner persona to appeal to him on a softer level. "I wondered if you and I could have a few words. In private."

My hand rests on Alexander's chest, possessively.

"Whatever you've got to say can be said to us both," he tells her.

She looks smaller and more vulnerable out here in the

open, without her iPad and her brigade of caterers. "It's just that I was hoping we could talk. But I suppose you're right. Maybe this weekend isn't the time and place. Maybe we could meet this week in the city, for a drink. I really have some things I wanted to talk to you about. We could go to that place we used to go near Rockefeller Center, remember?"

"Why don't you just tell me now, Margot." He sounds bored. With that edge of misery inking his words.

I slide my arms around Alexander's waist. *He's so big… and hard. Everywhere.* "We're actually going away later this week," I gush, putting on an upbeat personality. Not that my usual personality *isn't* upbeat, it's just not *this* upbeat. "I'm *so* excited. Alexander's always surprising me with impromptu little trips, aren't you, honey?" I glance up at him, blinking.

They're both staring at me, Alexander with mild amusement, Margot with unbridled jealousy. "I sure am, sweetie," he replies.

"Where are you going?" Margot asks tentatively, like she's not sure she wants to know.

I'm making this up as I go. "To the South Pacific!"

"You *are?*" Margot sounds almost breathless.

I don't want to be mean. I feel for her, I really do. But I can't change the fact that Alexander wants nothing to do with her—so much that he's willing to shell out a shit-load of cash to send her that direct message.

It occurs to me that Alexander is actually being kind

by staging this tedious charade. He's genuinely trying to let her down as gently as possible. He's *told* her he's not interested. It's not his fault she won't take no for an answer. And I want to get it through to her, for his sake and for hers—and mine—once and for all.

"I told Alexander I've always wanted to go to Tahiti because I read about it online and the next thing I know he's booked us two tickets! For two weeks in a little seaside bungalow that's actually perched over the water, so you can dive straight in from the deck. Can you *believe* that? He's *so* sweet." I don't even know if they have those huts in Tahiti—I think they do—but I smile at him, standing on my toes to kiss his lips, which are almost smiling back.

"Sweet," Margot repeats, as though she's unfamiliar with the word and Alexander's name in the same sentence.

"I don't know *what* I've done to deserve such a fabulous gift." I beam up at Alexander lovingly. Hell, maybe I've missed my calling. Maybe I should go to freaking Hollywood.

"You know exactly what you've done to deserve it, sweetheart." His sneering reply is sort of…absolutely filthy.

I blush—for real—and giggle coyly, pushing at his chest. "You are *so* bad." To Margot, conspiratorially: "Men. They have *such* dirty minds, don't they?"

"Mmhm." Her frown is testing the limits of her

Botox. Admitting defeat, at least for now, she turns to head back to the party. "Please take your seats. Dinner is about to be served."

15

ALEXANDER

The night has become a strange kind of slow-motion torture. I'm addicted to this sweet and sassy girl on my arm who has more power over me than anyone ever has. I don't even know how that's possible.

I can't analyze it tonight. All I know is that something in me has shifted and it feels monumental and out of control. I'm trying to get a handle on my new obsession, but then I watch her amber eyes catch starlight and I'm spellbound all over again.

It occurs to me that I spend most of my life surrounded by people I don't actually like. Employees who were picked for their ability to predict the market and not at all because they're fun to be around. Or decrepit old board members who are more ancient than my father was. Most of them are grumpier even than me. Or women who endlessly pursue me, not because they know me or because we have anything in common, but because they like the way I look and most of all they love my money.

My brothers are the only people I know whose company I genuinely enjoy, but I don't see enough of them. Besides, that's different. They're family. I love them *because* they annoy me.

It's so rare for me to…have *fun*, if that's what this is. To smile because her laughter is so fucking cute. To feel mesmerized by the shape of her mouth as she makes up lies to convince my ex that we're in love.

The plan was ludicrous. But it's turning out to be my favorite mistake.

Is it possible to fall for someone this fast?

Of course it isn't. I've known her for a total of three hours.

Then why do I feel so fucking unhinged? Like I could kill anyone who glances in her general direction. Not to mention that I'm hard as fuck and can't seem to deflate. I want so badly to be alone with her so I can kiss that delectable mouth again, I'm going half insane with it.

First I have to get through an entire five-course dinner.

We're back at our table.

Ivy's chair is close to mine, at my insistence, and she's talking to a woman who's seated on her left. Ethan wisely moved to the furthest table from ours, trying it on with Samantha Bentley, a nightmarish heiress who I very briefly "dated" after Leah set us up at one of her strategic dinner parties. It might have been eighteen months ago.

I regret to say I went with it that night. I regretted it practically before it was over and I'm regretting it even more right now.

She's not the only one at this party I'm regretting spending time with.

I'm not proud of any of it. The soul-destroying one night stands. The serial leave-before-morning-and-never-call behavior that's accounted for 98% of all the "relationships" I've ever had.

I'm thankful Ivy is with me tonight for many reasons, but most of all because it actually feels *good* to be with her. Fake date or no fake date, it's the first time in a long time —or ever?—that I don't feel like I have to force it. I like her company. I've spent most of my time tonight enthralled by her gorgeous pixie-cute face, her full, pink lips and her golden eyes that scold me and watch me, *seeing* me. Reading me. Calming me with that glittery effect she has.

What happens on Sunday afternoon, when she walks away and takes all that soft, magical gorgeousness with her?

I push the thought out of my head. We'll get on with our lives, that's what happens. She'll forget she ever met me except for the quarter mil she'll have sitting in her bank account, a reward for having to put up with me for two solid days.

That's when an idea comes to me. A plan. To buy myself a little more time.

Two days won't be nearly enough.

"I'm Astrid, a friend of Leah's from high school," the woman is telling Ivy. "And trust me, I know who you are. It was Leah who introduced me to your music. That was right after I went through this *horrible* break-up and all I can say is it really helped me get through some shitty times. I'm *such* a fan. I follow you on all your social media platforms."

Here we go again.

I'll put up with this for exactly as long as it takes to send a message to Esther. I hardly recognize this compulsion but fuck it. I'm going with it tonight.

I need two first class tickets to Tahiti

Three dots immediately hover.

Tahiti? Isn't that in the South Pacific?

Yes

One room or two?

It's a fair question, unfortunately. *Will she even agree to it?*

One. Leaving a week from Thursday. For two weeks. To whatever the best resort on the island is. Actually I think I'll take the Gulfstream. Let Marco know

Of course I'm aware that I've never taken a vacation in my goddamn life, that my work schedule is as full as always over the coming weeks, and that Ivy might not be able to take off for that long. I don't care about any of these details. When you have as much money as I do, you tend to be able to make things work if you really fucking want them to. And I'm determined to spend some time alone with the unicorn that just landed in the middle of my life. She said she wants Tahiti, so she gets Tahiti.

I can almost predict the next question. Esther knows better than anyone that I basically live in my office and have since she was still my father's assistant.

Two whole weeks?

Yes. Try to get one of those little huts, if you can find one that's rated five stars

Huts?

The ones that are perched over the water and you can dive off the deck directly into the ocean

Oh ok. I'll see if I can find one

Thanks Esther

I wouldn't usually add that last text, I realize. Something about the way Ivy is *grateful* is rubbing off on me. It doesn't feel entirely terrible to actually be aware of appreciating things now and then.

"I'm so glad Ethan wanted to swap seats," the woman is still gushing to Ivy.

"Ethan? Oh. Yes, I saw his name on the place card."

"He said since you're obviously taken, he's going to try his luck with some socialite he's got his eye on. Of course Margot almost had a conniption when she saw that we'd swapped, but I'd much rather sit at this table. I mean, getting to sit next to *Ivy Laine*, are you kidding? I can't wait to tell my book club about this. Margot's been evil-eyeing us in this direction ever since I sat here, though. It's hardly *that* big of a deal. Do you have plans to release any new music any time soon?"

I loop my arm around Ivy's shoulders, pulling her closer, bored by the woman who's monopolizing her attention.

She's mine.

I let my thumb rest against the delicate skin of Ivy's neck and she turns to me. I like to think it's not a demand but more of a request.

The woman sitting next to Ivy reads the room—or my scowl—and turns to the man who's sitting on her left.

Ivy gives me a look, and that gentle scolding sends another rush of blood to my already painfully thick cock. But my girl remembers the assignment. She touches my hair, leaning her mouth close to my ear. The light scent of her tropical shampoo makes me want to do something downright depraved. Like take her away with me and keep her all to myself until I can get my fill. *Taste her and eat her sweet pussy until she's coming on my tongue. Feast on those ripe little nipples that are poking against her thin dress.*

"Margot's watching us again," she whispers. "Pretend I'm saying something really dirty to you right now."

Fucking hell. If she sat on my lap I could practically come. If her wet pussy softened to the shape of my raging erection like it did before, this time I could position her, moving her panties to the side… "My imagination's not that good. You'll have to give me some material to work with."

I have a very real problem. Because there's nothing fake about my throbbing lust. I lean close to her ear, breathing in more of the heady floral scent of her.

"I'm waiting, Jones."

"I don't know how to talk dirty," she giggles. "I've never done it."

"Try."

Her nose crinkles and it's almost unbearably adorable. She leans closer, cupping her hand like she's telling me a secret. "I liked our kiss."

"I'm sure you can do better than that." I can barely control the yeti of my lust, who wants nothing more than to sling her over my shoulder and carry her back to our room, to peel off her little dress and taste every inch of her perfect skin. "Kiss me again."

Someone taps on the microphone. *Damn it.* Blake is getting ready to make a speech.

"I just wanted to say a few words," he begins. "First of all, I'd like to thank all of you for being here this weekend. You're our family and we love that you're here with us to celebrate this very special occasion. Leah and I also want to thank Margot Russo, our amazing wedding planner. Margot, we couldn't have done all this without you and we're lucky to have you." There's a smattering of applause and Margot smiles rigidly. "And finally, enjoy tonight, but the real festivities are tomorrow night and if any of you are too hungover to party, you're officially off our Christmas card list haha. To my groomsmen, I'm ordering you to meet me in the hotel bar after dinner for a run-through of the day tomorrow. Leah's bridesmaids will meet with her in the pool house for a final nightcap. So, please enjoy the outstanding food, provided by our caterers, Elite Catering. Margot will say a few more words once dessert is served. Cheers, guys. We love you."

Fuck it all. That means we'll be apart for at least a few hours.

Blake and Leah take their seats at our table and the rest of the dinner goes smoothly enough. Everyone's intrigued by Ivy. She dodges the more personal questions gracefully.

I'm paying attention, but I learn very little about her that she hasn't already told me. She lives in Soho. She writes her own music and performs in small clubs, mostly around Manhattan. Her admirers around the table are in awe of her "content," the stuff she's posting through social media, which she laughs off as a way to make a living. She has a younger brother whose name is Josh. I learn he's headed to Columbia at the end of the summer.

She tenses when she talks about her brother and her breezy façade slips. I guess it's not surprising. She lost her mother and her father doesn't seem to be on the scene. Which means she's responsible for her teenage brother. It can't have been easy.

But she plays her part like a pro, continually circling me into the conversation, making up little stories about our two months together that thoroughly convince our rapt audience.

"Last Saturday we went to the Met," she tells them. "We wandered around for hours and then Alex took me to this little rooftop bistro on the Upper West Side that I never knew was there. A jazz trio was playing live music and it was just one of those perfectly romantic New York afternoons, like something out of a movie."

"What was the name of the bistro?" asks the woman who took Ethan's seat, whose name I've forgotten.

"It had such a cool atmosphere, and the food was amazing." Ivy turns to me. "Can you remember what it was called, sweetie?"

Thankfully Leah intercepts the question. "Our workaholic Alexander Maddox taking an entire afternoon off?" Leah laughs, saving me from answering the question.

"We've known Alexander for years and he's always got some excuse why he can't join us for things like that, because he's always working on the weekends. I'm just amazed he was able to keep this from us for so long."

"He's told us absolutely nothing about you," Blake adds. "Although this does explain the reason why he was too busy to come to my bachelor party in Vegas."

"We were buying a fund." I've already told him this, more than once. "I was needed for the negotiations."

Ivy's bare thigh is flush against mine. I'm trying to ignore my perpetual fucking hard-on, which throbs hotly. I'm going to have to do something about this problem before we share a bed tonight, but I'll worry about that later.

Dessert is finally served and Margot makes the announcement about the rest of the evening.

People start to get up from their chairs.

"Ivy," Leah says, "you're welcome to join me and my bridesmaids in the pool house. We're just going to go through a few more details of tomorrow's schedule."

"Thank you, but I think I'll call it a night. I've had a crazy week."

"Of course. But we'll see you tomorrow." Leah gives Ivy a hug. "Thank you so much for singing."

"Of course. I'm so excited for you."

Leah smiles at us both, but it's me she's talking to when she says, "I'm so excited for *you*."

"I'll walk Ivy back to our room, then meet you in the bar," I tell Blake.

"Don't even think about not showing up. I'll have a Jack Daniels on ice waiting for you," Blake grins, like he knows how tempted I am. "Goodnight, Ivy."

After everyone starts making their way from the tables, I offer Ivy my arm and we head toward our suite. "Our room is 212."

"My lucky number," Ivy says.

"Is it?"

"Yeah. It's my birthday. February 12th."

I don't know why this makes me so fucking happy.

We get to the door and I open it. Inside, the suite is expansive with a view that opens out over the water. Blake and Leah know I have expensive taste. "Are you going to be okay?" I ask her.

"I'll be fine. I'm going to take a long, hot shower then fall into a blissful sleep."

"I'll try not to wake you."

Ivy blinks at me, and there's an edge of nervousness to her. I've just reminded her that we're sleeping in the same room. In the same bed.

We stand there like that for a few seconds and I can't help myself. I lean in, placing my palm flat on the door behind her, trapping her with my body. Her eyes round and her lips part. *I need it.* I brush my lips against hers, drowning in the sensation of her. Dipping my tongue into her mouth, I slide deeper. *Holy fuck, she tastes good.*

She pulls back, breathless, putting her hand on my chest. I feel another crazy surge of this new feeling—*happiness*—that we're this familiar with each other that she does this without hesitation. "No one's even watching us, Maddox. I'll see you later. I won't wait up."

"Goodnight, Jones."

She shakes her head a little, laughing lightly. Then she closes the door in my face.

You fucking owe me one, Blake. Then again, if it wasn't for Blake and Leah's wedding, I probably never would have met Ivy.

I'm walking toward the bar when someone approaches me. Even in the dark, Margot is easy to recognize. "Oh, good, I was hoping I'd run into you without your…entourage."

This is the thing about Margot. Every damn word she says is bitchy. "You mean my date?"

"Isn't she a little young for you?"

I'm not interested in having this conversation. "Is there something you need, Margot?"

"I was hoping we could talk, Alexander."

"About what?"

"Could we meet for a drink this week?"

"I told you. I'm busy this week. And I don't want to meet for a drink."

"I thought maybe we could talk about…giving us another chance. Please, Alexander. Please don't give up on us so easily."

"I've already given up on us. A long time ago. I gave up on us because I was miserable the entire time we were together. This is the problem with you, Margot. Our 'relationship,' if that's what you could even call it, is over. Done. Finished. We've moved on. *I've* moved on. Obviously. I've explained this to you a dozen fucking times and you refuse to listen."

She even summons tears. "It's just that…we were so *perfect* together. *Everything* was a match."

Holy fuck, the woman is relentless. "We were terrible together, Margot. Absolutely terrible. Just deal with the fact that I'm with someone else now."

She blows her nose. "Honestly, I get it. She's young— and I mean *young*—and cute, in a slightly rough-edged kind of a way, if you're into that kind of thing. And she's sort of famous, if that's to be believed. But it's hardly even *appropriate*, Alexander. What is she, like, ten years younger than you?"

"Who gives a fuck."

"She basically sells pictures of herself half-dressed for money. Is that *really* the kind of person you see yourself ending up with? I heard one woman describing her as an 'Instagram whore'—I mean, *I* didn't say it, but it's kind of true."

I step around her, resisting the urge to shove her aside. If she was a man, I'd have punched her in the face for that one, but I don't really feel like going to jail just for

Margot. She's probably hoping I'll react, so she can gloat about it. "I'll put this as politely as I possibly can, Margot. Fuck off."

With that, I walk away, more than ready for that drink Blake promised.

16

I SIT on the gigantic bed for a minute, to catch my breath. It's nice to have a moment alone, after a very intense few hours. I'm tempted to call Cleo because I feel like talking to someone, but then she'd want every detail and it's not good timing. She'll ask too many questions about the *sleeping arrangements* and I can't even go there yet.

The room is palatial. An entire wall of windows showcases the view of the water, shimmering with silver moonlight and dotted with a few anchored boats.

A high-vaulted ceiling has painted white beams, and a dark-wood ceiling fan shaped like palm fronds spins slowly. Expensive-looking table lamps give the space a low, golden light. I turn off all but one. It's the kind of over-the-top luxury that takes a little getting used to.

I unlock the sliding glass doors and open one halfway,

to let some air in. I can hear music playing in the distance.

Then I contemplate the bed I'm going to be sharing with Alexander Maddox, investment mogul, CEO of Maddox Enterprises, elusive grump, and one of Manhattan's most eligible bachelors. It's a little daunting, but at least the bed is big enough to sleep a family of six.

I honestly didn't see him coming. I already feel like I've changed. Something about being around him makes me feel…powerful. Feminine. The way he looks at me with that dark fascination. *The sound he made when I sucked gently on his tongue.*

He's a force to be reckoned with. The most infuriating man I've ever met. I can admit he's also the most gorgeous, by a country mile. Magnetic and bossy as hell. Built like an elite athlete. *A very well-hung one.* Not that I have a lot of experience with things like that, but I haven't exactly grown up in a vacuum. The man is obviously exceptional, on every level.

I still haven't recovered from the feel of that gigantic *thing* he's packing from when I sat on his lap.

The goodnight kiss ramped up the memory, igniting my body like he's lit little fires along my bloodstream—*and between my thighs, where I'm wet again.*

I've never experienced this kind of reaction to a man before. I feel flushed and strangely reckless.

And I'm relieved to see that there's a mountain of pillows I can discreetly use to make a barrier between us.

Do I want to?

Of course I do. It's ridiculous to get carried away by a staged kiss with a total—okay, not *total*—stranger.

He's not a stranger when you know what the ridges of his cock feel like pressed up against your softening pussy. And that his tongue tastes like whiskey and mint when it sinks into your mouth and tangles silkily with yours.

I've already been more intimate with Alexander Maddox than I've been with anyone else in my life.

But I remind myself that it's an act we're putting on, and nothing more. It doesn't *mean* anything. He's probably out there flirting with a flock of socialites as we speak.

Can a man get a colossal hard-on as an act?

I mean, I don't *think* so, but what do I know?

It makes me wish I wasn't so inexperienced. I'm pretty sure you can't fake chemistry like that, though. Sparkling, magical chemistry that's playful but at the same time… *scorching hot.*

But maybe that's just another part of the act.

It's confusing.

I'm flustered by the crazy reactions of my body, especially when my common sense is telling me to get real. He paid a lot of money to make this whole charade convincing. Most likely that's all that's happening here.

I get up to check my phone again for messages from Josh. Or anyone else, including detectives and whatnot.

The only texts are from Cleo.

Hope you're having fun!!!

Txt me if he's being an a-hole and I'll get
Noah to do some damage control!

Txt me when you get a chance!

Hope it's going well!!

I text back a quick reply.

> He's not being an a-hole. Everything
> is fine

> The venue is OTT beautiful and so far
> we've managed to successfully trick the
> evil ex. I'll msg you tomorrow xx

Then I go into the bathroom and turn on the shower, peeling off my dress. I'm slightly mortified to find that my tiny lace panties are absolutely saturated. *Yikes.*

The shower is heavenly. Three shower heads offer various levels of massage, releasing a fraction of the tension knotting my shoulders. I let the water sluice over my skin. Over my breasts and the tight peaks of my nipples. Down my stomach and over my hipbones.

Between my legs.

God, I'm so sensitive there. I almost feel like I could…*get there*, just from the sensual flow of the water.

As horny as I might be, I'm not going to get myself off in the shower when my fake date could walk in any minute. Most likely he'll be another hour or more, but still. I'd rather be safely tucked into bed, hopefully sound asleep.

I turn off the shower, grabbing a fluffy towel and wrapping it around myself.

My small suitcase has been placed in the corner and I flip it open, searching through the clothes Cleo packed for me.

Cleo, what the hell?

Not only are the only pajamas a tiny, tight-fitting, slinky little white satin and lace number, it also barely reaches the tops of my thighs.

I keep searching.

Cleo!

She didn't pack a single pair of panties.

There are two tiny bikinis but I don't really want to wear my bathing suit to bed. I almost tell her off by text message but I'm very aware that Alexander could swan in at any moment and I'm standing here dressed in nothing but a very see-through piece of lace and nothing else.

I quickly dry off my hair, running a brush through it. Then I brush my teeth before padding back into the bedroom, fishing around for my charger to plug in my phone and crawling between the soft sheets.

The minute my head sinks into the plush pillow, I can't help it. I sigh. This bed is ridiculously comfortable.

My heartbeat starts to even out and I turn on my side, facing away from Alexander's side of the bed, curling into the fetal position. Which makes my tiny nightie ride up, exposing my ass.

Cleo!

I tug it back into position as best I can.

And I forgot to put up the pillow barrier next to me.

But it's fine. I've never slept in a Californian king before. There's plenty of space between his side and mine.

This is going to be fine.

Except that the tiny pulse is back again. There.

What if…I mean, when you think about it, it could be…maybe…*a very convenient scenario to…cash in my V-card.*

There's no doubt he's the best candidate to come along so far. He's beautiful. He's allergic to commitment, so I won't have to deal with an actual relationship, which I'm not ready for anyway. *And, if that giant cock I felt through my dress is any indication, he's ready.*

I could have a very brief fling with the hot billionaire then make a run for it at the end of the weekend. Then I wouldn't have to wonder anymore. I could rip off the band-aid, so to speak, and re-emerge into the real world armed with experience, a nicely padded bank account and a brand new outlook.

It's a win-win. Isn't it?

Do it, whispers the newly voracious little devil on my shoulder. *Cash it in. He'll be rough. Punishing, in the best kind of way. And very, very thorough.*

The thought makes my body feel warm and softly electric.

It would be so easy to tempt him. Just roll over and kiss him again.

Would he let me?

Of course he would. Gently suck on his tongue, like you did when you were sitting on his lap. When he groaned like an animal. This time, when you touch his chest, he won't be wearing his suit. His big, buff body will be warm and hard and hair-dusted.

God. I'm hot. I feel so restless. My pussy feels slippery and lightly swollen.

Get a grip, girl!

It takes a while, but I gratefully drift into a soft, dreamy sleep.

I dream of that dark challenge in his blue, blue eyes.

17

ALEXANDER

"Dude, how the hell did you manage to score *Ivy Laine*? She's *insanely* hot." Blake's younger brother Freddie is obnoxious at the best of times. He used to come visit us at Harvard from Cornell all the time. Always loud and borderline inappropriate, I never really warmed to the guy. The only thing I'm fucking warming to right now is the idea of throttling him if he so much as mentions her name again.

Blake picks up on my tension and steers the conversation in a different direction. "I booked us a charter fishing boat tomorrow morning for a few hours. So we don't have to stand around twiddling our thumbs while the girls get ready. How hard is it to put on a tux, am I right? All we have to do is show up and be standing there by two o'clock. Shit, don't let me forget the ring."

What makes the fact that most of these guys have heard of Ivy Laine even worse is that they can go back to their rooms tonight and scroll through the photos of her barely dressed.

There was nothing extreme about the way she was posing, or what she was wearing, but knowing half the men in this bar are probably going to be helping themselves later tonight—I can't even fucking think about it without wanting to bend a crowbar in half.

When she's mine, we're going to have to have a conversation about this. She won't need to post photos of herself half-dressed for the money. She won't have to "create content," or whatever the fuck they call it. I'll take care of her. She'll be free to write her music, without having to rely on the influencer sideline.

With the kind of talent she has, it makes me wonder why she hasn't done more with the music. She said she performs around Manhattan but rarely goes further.

But then I remember. The brother. She needs to stay local to make sure he's not getting into trouble. She mentioned he was seventeen. Growing up with three younger brothers, I know only too well that seventeen-year-old boys are always a handful.

Is she okay? How is she managing to hold it all together?

And she *must* be holding it together. Very well. The kid got into Columbia.

How's she paying for that?

It occurs to me then that the two hundred and fifty grand is probably going a long way toward helping with that. But not *all* the way.

Will she have enough for the other things she needs or is every spare penny going toward the college fund?

She agreed to be my fake date only because she wants to get her brother through college.

I pull out my phone and make a note of it. *Pay for Josh Laine's entire four-year tuition at Columbia.*

Easily done.

I think of her now, alone in the room, taking that long, hot shower.

Damn it.

I do my best. I make polite conversation. I agree to meet them in the morning to go out on the charter. But I'm insanely grateful when Blake finally announces we need to have an early night so we're not too hungover to make the most of tomorrow.

We wrap it up and I head back to the room.

I'm careful not to wake her. She's curled up under the covers, facing away from my side of the bed. She looks so small in the huge bed. My protective instincts flare.

It's been so hard for her, handling so much on her own. *Now she's got me.* I can't overthink it, but I'm already in deep.

When you've spent a lifetime mired in a kind of quicksand of discontent like mine, so that it takes all your effort to breathe on a daily basis, when pure beauty in the form of a tattooed little musical unicorn walks into your life, you don't just let her walk out again without fucking fighting to keep her.

It's burning in me along with my heartbeat. *She's mine.*

I go into the bathroom and turn on the shower. To ice cold. To ease the wildfire that's taken over my cock since the minute I saw her. I fist my rock-hard length but I don't get myself off. I can't.

I don't want to be the grumpy grouch Cleo warned her about. Or the cold-hearted prick women always accuse me of being.

I want to make her happy. *Can I?* Am I capable of something like that?

I fucking want to try. I want her safe.

She'll have bodyguards and drivers. I'll find out what she dreams about. I'll use all the resources I have—which are significant—to please her.

Would you fucking listen to yourself?

I don't care.

I turn off the shower and dry myself off. The cold shower did nothing to tone down my colossal hard-on, but it can't be helped. I pull on a pair of boxers, doing my best to stuff myself into them.

She's still asleep.

I turn off the low lamp. The moon is full tonight, flooding the room with silver light, but I leave the door that leads out onto our private patio open. The air feels good.

I get into bed, careful not to wake her. I lay on my back, covering myself with only a sheet, to my waist. I'm hot.

Glancing over at her, she's curled up on her side, facing away from me. Her long hair spills over the pillow in glossy waves.

Is that sweet pussy wet for me?

My cock surges, leaking pre-cum. I try to ignore the agony I'm in right now.

The skin of her shoulder is so smooth. There's another tiny tattoo, one I haven't seen yet. It's a simple heart with the word *love* inked into it.

I wonder if she's ever been in love.

I know for a fact I never have. Not until—

I stop myself from even thinking it. *You can't fall in love with someone in one day, you idiot.*

It's a mild obsession, that's all it is. It's lust, pure and simple.

I fight the raging urge to hold her. To run my fingers along her flawless skin. To sink my fist into that silky hair.

To rub my cock against her.

To cover her in my hot cum.

To claim her. I feel like a wild animal.

Never in my life have I watched a woman sleep, hypnotized by the details of her beauty. I've never felt this burning, visceral desire to be as close as it's possible to be.

I have no idea how I could be so fucking besotted with this gorgeous little stranger. All I know is that I can't move, because I can't trust myself not to reach for her.

I close my eyes. Count some sheep. Think about the fishing trip. Baseball. *Anything but those tight nipples. That nubile, squirming body. That slippery-sweet pussy. So close to me.*

Fuck.

THE LIGHT CLICK of the door as he closes it wakes me.

Alexander goes into the bathroom to take a shower. I try to fall back asleep but I'm suddenly wide awake.

He's not in there for long. The door opens and he climbs into bed next to me, keeping a distance between us.

I don't dare move. I'm frozen in place, but I can feel the heat of his body. It's strangely…comforting.

His effect is seeping into me like a physical force. A warmth settles, that awareness of being watched. It sprouts slow-moving tendrils that bloom through my body like hothouse flowers of sweet, ripe heat.

Whoa.

A warm pulse centers in my clit and I can feel a slickness *inside*. My body is flaring with soft, tingling need.

My eyes are closed. My mind is quiet. But my lust is

vibrantly rampaging through my core, igniting me from my thighs to my belly. I'm so wet, I can feel the trickle of moisture on the high skin of my inner thigh.

I'm listening to his breathing, which evens and deepens. Only then do I dare to very carefully turn, stealing a glance at him in the moonlight.

His black hair is still damp, sticking up in silky disarray. His brawny shoulders are gracefully sculpted. Muscular in a way that's somehow ideal, like a work of art just crawled into bed with me.

I'm surprised to see that he has a tattoo on his chest. Of a dragon. I don't know why, but this…charms me. Alexander Maddox has layers I didn't know about. Hidden depths to his character that intrigue me.

His face is peaceful. He looks younger in his sleep. Relaxed. That visceral, male aggression that clings to him is softer now, but the innate arrogance is somehow still there. In the curve of his mouth. In his strong features and the stripes of his eyebrows.

I watch him sleep for a few minutes, fascinated by his mesmerizing *male*ness.

I could touch him, with feather-light strokes across his shoulders. I could kiss his perfect mouth, like I did earlier, when we were performing for the crowd. But this time, I could do it for real. And not because we have anything to prove.

His chest is dusted with dark hair. The quilted six-pack of his abs is defined. A tantalizing trail of dark hair disappears under the sheet.

It's then that he stirs. He doesn't wake, but his movement causes the covers to slip lower and…*holy shit.*

I can only stare for a few seconds. His cock is…*huge.* Like, *freaking gigantic.* And hard, even in his sleep. It's sticking out of his boxers and it's…*wet.* Glistening with moisture at the round tip.

I wasn't expecting it to be so…appealing. So freaking mouth-watering. I have the craziest urge to lick it.

Do it. Lick that bead of wetness. Drink it. Suck on that giant manhood.

Holy hell, my inner sex goddess is totally out of control. I mentally discipline her by turning and laying on my side again, facing away from him, grasping for self-control.

This is a fake date, I remind myself. Fake. Not real.

But my body has a mind of her own. I'm so freaking turned on, I squirm a little, trying to deal with it. My pussy is throbbing. My thighs are wet. My see-through nightie is bunched up around my waist.

I close my eyes and try to meditate. To put the loudly echoing image of his *giant glistening cock* out of my mind.

I take a deep breath. And another one.

That's better.

But my back arches a little, almost involuntarily, like it's seeking him.

Alexander sighs, and moves. He turns, laying on his side. Facing me.

I freeze.

Oh god oh god. Is he awake?

But his breathing deepens again.

God, he's so close to me. That massive cock is right there. It's sticking out of his boxers. It's almost touching me, skin to skin.

My back arches a little bit more and I feel a deep warmth spread. My clit is pulsing. My inner muscles clench lightly, wetting my pussy even more. I feel warm and ripe and greedy.

Oh god, I'm so close. I think I'm about to come.

The hot, melting glow is honestly the most pleasurable feeling I've ever had. It's dark and sweet and *I need it.* I need it so much. I barely squirm and that's when I feel it.

The brush of his hot hardness against my skin.

I go very still. His breathing is faster now. *I think he might be awake.* I don't dare move.

But then the ache clenches again and I *have* to writhe. I'm going to come if I don't do *something.*

I squirm and this time his hot, hard length presses against me.

Oh.

Oh my god.

The pleasure swells. It's about to…overflow.

I need it to.

I need it more than I need to breathe.

If I could just get a little closer…*if it would just touch me…right there.*

Alexander sighs a low groan.

The head of his cock slides against me more strongly and I'm so slick with moisture, he slides *along my pussy, pressing.*

God, this is way too much. It's too fast. I should stop this. He's very, very close to…*oh my god.*

I don't even *mean* to do it. I don't have full control of my own reactions. It's like my hormones or instincts or whatever have taken over and they want *more* of the giant hunk of man whose cock is positioned in a way that if I move the tiniest, tiniest bit, he'll be *inside me.*

My body moves, independently of all thoughts, just the tiniest bit, and it's enough. His hot, thick bulk is *right there*, sliding against an insanely pleasurable trigger. I'm going to come. *I'm coming.*

I lose all sense of reason. The only thing I *need* is for his big cock to give me more of his pleasure-heavy hardness. Thickness. Heat. *He feels so damn good.*

I arch again, *so close*, and the head of his cock slides just inside my writhing, slippery body.

His strong hand grips my hip, like he's trying to warn me. "Ivy—"

"*Please. Please.*" I don't want him to stop. I'll die if he stops.

He's stretching me, forcing his way inside, igniting a tidal wave of pleasure that makes me rock back against him in a needy, silky rhythm. I arch against him, inviting more. He's so big and I'm so tight but so wet and *nothing has ever felt this fucking good.*

His cock slides even deeper and he groans. I arch back against him and my body opens to him as he drives deeper. The pleasure reaches a wild peak, tipping me over into a rush of pleasure so extreme, I cry out. A molten explosion of clenching rapture consumes me. The spasming waves milk his big cock lusciously, pulling him deeper. Alexander grips me and thrusts into me. A thread of pain is engulfed by an even bigger wave of pleasure.

Oh my god. He's all the way inside me. *He's fucking me with that gigantic cock and I'm going to come again. Even harder.*

His hand cups my breasts, one then the other, pulling the soft elastic of my nightie down over them, giving him full access. His fingers squeeze my nipples, making me moan. His other hand slides down my stomach. Between my legs. His fingers swirl around my clit and squeeze in sync with the play of my nipple and the thrust of his impossibly huge cock. I can *hear* the wet thrusts as he drives deep, impaling me, his thickness sliding deep, deep inside, shattering me.

I lose myself completely. We're rocking and bucking, gripping and fucking, mindless with it. I come again, *hard.* The physical bliss swells and breaks through me in jolts of ecstasy that tug lovingly at his deeply-rooted cock.

Alexander growls like a bear and I can feel the

rushing flood of warmth inside me, filling me with milky, lustrous heat.

It lasts a long time. The surge of his cock inside me throbs in perfect harmony with the fluttery clench of my inner muscles around him. Our bodies are locked in a secret dance that holds and plays.

His big body is wrapped around mine. His still-throbbing cock is wedged deep inside me. His overflowing cum coats my thighs.

And I start to come down from the best feeling I've ever experienced in my life.

I don't allow my brain to think, but the whispers knock on some door behind my sated endorphin rush. *I just lost my virginity to my fake date. I just got fucked by a total stranger. Without protection. And he's still inside me.*

But I don't have room for logic right now.

The only thing I have room for is a deeply-fulfilling happiness. Because I have never in my life felt this safe or this good.

19

ALEXANDER

FUCK.

I slowly pull out of her and a gush of my cum spills. What's really fucked up is *I don't want it to spill.*

Christ. "Ivy?" I carefully roll her onto her back, crouching over her, gently smoothing her hair back.

Her eyes are bright but sort of lust-drowsed, her face flushed and so sweet, I silence all the thoughts rampaging through my head just so I can kiss her perfect lips.

"Are you okay, baby girl?" I was so fucking overcome with lust that I just spent myself inside her. I could never have pulled out of that tight, juicy little heaven on earth.

Goddamn it. It didn't even *occur* to me to put on a condom. I've never had sex without a condom in my life.

As soon as I felt her writhing little body backing up to me, her pussy so wet and ready for me, my brain took flight and left the building. Leaving my goddamn cock in charge, and he just had the night of his fucking life.

Little Ivy Laine was a *virgin*. I *felt* it when I broke through the thin barrier. My cock had never been more engorged, hot and rock-hard. "Did I hurt you?"

I *would* have hurt her. But I couldn't have stopped myself if a herd of wild horses was trying to drag me away. "Why didn't you tell me, sweetheart?"

Even as I ask her this, I think we both know it wouldn't have slowed either one of us down.

"You didn't hurt me," she says softly. Her dark, light-catching hair spills over the pillow in a silky cascade. I was rough with her. Is she bruised? She'll be sore.

I get up, pulling my boxers mostly back up since I never managed to get them all the way off, and I go into the bathroom to run some warm water.

Fuck, I'm already half-cocked again. The little goddess is giving me superpowers.

I grab a small towel and make sure it's the right temperature before squeezing out the excess.

Going back into the bedroom, I turn on one low lamp so I can see her. She hasn't moved. She's laying there sort of blissed out, like an angel who just got her first taste of the devil and fucking *loved* it. I've never seen anything more stunning in my life as this girl and especially now.

The lacy lingerie she's wearing is pulled down over her breasts, plumping them high and close. The nonexistent skirt of it is bunched up around her waist. She's completely bare and her pussy is pink and wet with my cum.

Holy fuck.

I can't get over how gorgeous she is. I'm also struggling to deal with how obsessed I am with this sultry vision of beauty and lusty lost innocence.

I sit on the bed between her legs. There are faint streaks of blood on her thighs, along with shiny moisture. I use the warm washcloth to carefully clean her skin, not touching her pussy yet.

She lets me do this, calm and golden-eyed, like she's still coming down from her high.

And I can't help myself. With my fingers, I swirl some of the cum that still spills, over her pussy, gently pushing some of it back inside her.

What are you doing, Maddox?

Claiming her. I want her.

You want her knocked up? Because it sort of seems like you're trying to make that happen right now.

My own internal dialogue is pissing me off.

I don't know. Maybe. Just recently I was thinking about how alone I am and always have been. Brothers don't count. I thought maybe it wasn't in the cards for me to *feel* so much I could actually bear to think about a future with someone.

Well, you might have a whole lot of future with this little minx if you don't figure out how to control this situation.

I don't want to control it.

She's watching my eyes and something visceral passes between us. We're in this together now. There's a bond here we're choosing to make more profound by letting this happen. By just going with how good this feels.

I paint my cum over her clit, using the silkiness of it to gently caress her. A soft moan escapes her as she barely writhes into the pleasure. My cock gets instantly rock-hard again.

When I'm satisfied, I use the warm cloth to clean some of myself from her, so I can taste her and only her. I toss the damp cloth aside, pushing her legs wider. I lean in, kissing her perfect pussy, gliding my tongue over her clit, sucking gently, then dipping my tongue inside her.

"*Oh*," she gasps.

Fucking hell.

She tastes like nirvana. As sweet as honey. Like she spends her days wandering through sunny summer meadows with wildflowers blooming, while eating peaches. I don't fucking know. All I know is that I *need* to feast on her.

I suck on her like she's a ripe fruit and I'm a starving man. It's depraved, almost, the need and greed I feel.

She squirms and moans, letting her knees fall wider.

I am so far gone. I'm whipped like nothing I've ever known.

I've been a straight-up, high-achieving, mostly-respectable workaholic my entire life. And I've tripled the value of my father's and grandfather's company, through sheer grit and hard work.

But *this girl* makes me want to fuck everything up. I want to mark her and claim her and fuck her with a desperation I don't even recognize.

Ivy's willingness only compounds my manic need. Her hands are in my hair. I play her with my tongue, easing two fingers inside her. I know she's sore. I try to be gentle.

"*Alex*," she moans.

I'm shocked by my own reaction, by how much I *love* that sound. Of her, calling my name, the version of it only the people closest to me use, in that dreamy exhale, like I'm a mythical creature she can't believe. Like I'm too good to be true.

She's starting to come, and there's no way I can *not* be inside her when that happens. I climb up her body, licking and roughly sucking her rosy nipples before laying myself over her. I ease myself into her, letting the spasms of her pleasure draw me deeper, until I can't hold back and I thrust all the way to the hilt, making her cry out.

Her snug, quivering pussy is so tight and so sweet, squeezing my cock in tight, silky pulls, until all my restraint is milked from my body, leaving me no choice. I couldn't stop this from happening even if I tried.

I don't try. I fully surrender to the perfect bliss of her. She feels so pure and so good, I might as well be pumping my whole soul into her along with my cum.

I kiss her as the waves begin to calm, licking into her

mouth as her gasps begin to ease, smoothing her damp hair from her angel's face. I gaze down at her with something close to rapt adoration.

I'm in real trouble here.

Because I've found my weakness. I already know I'll do anything to keep her. Already, the thought of her leaving me and walking out of my life like she's not the most magical thing in the fucking world is unbearable.

This is what I want, right here. This perfect girl. I'm addicted, besotted and obsessed.

Mine.

20

I open my eyes. I wait for the familiarity to settle, used to feeling a little unsure of my surroundings. *I live in Soho now.*

But I'm not in Soho. A ceiling fan circles slowly above me and everything comes rushing back.

I'm in Alexander Maddox's hotel room. In the Hamptons.

My fake date.

Oh my god. We spent most of the night…having hot, crazy sex.

Very unprotected hot, crazy sex.

I'm going to need to think about this, about what I'm going to do. My period is due in a few days. *Maybe it's too late in my cycle. Maybe it takes more than…four times.*

Oh shit.

I groan even though I can't summon even a single iota of regret. Even though I really, really *should* be able to.

This is bad.

I turn to his side of the bed, gasping at the new aches and pains in my body. I'm very sore. My virginity has been well and truly cashed in. Repeatedly and extremely thoroughly.

God, it was so amazing.

Alexander's gone. There's a note on the pillow and a single red rose.

> *Good morning gorgeous,*
> *You looked so peaceful I couldn't bear to wake you. I've gone fishing with Blake and the others. I'll be back in a few hours. Call room service when you're ready and they'll bring you breakfast. You'll be hungry. Then I'd like you to sleep some more, or relax by the pool, swim, order more room service and wait for me.*
> *P.S. You're the most beautiful, sexy, perfect and delectable woman in the world. I'll spend the entire fishing trip thinking about you and counting the minutes until I can see you again.*
> *A*

Wow.

The hot, grumpy billionaire is…sweet. And romantic.

Yesterday, I wouldn't have believed it. But now I know better. I'm not surprised that Alexander Maddox is as insistent and ruthless in bed as he is out of it. But he's also a very attentive, tender and dedicated lover. He lavished me with so many orgasms I lost count.

He made sure he got his way, but he *felt* me so deeply. He made sure *my* pleasure was the priority, and that my pleasure *worked* his. He played my body like Yo-Yo Ma plays his freaking cello.

My stomach growls.

He's right, I am hungry. Starving, in fact. I feel like I've run a marathon.

Gingerly, I sit up. I'm sore in places I didn't even know I had muscles. I climb out of bed, adjusting to my new body. The one that's been made love to so thoroughly I feel like a completely different person. A freer one. A more powerful one.

The bed looks like a three-day orgy took place in it. There's a light smear of blood on the sheets.

Yikes.

How many times did he come inside me? Three? Four? *Five?*

I really can't believe we got so carried away. I can't believe *I* got so carried away and I can't believe Mr. Control Freak did either. I only just met him, but it seems out of character for him. I mean, who *does* that?

Who jumps into bed with an almost-stranger and has unprotected sex with him all night long, throwing all caution to the wind just to have simultaneous multiple orgasms for the very first time in her life?

Me, apparently.

That's not okay. You need to deal with this.

I will. But I carefully slide the a-lot-of-very-real-issues-to-worry-about circular thought process into a file near the back of my brain labeled I Definitely Will Worry About All Of Them, In Excruciating Detail, Maybe Even Later Today, But Not Right This Moment.

There's a white terrycloth robe in the open closet. I put it on, tying the belt. Then I pick up the hotel phone. *For reception, press 1*, it reads.

They pick up on the first ring. "Good morning, Miss Ivy. We've been waiting for your call. We hope you've had a restful sleep. Do you prefer coffee or tea?"

"Um…coffee please. And could I please order some fruit?"

"Do you have any special dietary requirements, Miss Ivy?"

"No, but if you have any fruit—"

"Mr. Maddox has selected a wide variety of dishes for you, Miss Ivy, among them a platter of fresh-cut organic fruits sourced from ethically-selected growers worldwide, including Hawaiian pineapple, locally-grown water-melon, New Zealand kiwis, coconuts imported earlier this week from Thailand, Georgia peaches, and seventeen others, which I'd be happy to list for you if you'd like."

"Oh. No, that's fine."

"Wonderful. We'll have your nutritious and rejuvenating breakfast delivered to your room within ten minutes."

"Okay. Thank you."

Wow, this place has amazing service.

I use the ten minutes to take a quick shower. It's strangely emotional watching the rivulets of water on the white stone of the shower floor, tinted with my own blood and the evidence of our lovemaking.

It was as beautiful as it possibly could have been. I wish we could do it all over again.

I'm glad I waited for him. Even if I never see him again after tomorrow, I'll always have this piece of him, this memory of what I can only describe as…well, the best night of my entire life. It sounds dramatic and it is. It felt so good to be *treasured*. To feel so beautiful that a man like Alexander Maddox couldn't control himself and didn't want to. There's a power to that that I'll take with me. I'll hold it—and him—close to my heart for the rest of time.

That might not be the only thing you're holding.

I'll deal with everything I need to deal with, like I always do. And I'll get on with rest of my life.

Hot sex with my fake date was…incredible. But I can't let myself be deluded into thinking it was more than that. Maybe sex *is* that connective. How would I know? Maybe it's one of those things that bonds two people just because it's the most intimate act of them all.

It felt like more than that.

It felt life-changing and extraordinary. I feel like I could…fall for him. He was so beautiful, so big, so freaking good at—

There's a loud knock on the door.

I turn off the shower, quickly dry myself and put my robe on, padding to the door—making a small detour to pull the duvet up over the sheets—to open it.

"Greetings, Miss Ivy." Three waiters are standing there with rolling trays full of silver domes covering at least twenty different plates, as well as juices, coffee and a bottle of champagne on ice. They start wheeling them into the room.

"Wow, this is so much food."

"At Mr. Maddox's insistence, Miss Ivy. He wanted to make sure you had enough to eat."

A woman dressed in a hotel uniform follows the waiters, carrying a huge bouquet of gorgeous pink peonies. She sets them on the table. "For you, Miss Ivy," she smiles. "From Mr. Maddox."

They unload all the plates, removing the silver domes and arranging everything sort of artfully, then they wheel the carts to the door. "Have a wonderful day, Miss Ivy."

"Thank you."

I've never seen so much food in my life. There's the fruit platter—which alone could feed me for a week— scrambled eggs, bagels with cream cheese, smoked salmon and capers, an antipasto platter, fresh bread with butter and jam, rashers of crispy bacon, hash browns, a basket of croissants, donuts, little cartons of different flavored yogurts, granola, French toast and waffles with maple syrup.

I couldn't eat all this in a month, but it does look delicious and my stomach growls again at the sight.

I pour myself a cup of coffee and make a small plate of fruit, adding a few pieces of bacon and a chocolate croissant, carrying it out to the patio, grabbing my phone on the way to check my messages.

It's a clear, perfect day and very warm. The water is calm and a few boats are out, making wakes. In the distance, along the shore, I can see the rows of chairs lined up in front of the altar and hotel staff busily getting ready for the wedding.

I have one message from Cleo.

CALL ME

And none from Josh. *Damn it, Josh. You better have taken care of it.*

I take a selfie with a backdrop of the view and send it to Cleo.

My phone immediately rings with a FaceTime call.

I almost don't answer it, but then she'll worry and there's no point putting off the inevitable. "Hey, Clee."

"I want to hear about *everything*. How was your night?"

"It was…good." I almost smile at the understatement, but I make a point of not being too obvious. *It was extremely hot and exceptionally orgasmic. It was also somehow abso-lutely perfect.*

"How did the whole sharing one bed thing go? Was it awkward?"

What to say? "No. No, it was fine. I slept really well, actually." Not a total lie. Those last few hours of sleeping in were the restorative REM kind of sleep.

I *will* end up telling Cleo at least most of what happened, but I can't do it now. I'm still only halfway through the weekend and at this point, anything could happen. Plus I'm not quite ready to talk about what happened last night. It's a monumentally big deal and I need to process it before I can provide a detailed tell-all to my very inquisitive bestie.

"Is he being nice?"

"Yes, he's being nice. He's actually not as grumpy as I was expecting."

"That's good. Is he there? Am I on speaker?"

"No, he's gone fishing with the groom and a few other guys from the bridal party."

"I'm glad he's being civilized, Ive. I give Alexander a hard time because he's always scowling at everyone when he comes to meetings at IE, but I've always thought there's a lot more to him. His brothers always say his bark is worse than his bite and that he's carrying the weight of the world on his shoulders, but somehow his heart of gold remains intact."

It's a nice description, and it fits.

"He's just a hard nut to crack," she adds.

Actually not that hard. "You should see the breakfast he ordered for me." I wander inside and point my camera at the table full of food.

"Holy shit. And flowers? Wait…did you guys… hook up?"

"What?" I laugh. "Of course not. He was just saying thank you. For doing this whole fake date thing." I hate lying to her but she'll go absolutely apeshit if I tell her the truth, and I'm still figuring out how to navigate this whole situation. It's hard enough to come to terms with the *thought* of what I've just done, I can't yet deal with the reality—and saying the words will make the whole thing much more real.

Oh and by the way, Clee, Alexander Maddox just boned me into next week. It was my very first time and my very first orgasm—as well as my second, third, fourth, fifth and sixth—and now I can barely walk. Oh, and we also didn't use protection of any kind whatsoever so I could possibly be dealing with ten different kinds of fallout from that, any one of which could completely change my life, and not necessarily in a good way. But how are you?

It's a lot. So I choose the more forgiving path, at least until I can talk about it with her in person. "He's been a complete gentleman." *In public. In private, he's a well-hung caveman with mad skills and a dirty mind.*

"What time's the wedding?" she asks, totally buying my lie.

I know she'll forgive me when I get a chance to

explain everything. "Two o'clock. Until then, I'm going to go work on my tan by the infinity pool."

"Wear that little animal print bikini I packed for you."

"Thanks for not packing me any undies, by the way."

She giggles. "Sorry. I might just be veeerrry secretly hoping that you two will fall madly in love and ride off happily into a beautiful sunset together."

"Yeah right." My heart skips a beat at her description. I have to remind myself that isn't going to happen. Alexander is not my handsome billionaire boyfriend and —hot sex or no hot sex—I'm still here to play a role. I pull the tiny shred of animal skin fabric out of my suitcase. "You mean this one?"

"When he sees you in that…all bets are off. You're going to totally scandalize the Hamptons. God, I wish I was there to see their faces."

"Do I really have to 'scandalize' anyone?"

"Of course you do." There's a beep at her end. "Oh, Sam's calling me, sweetie, I have to go. Send me a picture of you by the pool and have fun. Call me later."

"Bye, Clee. Tell Sam I said hi."

We end the call and I stand in front of the full-length mirror. I let the robe drop and pull on the minuscule bikini.

Cleo's not wrong. This bikini really *might* scandalize the Hamptons. Two small triangles of fabric barely cover my nipples, revealing the rest of the fullness of my breasts almost completely. The lower triangle barely covers the parts it's supposed to cover. *And* it's a thong.

I turn, getting a view of myself in the mirror from different angles. I'm really not sure this is a good idea.

As though Cleo's reading my mind, I get a text at that exact moment.

Don't second guess it. You look freaking hot and you know it. WEAR IT. And work it, girl! You're a smoke show and everyone wishes they were as gorgeous as you. Love u xx

I sigh. I love my best friend more than anyone, but she really can be infuriating.

I finish my breakfast, brush my teeth, grab my bag and sunglasses and head for the pool.

21

I'm WEARING my high-heeled sandals because they're the only pair of shoes I brought with me.

Several other women are at the pool, chatting in lounge chairs. I don't recognize any of them from last night. They all look up as I walk past them, murmuring to each other, and I smile, finding an empty lounger a few seats away from them.

I spread my towel out and take a few minutes to put my Sun Tropez Bronzer sunscreen on, a gift from one of my clients. I lay back, taking a selfie with the tube of sunscreen visible. Then I post it, tagging them and the swimsuit company.

The perfect sunscreen to go with the perfect bikini on a sunny day in the Hamptons #ad #hamptons #wildswimcali #suntropezbronzer [splashing water emoji] [bikini emoji] [sunshine emoji]

Then I enjoy the sun for a while, letting myself completely relax. I have a lot of things I *could* worry about right now, but I give myself exactly one hour to bask in the beautiful day in this stunning place, my body still humming from all the orgasms. I figure that's forgivable. I mean, who knows when it'll ever happen again?

I'm grateful to be here, by this glittering pool. I know how lucky I am, to get to spend the day like this.

I'm grateful people liked the song last night and so many people complimented my music.

I'm grateful I got to meet Alexander Maddox. It's a crazy scenario that led me here and I have no idea what will happen, but I'm grateful…it was him. I'm grateful he felt so freaking good. He was so big. So hard. God. The way he felt when he came inside me…it was like the jets of his cum were a kind of trigger, like my body couldn't get enough of the warm, pulsing force of it.

I'm supposed to be doing my gratitude practice and instead all I can think about is my fake date's gigantic cock.

I'm getting wet just thinking about him. My pussy's tingling and softening. Like it did when he swirled his cum all over it, pushing some of it back inside. Why did he do that?

I decide to take a dip in the pool, to cool down a little. I go over to the far end where the steps are and wade in until I'm up to my neck. I let my arms rest on the edge of the infinity pool, looking out over the view of the ocean.

It's then that I hear more voices.

The men are back from their fishing trip. I can see

Blake, Alexander and a few others entering the pool area. They're followed by Margot.

I swim back to the steps and, dripping wet, head to my lounger.

When they see me, every single one of them stops in their tracks and they all go completely silent. Staring at me. From my toes, up. Lingering on each one of the triangles. Not even reaching my face.

One of the men covers Blake's eyes with his hand. Another guy, who looks a lot like a slightly younger version of Blake, glances at Alexander before covering his own eyes with his own hand.

Margot, dressed in a new beige outfit and clutching her iPad, looks pissed off.

The expression on Alexander's face is one of stormy, layered fury.

He walks toward me, grabbing my towel on the way, which he carefully wraps around me. In fact his carefulness clashes with the fire in his eyes. He leans close to my ear and growls, "I'm going to request that you come back to the room with me immediately, Jones. Please, don't protest. Because you're coming with me even if I have to carry you over my shoulder."

I glare at him. If it was any other weekend, under any other circumstances, I'd do what I want and return to my lounger. But we had a deal. "Fine."

"Good." His arm is around me. I step into my shoes

and he grabs my bag, leading me out of the pool area, as the cluster of people watches us.

"What's your problem?" I ask him, once we're out of earshot. I probably should have said what's *the* problem, but it's too late. The way I've phrased it sounds like we're familiar. It's a petulant question you'd ask a friend or a sibling or a lover.

But to hell with it. He *is* familiar—in some ways more familiar than anyone else in my life has ever been. He *is* my lover. Or he was. And he's pissing me off by dragging me along with him like he owns me.

We get to the door of the suite and he opens it, ushering me through it before basically slamming it shut, trapping me against it with the cage of his big body. "You want to know what my *problem* is?" he seethes.

"Yes! I don't appreciate you treating me like some kind of possession!" I don't care if he paid for my time. He didn't pay to boss me around like he's my damn CEO.

"I'm not treating you like a *possession*, but if I have to watch ten feral men ogle you in that…that *bikini*, there's a very real chance I'll kill one of them, and that would really ruin the fucking wedding day, wouldn't it?"

He's so freaking *bossy*. "They weren't *ogling* me."

"Oh yes they were! Every single one of them was fantasizing about taking you to bed!"

"Who cares? It happens."

"It *happens*?"

"Yes! All the time! And you *told* me to put on a show,

so here's your show!" I let the towel drop, noticing then that the bed has been made by housekeeping. The flowers are still on the table, the champagne has been freshly iced and some of the food is back under its silver domes.

But Alexander doesn't notice any of it. His eyes are on me. On the tiny triangles of animal skin fabric, and more specifically on the areas *not* covered by the tiny triangles of animal skin fabric.

I'm a little shocked when he drops to his knees. His warm palms slide down my thighs. "I can't fucking handle this. I spent the whole morning going insane because I'm addicted to how fucking sweet you are. Let me taste your pink pussy again, baby girl. I need my fix. You can't tease me like that and not give me more." He presses his mouth between my legs, kissing me through the thin layer of my bathing suit. Gently *biting*.

I gasp, grabbing fistfuls of his thick hair. I should refuse him, of course. He's an overbearing jerk. And this is definitely not part of our "deal." We should be sitting down and talking through what we're going to do about the very real consequences we might have on our hands from last night's sex-a-thon.

But he's pushing my bikini to the side, licking me in lewd, delving swipes. *Eating* me in lusty mouthfuls. Sucking on me until the pleasure waves are already close to pushing me over some crazy edge.

"*Alex*," I protest, lightly pulling on his hair. I don't know if I'm trying to push him away or pull him closer.

"You want me, Jones. Your pussy's so fucking wet for me. I can *taste* how bad you want me." He licks me again with a growl.

Holy hell. I'm about to come.

"Say it."

"Say w-what?" I manage to gasp.

"Say fuck me right up against this door, Maddox, because I need to ride that big cock until I'm coming hard."

Oh god, I'm going to come if he keeps sucking on my clit like that.

He stands, lifting me as he does, freeing my nipples from their ridiculously small coverings and I have no choice but to wrap my legs around him. He's so tall. So damn strong. His expression is stern, full of heat and also laced with a hint of vulnerability, like he *needs* me to want him as much as he wants me, and this detail almost clashes with his alpha, hard-bodied, billionaire vibe.

"*Please*," is the best I can do right now because his gigantic cock is pressed up against the *exact* place that if he started doing that with any kind of rhythm, I'd shatter in the best kind of way.

"Does 'please' mean you want me to pump you full of my hot cum right here up against this door?"

"*Yes*." In fact it does.

He's unfastening his pants and kissing me. His big cock springs free and rubs up against my slick wetness and *damn him.* My traitorous hips tilt forward, seeking more of him. *All* of him.

I mean, we've already done it with no barriers several times. Once more is hardly going to matter. Then we'll talk.

What, after you're knocked up?

My common sense is screaming behind some wall of pleasure that's so beautiful and so powerful, it washes away all my sanity. Common sense is no match for animal biology when it comes to Alexander Maddox, I'm learning. Something in me wonders if it's because he's basically perfect in every possible way. He's an A-list alpha male apex New York predator. He's also so gorgeous and hot and beautiful I literally can't resist him.

I love his big muscles. I love the dark burn in his blue eyes. I love his thick black hair that never quite behaves like a CEO's should. I even love his grumpiness, which is sexier than I know what to do with. *Oh god.* And I *love* how he feels when he teases my clit with his huge, rigid, silky length.

"Tell me what you want, Jones. Tell me you want me to fuck you hard and deep, just the way you like it."

Damn it! "*Yes. Please. Please fuck me,*" I hear myself plead because I'm already starting to come and I've never experienced the kind of pleasure he coaxes from my quivering body. I cry out as his thickness forces entry, stretching me open and sliding deep, the hard, veined ridges of him rubbing against the soreness and most of all the sweet, perfect trigger that's already tipping me over the edge.

He grips my ass and starts thrusting in a slow, in-out rhythm that feels so damn good all I can do is moan into his mouth as his tongue tangles with mine.

The thick, slippery friction is too much. The pleasure is crazy, crashing through me in luscious clenches. My whole body is coming, milking his throbbing length in tight tugs, over and over. He groans a low oath as his release explodes, pumping his flooding heat deep inside me in rhythmic bursts until it's dripping down my thighs.

We're both breathing hard. I'm dazed and over-whelmed.

My head rests on his shoulder as he carries me to the bed, somehow keeping himself inside me. Only when he lays me down does his huge, spilling bulk slip from my body.

Alexander climbs up the bed and lays next to me. We stay like that for a while, face to face on the bed with his arm around me, just staring into each other's eyes as he smooths my hair. "It's okay," he murmurs. "Everything's okay."

Is it? I feel the sting of tears because this is all happening so fast and we're both losing control and I don't know how to stop it or slow it down. We need to talk about it and I don't know how so I just blurt it out. "I'm not on the pill."

He wipes my tear with his thumb sort of contemplatively. For a second I wonder if he heard me. "We're going to go to this wedding," he says. "Then tonight I'm going to hold you in my arms and tell you how beautiful you are. Tomorrow you're going to come home with me. You're going to stay with me and we're going to talk everything through and figure this out."

"Come *home* with you? I can't come home with you." That wasn't part of our deal.

"You said Josh won't be back until Monday."

I told him that? I must have been rambling when I was trying to make small talk with the people at our table last night. Just hearing Alexander say my brother's name somehow makes this whole thing feel much more real. "I can't come home with you," I say again.

That would be breaking our rule. The one where this is a fake date and we're strangers and we play our roles and then we go our separate ways. That's how this was supposed to play out.

Besides, tomorrow night I'm going to be scrambling around trying to find a pharmacy or an emergency clinic that can provide me with a Plan B because I keep getting so carried away, I've now had unprotected sex with a man I've known for one day at least five times.

"Ivy." Alexander traces the wing of my eyebrow with his finger. "I know this is going to sound crazy, but I'm going to say it anyway. What we're doing doesn't feel like a mistake. It feels like it's something we shouldn't take for granted. I've never had sex without a condom. I've never felt like a Sasquatch capable of murder when another man checks out my date, who happens to be the most stunning girl I've ever seen in my life. I somehow got lucky enough to go on a fake date with a perfect little goddess who walked out of my wildest fantasies. When you get *that* lucky, baby, you don't just let her walk away. You do whatever it takes to get another date with her. A real one, this time."

Wow. "I bet you say that to all the girls."

"I don't have other girls. You're my only girl. You're the girl I want."

"You can't know that after one day," I whisper.

"It's not one day. It's almost thirty years of feeling totally fucking empty."

I have to ask it. "You don't feel empty now?"

He pulls me closer, so my body is flush against his. His eyes are deep, the blueness of them almost surreal. "No. I don't feel empty. What I *feel* like is that a supernova of beauty just landed in the middle of my life and I'm trying to figure out how to keep her there, because I'm addicted to her sweet smile. I feel like, after a lifetime of running, I might actually be *trying* to knock you up just so I can keep you. I don't know what to do with all that, Jones, except whatever you need me to do to look at me and begin to see a future."

22

Alexander escorts me to my seat, which is at the outer edge of the first row. He leans down to kiss me—a *real* kiss, his tongue touching mine, like a claim.

Then he makes his way up to the front, to the altar, where Blake, Margot, the minister and the other groomsmen are already waiting, watching us both.

They're not the only ones whose heads turn toward me. I'm wearing a fitted sleeveless gold dress that hugs my curves and my gold high-heeled sandals.

But I'm hardly worried about my outfit.

I'm still flushed from all those things Alexander said to me. And from the confusion I'm feeling. The lust that's digging into me, burrowing its power into my soul with shards of something else altogether. Something new and hopeful.

Do I *want* a real date with Alexander Maddox? Do I

want to spend the night with him tomorrow night…for real? As two people who aren't faking it at all, but are instead choosing to enter brand new territory that includes both emotion and reality? We already know we have a crazy chemistry and an intense physical attraction to each other. But can you build a relationship on that? Do I want to?

Of course you do. Look at him. Standing there in his tux like a freaking Spartan or a god among men. He's extraordinary.

I don't feel even remotely ready for any of the decisions I need to make within the next day and a half. Which means I'm probably not remotely ready to say yes to any of them.

It's not helping that Alexander is so damn gorgeous. Eyeing me sternly like all he wants to do is carry me back to the room and have his way with me again.

I'm in big trouble. For around ten different reasons.

Margot is saying something to Alexander and Blake, but the ruse we were putting on for her is inconsequential now. Within the intensity of our whirlwind fake-date-turned-wild-love-affair-on-steroids, Margot got cut loose. Alexander isn't interested in humoring her or listening to what she's saying at all. She lost him a long time ago, but now he's aggressive about it, and cutting.

She retreats to her seat on the other side of the front row, looking dejected and hurt, but I can't help feeling that she's sort of asking for it at this point. There are only so many times a person can say no. Eventually you have to listen, no matter how badly you wish you could change their mind.

He's mine now.

I don't analyze the possessive flare burning inside me. It feels good there. It's warming me with hope. It's not an emotion I allow myself to indulge very often. I'm usually too focused on getting shit done to improve my brother's life and my own.

Now, I let it simmer.

Alexander's eyes find mine. My heart skips a beat as I see the way he lights up—a small but unmistakable *happiness* in him. Because of me.

It's powerful.

He looks so damn hot and at the same time sort of spellbound by this connection we're both feeling, it stirs something in me. Against this backdrop of romance and undying love, I let myself imagine for a split second what it might *feel* like. To fall in love with him. To trust him to be loyal and kind and faithful—things I have no experience with. My baggage is all about abandonment, infidelity and divorce.

But those things were never mine. They belonged to my parents, not me. And I don't have to be defined by them. In fact, I *refuse* to be defined by them. *I* get to decide my own story.

A string quartet starts to play. Everyone turns to look at Leah and her four bridesmaids, who are all dressed in yellow silk.

Leah's dress is classic and beautiful, with a long, lacy train that trails behind her. Her blond hair hangs over her shoulders. She looks absolutely radiant.

We all watch her walk down the aisle to where Blake is standing. As the ceremony begins, I only vaguely hear their vows. I'm too busy staring at my hot fake date.

Alexander is a head taller than the other men and his jacket clings tightly to his muscles.

The width of his shoulders is impressive, almost imposing. The squareness of his jaw reminds me of the scratchy feel of it on the sensitive skin of my thigh *as he feasted on me so lustily. Licking into me. Drawing pleasure from my body with the greedy draws of his mouth.*

Alexander's watching me, like he can read my dirty mind.

I bite my bottom lip, imagining being back in our hotel room, undoing his belt, taking his massive length in my hands and gripping him with my fist. Kissing him.

Sucking on him.

I want to do it.

I blush, but Alexander holds my gaze, as if daring me to look away first.

He mouths a single word.

Mine.

Very subtly, I shake my head.

Very subtly, he nods, barely narrowing his eyes at me.

Maybe I could love him. Maybe I'm already falling just the tiniest bit.

Maybe sometimes you just click with someone and it happens in a wild rush that feels star-studded and full of optimism. Maybe it makes you believe that love at first sight could be real. That white-hot lust can bloom and grow into a lifetime.

As Leah says the words, "I do," through tears of joy, I let myself, for a moment, *feel* him.

Our gazes are still locked. Very subtly, I nod. Alexander's slow smile causes the smallest fissure in my heart to open a fraction wider.

He's outrageously beautiful. And I remember his words.

I somehow got lucky enough to go on a fake date with a perfect little goddess who walked out of my wildest fantasies. When you get that lucky, baby, you don't just let her walk away. You do whatever it takes to get another date with her. A real one, this time.

Maybe one more night with him wouldn't be so bad.

One more night, and then I'll figure out what to do.

"WHY ARE you're such a good dancer?" I ask him, laughing. The band is upbeat and they insisted the whole crowd pile onto the dance floor as soon the bride and groom had finished their first dance.

"Boarding school. All well-rounded young men should be able to lead a woman around the dance floor."

"Who says you're leading? Your hands keep wandering," I tell him.

"Of course they do. *Look* at you." His hands are on my waist, holding me against his big, lean body. He leans close to my ear and growls, "You look so fucking gorgeous I could eat you."

"Didn't you…already…?" I whisper back, blushing.

The blue heat in his eyes is becoming familiar to me by now. "Don't mention eating your perfect pussy to me,

Jones," he murmurs, "or I'll have to drag you back to our room and ravage you again."

I laugh again. It's been a while since I laughed this much. My grumpy fake date is not only infuriating, he's also surprisingly charming. He's got a wry, filthy sense of humor and he insists on having his arm around me at all times. He's funny and attentive, and I'm having more fun than I've had in a long time.

The ceremony was beautiful and so far the reception has gone without a hitch. Sour-faced and sporting another beige outfit or not, I have to give it to Margot. She plans a good wedding.

Huge, full-bloom bouquets of white peonies and roses fill the marquee. Floral notes mix with the sea breeze, giving the whole place a magical atmosphere. Crisp white linen tablecloths, gold silverware and green sea-glass candleholders add to the luxury and romance of the setting.

Alexander brushes his lips against mine.

He doesn't *need* to do this. No one's questioning whether the two of us are legit anymore, if they ever did, and Margot seems to have accepted defeat once and for all. She's distracted, busy ordering her minions around. She's hardly a blip on our radar at this point.

I think Alexander and I have both decided to just enjoy the rest of our weekend and lean in to…this. This connection. This wild attraction. This crazy intensity.

The touch of his tongue sends a zing of electric

warmth down my spine, settling lower, centering in that secret place. I can still feel the soreness…*from his punishing, spilling cock.*

"I'd kiss you properly," he says, his voice low, "but I have to give a speech soon and I don't want to scare anyone away with my gigantic hard-on."

A giggle escapes me. "I can say from experience that it *is* in fact very scary. I can still barely walk." The playful banter comes so easily. I stand on my toes to whisper in his ear. "I guess in that case I shouldn't mention that I'm not wearing any panties."

He groans. "Fucking hell, Jones. Are you *trying* to kill me?"

I can't help laughing at his pained expression.

The band plays a final chord and Margot steps up to tap on the microphone. "Please take your seats, wedding guests. We'll now begin the speeches as our third course is served."

She motions to Alexander. He's on the schedule to give the first speech.

He escorts me back to our table and pulls out my chair for me. Then he tops up my champagne from the ice bucket next to our table. He kisses me again, maybe more lustily than the occasion calls for, until a few people whistle and cheer.

Then he buttons the jacket of his tux and heads for the stage.

I'm a long way from *acting* as I gaze up at him, as rapt

as everyone else here by his larger-than-life stage presence.

My first impression of Alexander Maddox was that he's a powerful man who's serious and reserved in everyday life. I wouldn't have guessed that in his own way, he might be described as—if not the life of the party—definitely the magnetic force of it. Everyone watches him and wants to get close to him. He's so darkly glamorous, so outrageously good-looking and has that smug humor that only comes out to play when he's relaxed. And I happen to know by now that hot sex takes the edge off his darker moods.

"For those of you who don't know me, I'm Alexander Maddox, Blake's best man," he begins.

Listening to him talk, I can see the part of him that's the showman. The professional. The great leader. The boss.

His speech hits all the right notes. He tastefully compliments Leah and talks about how she's added so much joy and love to Blake's life. He adds a few funny anecdotes about the early days of his friendship with Blake that are genuinely funny.

Alexander's speech is sincere and meaningful, and it gives a gravity to the whole event. It's the kind of speech you actually listen to. With his dark good looks and his stormy allure, you can't help but hang on his every word.

Turns out the grumpy billionaire is downright dreamy.

Stop falling for him this hard.

Alexander finishes the speech to loud applause. He goes over and shakes Blake's hand and kisses Leah on the cheek.

And then he walks back to me, his eyes on mine. My breath catches.

Don't you dare let your mind wander in crazy directions, girl, like the ones where you start to picture more than a weekend.

"Well done, Maddox," I smile, congratulating myself on not sounding breathless.

"Thank you, Jones." He sits and pulls me onto his lap. We fall into our rhythm, the one that started out as an act but has quickly evolved into an avalanche of feeling. I let my fingers weave through his thick hair because I want them to.

The rest of the speeches are given, some verging on awkward, others emotional and heartfelt. The food is outstanding, the champagne endlessly topped up. Blake and Leah cut the wedding cake. I'm high on sugar and Moët and the hard body of my suddenly not-so-fake date.

"You want to dance?" he drawls.

I nod and he pulls me onto the dance floor.

Alexander holds me close, his big hardness pressing against my stomach. I try to ignore the fact that I'm wet for him, that I'm not wearing panties and that something inside my heart feels light and airy, like the weight of the world isn't quite so heavy in this sea-scented candlelit night.

I don't know what will happen tomorrow or the day after. But tonight I allow myself to be just a little bit in love with Alexander Maddox.

"Leah and Blake seem so happy," I say.

"I was there the night they met. Blake couldn't take his eyes off her, from the very first time he saw her." My hands instinctively curl around his neck, slowly and intimately. "I didn't believe love at first sight was a real thing," he adds, his gaze wolfish but also almost unsettlingly sincere. "Now I know better."

I smile at his joke, but my throat feels tight.

One of the other groomsmen hovers near us for a few seconds like he's thinking about breaking in for a dance, but Alexander turns us so his back is to the man, who eventually wanders off.

I don't know what's happening to me. I feel so *safe* with him, so protected. Some buried, primitive instinct in me *loves* this. It's a feeling a girl could get used to.

I don't *need* a man, of course I don't. I've never had one and we've managed just fine. I'm a capable, empowered, modern woman. But I haven't spent a lot of my life feeling *safe*, and in this moment I can admit it's wildly comforting.

I stare into his eyes, my body molten with his effect.

Alexander's thumb brushes over my bottom lip. His kiss is gentle at first, but as his hands wander over my body, he presses harder against me, devouring my mouth.

Our tongues tangle and slide. I can feel his cock pushing against me, thick and hard between us.

"I never thought I'd see the day our Alexander would fall so hard," laughs Leah, and we break the kiss. She and Blake are dancing nearby, sort of drunkenly and very in love.

"Who can blame the man?" Blake laughs and Leah swats him playfully before they disappear back into the crowd.

"Come on," Alexander says, taking me by the hand. "Let's get out of here. It's getting late."

The party is really underway now. We're not even halfway back to our table when I feel someone's hand on my arm.

"Could I have this dance, Miss Laine?" a man asks.

Alexander and I both turn, and Alexander eyes the man aggressively. His eyes go dark and his whole body tenses. "Not a chance, buddy."

The man isn't smiling. He's also not wearing the typical wedding outfit. It looks more like a business suit, like he stopped by after a long day at the office. He reaches into his jacket pocket and angles an ID card toward us. He does this discreetly. "My name is Jack Dempsey. I'm a private investigator, hired by your father to investigate a recent incident. May I speak to you in private, Miss Laine? I'm afraid I must insist."

24

My stomach drops, like I've just hit the summit of a roller coaster and now we're plummeting straight down.

Shit shit shit.

Alexander's grip tightens. To the man, he hisses, "What's this about?"

"I'm afraid I can't discuss the details here, sir. It's a confidential matter." Mr. Dempsey turns to me. "Miss Laine, if you could accompany me to a quieter spot, I can explain to you what your father is intending to do about the incident. He takes this very seriously and so should you."

Of course I'm interested in hearing what the man has to say, but I'm unnerved by the fact that he's followed me here to the Hamptons. It's creepy that he would even know where I was.

I shouldn't allow Alexander to overhear this conversation. But at the same time, I don't want to be alone with this man. I make a split-second decision I'll probably regret. "I'll come with you. My…boyfriend will stay with me."

It's a ridiculous way to describe Alexander Maddox, who's about as alpha as a man can get, but fuck it. Even if I told him to leave me alone with Jack Dempsey, I know he wouldn't. And I don't want to argue with him about it right now. I also wouldn't mind his strong, comforting presence as I contemplate jail time.

We follow the private investigator toward a deserted seating area down by the water. To someone watching, we might look like we're admiring the view.

Alexander's palm settles in the small of my back.

I stare out at the water and try to steady my voice so I don't sound…well, guilty as fuck. "What did you want to discuss, Mr. Dempsey? And couldn't it have waited until Monday?"

"Your father is somewhat impatient about the matter," Mr. Dempsey replies. "Plain and simple, Miss Laine, he wants his money back. It's gone from his account and no one else has his banking information. Only you, which you accessed after breaking into his house."

Damn it, Josh! You said you'd put it back! "I didn't break into his house."

"According to his security cameras, you did. You also took a photo of the bank statement in question. And emailed it to your brother—who, incidentally, is currently in Fort Lauderdale spending up large. I have all the paper trails, Miss Laine. And enough evidence to present to the police in what would likely be a fairly open and shut case."

My mind is spinning with visions of my brother being dragged away in an orange jumpsuit. *Goodbye, Columbia.* I don't know whether to admit to Mr. Dempsey that he's right or continue pretending we're innocent.

I take a deep breath, using my meditation muscle memory to calm myself. To let the worst of the stress bounce off my inner forcefield. It barely helps. "Mr. Dempsey, my brother has a job and has saved some money. I also give him spending money. He's a seventeen-year-old on Spring Break, of course he's living it up. As for the security camera footage, I went to visit my father, gave him plenty of warning and assumed his door was unlocked because he was expecting me. I went into his office to leave him a note. The only photo I took was of my two other younger brothers, who I've never actually met." It's a lie and Mr. Dempsey knows it.

"Lying will only extend your jail time, Miss Laine, especially if you do it under oath, which is a situation you'll soon find yourself in if your father decides to pursue this prosecution. He was hoping that could be avoided. If the money is returned *in full* by Tuesday at five p.m., he's agreed to drop this whole thing. If not, he intends to prosecute to the full extent of the law."

Fuck fuck fuck.

Alexander has been quiet until now. "Mr. Dempsey," he says, slowly, like we've got all the time in the world. "Even if Miss Laine happened to see a bank statement, if Ivy and Josh's names aren't on the account, they couldn't possibly have withdrawn the funds."

Mr. Dempsey stares steadily at Alexander. "I'm sorry, I didn't catch your name."

"Maddox. Alexander Maddox."

It's easy to see that Mr. Dempsey has heard of him. He straightens his tie and adjusts his tone. Then he offers his hand and Alexander briefly shakes it. "Mr. Maddox, are you aware that Miss Laine's brother Josh is an experienced hacker? Who has successfully—and very illegally—hacked into at least one complex operating system before, barely escaping juvenile detention? A Bahamas bank account would have been a test of any hacker's expertise, but the boy clearly has skills. He's also created an incredibly realistic-looking fake ID, which he's currently using to bar hop his way through Fort Lauderdale. Another detail we'll be presenting to the police if that becomes necessary. Miss Laine, what did you say your brother is going to be studying at Columbia this fall?"

"Um…computer science," I admit.

Alexander almost looks impressed. "We appreciate your time, Mr. Dempsey, and we'll take all of that into consideration as Ivy and Josh consult their lawyers. If you'd like to leave your card with us, we'll contact you at our earliest convenience and let you know how we'd like to proceed. We'll be in touch before five p.m. on Tuesday."

We.

It's a good answer. He's using his CEO's voice. And it gets Mr. Dempsey's attention. "Very well."

"Are we done here, then?" Alexander asks.

"Uh…yes." Mr. Dempsey hands Alexander his card. "We'll hear from you by Tuesday, then."

"You will."

"Enjoy your night, Mr. Maddox," Mr. Dempsey says, nodding to me, "Miss Laine." With that, he walks off into the night.

My champagne high is completely gone.

I lean against the railing, letting my face drop into my hands. *Oh, Josh.*

Alexander comes up behind me, stroking my hair away from my neck, his fingers settling on my shoulders. "You're okay, sweetheart. Whatever this is, we'll figure it out. I've got you."

Here he goes again with the *I've got you.* I turn to face him. "Thank you for buying me some time. But I don't actually *have* a lawyer. So I'm going to—"

"Luckily for you, baby girl, *I* do. A whole fucking brigade of them."

I begin to push past him. "Since there's a snowball's chance in hell that I can afford your *brigade*—"

"Ivy." He snakes his brawny arm around my waist.

I look up at his outrageously handsome face and I can't help it: I burst into tears. I really try not to, but it's no use. I'm not good at confrontation and I'm definitely not good at being questioned by a private investigator who's followed me here like some kind of stalker.

How the hell did I get myself into this mess? I'm lying to a guy my dad hired to chase after me, I'm lying about being in a relationship with Alexander Maddox, and I'm lying to the whole world about how glamorous my life is. Lies, lies, lies.

It suddenly all feels heavier than I can bear.

Alexander wraps his arms around me, pulling me against his chest. It's so tender, so disarmingly sincere that it causes more tears to stream down my face.

"Hey," he croons. "We'll work it out. You're okay. Everything will be fine. You've got me now."

It feels more like a spear to the heart than a reassurance. I've literally known this man for *a day*. Yes, it feels like we've fast-tracked this whole thing. We clicked, or whatever you want to call it. Our souls meshed from that very first moment and have continued to entwine with every glance, every smile—and every fucking orgasm. But that doesn't make him my prince in shining armor.

He can't just *make* promises like that. It's not fair.

I wriggle from his embrace. "I need to go back to the room."

His arm is still around me, supporting me. And we don't have far to go. When we get back to our suite,

Alexander faces me, holding my shoulders with strong hands. "I'm going to go out to the patio and make a couple of phone calls. You get ready for bed and I'll be back in a minute."

I wipe my tears.

I get ready for bed, searching through my bag and finding the other nightie Cleo packed for me, a pink cotton babydoll number that once again barely covers me. I slide under the cool sheet and the plush duvet and force myself to think only about the extreme comfort levels of this bed.

It doesn't work.

We'll figure it out. Josh will have returned the money by the time he gets back. He promised.

I'm so comfortable I've almost drifted off when I feel Alexander's warm weight settle in next to me. He feels so good, instinctively, I curl up against him. His arms wrap around me.

"Is it true?" His voice is deep, lightly graveled. Not accusing, just curious. When I don't reply right away, he says, "You can trust me, Jones."

I don't know if it's his top-shelf pheromones, which seem to be pulling all the little strands of my DNA toward him, like flowers seeking sun. Or if maybe it's just nice to hear the sincerity in his voice when he says the word *trust.* It's so new, this soothing, comforting effect he has on me, like he's carrying some of the weight of my burden.

And so I end up telling him everything. I tell him

about what an asshat my father is and how I was trying to reach out to him one last time. I tell him about how Josh has struggled with feelings of abandonment but has still managed to rise above it and get himself into Columbia, and what a huge accomplishment that feels like. How he's a good kid. I tell him about losing our mother and feeling so alone with all the responsibility of keeping both of us on track, I sometimes felt like I was drowning. I tell him about how I don't *love* putting all the details of my life on Instagram, but how, the more I shared, the more money I made. And about how it was the best feeling in the world and one of the best days of my life when I was able to buy us the loft in Soho.

Alexander listens to all of it, asking questions here and there. He gently coaxes every secret, every emotion and every lie, explained, out of me, until I'm sobbing in his arms. But as my tears start to ease I find that I feel lighter. *So* much lighter, like he's taken some of the existential weight I've been carrying and offered to carry it himself.

"God," I exhale a sigh of relief or maybe regret. "I'm sorry. Now you know everything about me. And here you thought your fake date would make your life easier, and not bore you to tears with my pathetic backstory."

"It's not pathetic," he says. "It's heroic."

It might be the nicest thing anyone has ever said to me. And it helps. I look up into his eyes and I make a wish. I'm scarred, but in this moment, he feels like a beautiful, magical gift.

I wish he was mine. I wish I could keep him.

I reach up to touch his face. I softly kiss his lips. "Thank you for listening, Maddox."

"Thank you for trusting me, Jones."

With the change in my position, it's then that I notice the massive, hot bulk of him, resting thickly between us.

"Ignore it," he says.

But I don't want to ignore it. I want to *feel* him.

I want to taste him.

Tentatively, I smooth my fingers across the dragon inked to his chest. "Why a dragon?"

He doesn't answer right away, but then he finally says, "To remind myself that I'm invincible. In the boardroom or when it comes to a deal or a negotiation I can't lose. And it would have pissed my father off to no end. He never knew about it."

So we both had fathers who let us down in ways that have affected us deeply.

I run my fingers over the tight grooves of his six pack.

He gives me time to explore him, to run my fingers over the textures of his body.

Slowly, I let my hand ease around his thick length, rubbing my palm across the silky bulk. A small gush of liquid seeps out the end.

Alexander groans.

A primal wash of longing floods through me.

"Can I kiss you?" I whisper. I feel loose and reckless after my emotional gush. I feel greedy and so desperate for him I can't get close enough.

His eyes are hot and lust-drowsed. "You're tired. You've had a scare."

That's part of the reason *why* I want to explore him. What if I never get another chance? What if my life comes to a screeching halt next week when my father presses charges? Right now, I want to *live.* "I want to taste you, Alex. Can I? Please?"

"You can do any damn thing you want, angel girl."

I slide both my palms gently along his slick, solid length. I finger the ridge of the crown. I swirl the bead of moisture that's leaking there and touch my finger to my tongue.

Alexander is watching me. "Fuck, honey. You get me so fucking hot."

I can see that what I'm doing to him is almost painfully pleasurable for him. I squeeze him gently, tightening my grip.

I hardly recognize myself. I'm *thirsty* for him.

So I do it. I lean forward and touch my tongue to him, licking lightly.

His head falls back and he growls some filthy words. So I lick him again. I put my lips around the broad end and take him deeper, sucking on him carefully.

He groans like his heart is breaking.

I love that this big, powerful CEO is at my mercy. *He's mine.*

It doesn't take long. His cock starts to jerk. Milky liquid jets into my mouth in hot bursts. I drink some but there's too much. It spills down my chin.

It's the most powerful feeling in the world. Me, drinking his seed, holding him as it pulses out of him. A sticky bond that's a part of us now.

He pulls me up to him and I'm lying on top of him. He wipes my mouth gently with his thumb. His eyes are lust-drowsed and awestruck. "Ivy, baby," he whispers. "*Mine.*"

Right now I can only agree.

25

ALEXANDER

Ivy's sitting on me, riding me, coming down from yet another unbelievably intense orgasm that's rocking us both. Her pussy's still quivering, milking the last throbs of my release. Her dark hair hangs long, the almost-blond tips of it feathery against my arms as I hold her, caressing her perfect breasts, cupping them, teasing the rosy peaks and exploring the silky smoothness of her skin.

"What would you do if you could do anything you wanted?" I ask her, so enthralled by her beauty I sometimes wonder if I'm dreaming her. "If you could just work on exactly what you wanted to work on without the stress or the worry of anything else, what would you do?"

She thinks about this for a few seconds, watching my eyes, still dazed with her lingering ecstasy. "I'd work on my music. I'd only post on social media when I felt like it. Or maybe not at all. I'd travel."

"Where?"

"To those huts."

This makes me smile. She's so fucking cute. "What if I told you I booked us into those huts. In Tahiti. Next week. Would you come with me?"

She gives me a look, thinking I'm joking. "Maybe."

I'm fucking in love with her. I know this as sure as I've ever known anything. Ever. I know it because I've never felt anything remotely like it and it's basically like having a wrecking ball of lust, obsession, tenderness, need, beauty, addiction and happiness—all wrapped up in one little golden-eyed goddess—crash straight through the middle of my life. I'd let my empire burn to the ground to keep her.

I'm already imagining her round with my baby as we swim in turquoise ocean water.

We haven't talked much about the elephant in the room. The fact that it's very possible I *have* knocked her up, already, if the stars are aligned for it.

It's absurd. It doesn't make sense that I could meet her and over the course of one single weekend know for a fact that she's the one.

But I do.

I can feel it in the beat of my heart.

I can also feel it in the surge and pulse of my cock, which wants to live inside this girl, spilling my soul and my seed into her until she's fully mine in every possible way. I want to fucking *breed* her with a primal need that's so sure of itself I can't argue or reason with it.

"Marry me," I say.

Her eyes get wide and she bites her lip. There's a light sadness to her smile that only makes my resolve that much more feral. "Sure thing, Maddox."

She doesn't know yet that I mean it, and that I'll give her all the time she needs until I can convince her. Or that I've booked a trip for us. Or that I've already talked to my lawyers, who are looking into the issue Jack Dempsey confronted us with. And doing a deep dive into Ivy's father's background, businesses and banking activities.

She doesn't know that I've got a bodyguard following Josh to make sure he's not in any danger. People can get touchy about things like having their offshore bank accounts drained, and if Mr. Laine would walk out on his own children, who knows what he's capable of. I've got enough information at this point to know that the man's a snake and coward, who chose to walk away instead of man up.

Ivy also doesn't know that I have my people looking into where she lives, the building where her apartment is located and the terms of its sale. Everything's for sale at the right price and I want it to be hers.

"Sing me that song you sang last night," I tell her.

"No."

"Please?" It's not a word I use very often. But for this girl, I'll grovel on my goddamn knees.

She narrows her eyes at me, her pussy squeezing as she does this and I'm already hard again. And so fucking besotted it's painful. I grip her hips and thrust into her slowly.

"Do you want to hear a new one I've been working on?" she breathes.

"Yes."

She starts singing to me as I'm fucking her and it feels so good to *know*. I *know* that I'll spend my entire fortune on her just to see her smile. I *know* that all those years and all the endless work was worth it. Because now I can use it to make this girl mine.

IVY

A BUZZING NOISE wakes me from a deep, deep sleep. It's the kind of sleep where you're so snug and you feel so secure, your dreams are magic-dusted and restorative and you wake up feeling like a better, calmer, more grounded version of yourself.

I'm not ready to open my eyes. I'm wrapped in the warm cage of his body. I wish I never had to move.

His phone is ringing.

"Fuck," he grumbles, reaching for it. "Yeah?" he answers. Not the usual *"Alexander Maddox"* I've heard him answer with before.

He listens and I can vaguely hear the man on the other end of the line. "Thirty five million cash," the man says. "There are seven apartments in the building. Do you want it?"

"Yes," Alexander says. "With the purchase made in the name I gave you."

"Yes, sir. The paperwork's in place and it can all be done today. They're just waiting for the call."

"Seal the deal," Alexander tells him.

"Yes, sir. I've also got all the intel on the individual you asked about," the man continues. "There's enough here to pin him to the wall."

"Good. Did you get a phone number?"

"Yes, sir."

"Okay, thanks, Bruce. I'll give you a call later today when I'm back in the city."

"Okay, boss."

Alexander ends the call and sets his phone back on the bedside table. Then he burrows his face into my neck, inhaling deeply. "Morning, gorgeous. You want to take a shower with me?"

"Okay. But not yet. I'm too comfortable. What day is it?"

"Sunday."

It's the last day of our fake date.

He'll fly me back in his helicopter after the farewell brunch and that will be that. I'll get the subway home, find a Plan B somewhere along the way and worry about Jack Dempsey's threat as I wait for Josh's return home tomorrow night. I know we talked about me staying with him tonight, but I can already feel the noose closing around my neck. I need to be ready for it.

"Ivy." Alexander says my name not like a question, but like he's about to say something serious.

"Yeah?" I finally open my eyes. And I'm greeted with a vision of tousled, relaxed, gorgeous alpha male perfection. I don't know if I've ever thought about "alpha males" so much before this weekend, but he's just so obviously that. Like a black-haired lion or a pirate king. His irises are so blue they look like stolen jewels this morning. His square jaw is dark with his stubble. I have never met such a physically beautiful person before.

He's watching my face with a look that could only be described as…caring. Invested.

Or maybe he's just about to let me down easy.

Which is fine. I'm expecting it. He said some very nice things to me this weekend. I think we both got a little carried away—or a lot, come to think of it. But the performance is over now. It's time for us to re-enter the cold hard light of reality. And Manhattan is very good at providing exactly that.

"I'm going to say some things to you right now," he drawls, "and I want you to let me finish before you say anything. Okay?"

"What things?"

He kisses me, like he can't help himself. "You're going to come back to my apartment with me tonight. And stay with me. You already agreed so don't even think of trying to back out of it. We're going to have dinner and we're going to talk about how we're going to navigate this."

"Navigate?"

"Yes, Jones. Navigate. It means find your way forward without getting lost." His hand slides over my breast, playing my nipples sort of absent-mindedly.

"I know what it means. And thank you for the invitation. But I have to—"

"I said wait until I'm finished before interrupting me." He burrows under the covers like a big bear, pulling them off me. He lightly nips at my nipple, which makes me squirm. I try to push him away.

But he won't budge. And he's sucking on me now, making me gasp. Getting me wet, like he so easily does.

He lets my nipple slip from his mouth as he looks up at me. "Nothing needs your attention tonight except me."

"That's not actually true." I pause for a second before saying it. "I kind of just want to tell it like it is, Maddox, so I'm going to. I'm not on the pill, as I mentioned. And I don't really want to raise a baby on my own, especially when I'm still basically raising another one who's still *navigating* trying to stay out of jail before he leaves for Columbia—*if* he leaves, which we haven't quite established yet."

"You wouldn't be raising it on your own."

I stare at him for a second. Then I exhale a frustrated huff, letting my head fall back on the pillow. He's watching my eyes sort of…hopefully. My tone is more serious when I continue. "Alexander, I've known you for *two days*. I'm not having a *baby* with you."

"Just imagine how beautiful it will be. Dark hair and golden eyes."

"Stop it." This is crazy. "I'm not even close to being ready for something like that."

"Then why did you have unprotected sex with me all weekend?"

An upsettingly good question. I stare at him for a second. "I don't know! Because I couldn't seem to control myself! But I can control myself now and I'm going to need to deal with it. So that's what I'm going to do. Tonight. We don't even *know* each other. It's ridiculous to even talk about."

"It would be mine too." Lazily, like he doesn't have a care in the world. "I *am* ready," he murmurs against my stomach as he kisses his way down. "I want you to know that." Like he's whispering to it. "The Maddox heir will have only the best of everything. Nannies. Chefs. Drivers. Penthouses. More money than a person could ever spend. A Harvard education."

This is way too much. But I ask it anyway. "Harvard?" Because I'm slightly obsessed with the Ivy League at this point.

"Every Maddox goes to Harvard. My grandfather. My father. Me. All my brothers. We give them a shit-load of money. We're one of their more generous donors. There's even a wing being built at the business school with part of my endowments. An 'investment incubator,' they're calling it, where students can learn how to invest with all the latest technology at their disposal."

I don't even know what to say to that. "Oh."

He continues kissing a line down my body. "We have a lot to talk about. Which is why you're coming home with me tonight. Give me one more night, Jones. Please?" He licks my pussy lightly.

But I push at his head. There are tears in my eyes now. *Fucking hell!* Because the way he describes things just isn't realistic. "Stop it."

He does stop, looking up at me, half-hurt and half-stern. "Don't cry, baby girl."

"You can't promise me all that. It's not fair. You don't know anything about me."

He's infuriatingly blasé about all this. "I know *some* things about you. Like how sweet you taste. And the sounds you make when you're coming *really* fucking hard. I know how your eyes light up when you talk about those little huts over the water. And you know what, Jones? It's not enough. I want to know everything. I want you to move in with me so I can *get* to know you. So I can learn what every single one of your dreams is and then make them all happen."

I blink at him through tears. "Would you stop? *No.*"

"Why not?" He's kissing my pussy again, ignoring all my protests.

"Because."

"Because why?"

Because I'm already half in love with you and if I start to believe the things you're saying and then you walk away, which you will because it would be the normal thing to do, it'll break my heart and also leave me on my own with an arrogant, gorgeous little blue-eyed baby to raise.

As he seems to have a knack for doing, he reads my thoughts. "I'm not your father, Ivy, let's just make that a very crystal clear point number one. I'm not *my* father either, thank fuck, because if I was, that baby would be forced to be a fucking CEO when it was five. That's not going to happen."

That doesn't really help. I grab fistfuls of his hair because I don't know what else to do in this moment.

"Point number two," he continues, licking me, "there might not even *be* a baby. Either way, I want to try this out because I'm fucking obsessed with you. I want you to move in with me and we can see how it goes. And I already know how it's going to go, Jones, because I'm going to shower you with gifts, make love to you 24/7, take you to those huts and all the other places you want to go, buy you jewelry and clothes and your own recording studio and whatever else it takes to convince you, and you're going to fall in love with me along the way. It's that simple. Instead of only always *earning* money, I'm going to fucking *spend* some. On you."

"*Alex*," I whisper. "*Please.* Please stop."

He doesn't stop. "Oh, and by the way, I bought your

building. With your name on the title. You own it free and clear. Or at least you will by the end of the day."

"You…what?"

"You heard me. Worst case scenario, you won't like me, you'll move back into your apartment and you can use the income from the other six to fund an extremely comfortable lifestyle. But most likely you'll never leave me. Because I won't let you." Another lewd, wet lick, *damn him*. "Just kidding. I'll let you, but you won't *want* to leave, because who would leave all this?"

He climbs up my body, laying himself and his giant, rigid cock over me, as though to prove a point.

"I'm too well-hung to walk away from, Jones. Admit it."

God, he's infuriating. He's pushing himself against my slippery core. *Inside* me. Teasing the silky, crazy pleasure. I'm a little in shock, or in awe, or maybe in love.

"All I'm asking for is tonight, baby girl. Then we'll take it from there. Say yes to me, Ivy Laine."

It's scary. It would involve trusting him so much. *Too* much. I look into his eyes and I whisper, "*Maybe*."

His grin is devilish and so sublime I'm almost coming already as he pushes himself deep, deep inside me, all the way to the hilt.

IVY

AND SO WE take a shower together—adding two more to my almost alarmingly high tally of orgasms accumulated over the weekend. We have brunch with the remaining wedding party guests and we say goodbye to Blake and Leah, who invite us to a dinner party next month. We're spared from any further confrontations with Margot, who seems to have been convinced enough by our performance and left early this morning. And we climb into the Maddox Enterprises helicopter to make our way back to Manhattan.

I don't know how to feel.

So I concentrate on the view of the Hamptons, which is just as beautiful as it was on Friday evening. But it looks different now. The whole world looks more vibrant and technicolored. Maybe because I'm a completely different person than I was three days ago. My body feels punished but enlightened in the best kind of way. After never having had a romantic relationship of any substance in my life, I've agreed to spend another night with my hot billionaire fake date. Because he's beautiful and sexy as sin and I'm not quite ready to walk away from the magic he infuses into everything.

I'm a realist because I've had to be and I'm not allowing myself to think past tomorrow, but right now I'm feeling *all* of it.

I think I'm sort of desperately in love with him, if that's what this is. It feels overwhelmingly good to be close to him. He feels like mine.

He's not mine, of course. He's a guy I met three days ago—actually two—who I barely know anything about except that he's a sweet-dirty talker, an extremely good lover and he might just break my jaded heart if I'm not careful.

Alexander is checking a few of his messages on his phone. Answering them. He seems to have a lot.

I watch him as he does this. It gives me a minute to just appreciate his magnificence without him being aware of it. That thick black hair that I know the feel of so intimately between my fingers. The handsome face that I once thought was stern and severe but now is relaxed and more endearing than I'd like to admit. The wide shoulders under the black cashmere sweater he's wearing. The broad chest and hard flatness of his abs. The way his black pants fit him…his muscular thighs and his long legs…it touches something primal in me. He's so impressive. So outrageously *masculine*. The swell of that gigantic—

"You're relentless, Jones." He's caught me staring at him. "You'll get more of that as soon as we land."

I turn to look out the window. "I don't know what you mean." But I bite my cheek to stop myself from smiling at him and I can feel the warmth on my face.

"What's your number, Ivy Laine?"

"We're exchanging numbers now? Do you think we're ready for that?" I joke.

"We've exchanged a lot more than numbers. I think we can handle it."

We certainly have. It's shocking to think about exactly *how much* we've exchanged. I give him my number and he keys it into his phone.

"I'll send you a text so you have mine." My phone immediately chirps with an incoming message from inside my bag.

I can see the city skyline now. We're getting close.

My heart beats faster because I don't know what will happen. It was easy in the Hamptons. We had the buffer of our charade.

Now, we have Real Life stuff to contend with. Including the very heavy threat of police investigations and criminal convictions. Not to mention the possible consequences of having unprotected sex so many times I lost count—which are about as Real Life as it gets.

Tomorrow. I googled it and I have three to five days, at the absolute most. I'll make that decision tomorrow and act on it. A hundred percent definitely.

Even if it's only tonight, even if the haze of our playful conversations, our blazing lust and our intense chemistry fades out under the burn of New York's glow, I'm grateful.

I'm grateful he showed me that an instant connection between two people can actually happen. I don't have to wonder anymore if there's something wrong with me because I never clicked with a man before him. I'm not broken. I'm capable of morphing into a sex goddess on steroids and I love that about myself. With him, I feel sexy beyond belief and it's empowering.

I'm grateful I just had the best weekend of my life. I'm grateful it was him I finally cashed in my V-card with. It was as beautiful and hot as it possibly could have been. That's something special. Not everyone's first time is so…luxurious.

I'm grateful we have one more night together. I'll stay with him tonight then I'll leave in the morning, without expectations. Expectations have gotten me nowhere in the past and I'm emotionally prepared for this to end whenever it ends. I mean, he's gorgeous and perfect, and I can hope that some of the things he said to me actually meant something. But chances are they were just words, spoken in the heat of a moment. Which is fine. It was a beautiful moment that's now almost over. My heart is locked up behind her fortified brick wall that's taken me a long time to build. I'll be okay, like I always am. Like I always force myself to be because I have no other choice.

I'm grateful Josh will be back in the afternoon and he'll have put the money back and everything will settle down. We'll deal with what we need to deal with.

Everything will be fine.

28

THE HELICOPTER DESCENDS over the helipad on the top of Alexander's building, touching down lightly before the engine revs down and the propellors begin to slow.

"Hey," Alexander says softly, brushing his thumb gently over the furrow between my eyebrows, smoothing it. He unfastens both our seatbelts and lifts me into his arms. "Whatever you're worrying about, don't."

"You don't have to carry me."

"Yes. I do. Over the threshold," he says.

"What?" I laugh a little. "What threshold?"

"The one where this stops being a fake date and becomes a real one. Starting right now."

It's…sweet.

It *does* feel meaningful.

He carries me across the upper level of the rooftop, allowing me to once again marvel at the extreme

269

opulence of the setting. All of New York City is laid out below us. And this time, I'm not just passing through to play a role. I'm here because he wants me here. And I'm here because I want to be here.

Alexander carries me into a glass elevator, which gives us a view of the lower level of the rooftop. I got a brief glimpse of it when we flew out, but now I can really take it all in. The huge, pristine pool surrounded by tropical plants is next-level. The wealth it would have taken to create something like this boggles the mind.

The elevator doors open and we enter the roof garden. Clearly no expense has been spared on the greenhouse or the outdoor kitchen and seating area, which is like a luxury lounge, framed by marble columns and folding doors that are pushed all the way open. Long white curtains have been tied back with gold tassels, giving the place a Roman Empire vibe. A giant flat-screen is mounted against one interior wall, playing a baseball game on mute.

Two men are hanging out by the pool. They're drinking beer. One of them is cooking burgers on a grill, the other one is just climbing out of the glittering water. They're both tall, muscular and shirtless, wearing only swim shorts.

They both look a lot like Alexander. At a guess, they must be two of his brothers.

They watch us approach. And both their jaws sort of drop.

"I don't remember inviting you two to help yourselves to my pool," Alexander says, but his tone is light. It's easy to read that he gets along well with his brothers.

"And I don't remember you being such an asshole," says the brother who's now drying his dark hair with a towel. He's got a mischievous glint in his blue eyes. "Oh wait, yes I do."

Both of them are intently watching the way Alexander is holding me in his arms. "Ivy, meet Noah. And Colton, who's the most obnoxious of my brothers most days."

"But today is not that day." Recognition flickers across Colton's smile as he checks me out. "Wait a minute. Ivy *Laine*? Your fake date is *Ivy Laine*?"

Alexander sighs, like he's tired of the question. "Yes. You've heard of her?"

"Of course I've heard of her. Hey, Ivy. Cleo plays your music in the office all the time. And why didn't Cleo *mention* she'd set you up with Ivy Laine?" Colton seems offended by the omission.

"Because it's none of your fucking business," Alexander explains, almost patiently.

Carefully, he sets me down on my feet, his arm settling around me.

"Hey, Ivy," Noah says. He visibly stops himself from stepping forward to kiss my cheek or shake my hand because of the growly *"mine"* energy practically radiating off Alexander.

"Hi," I smile, feeling a tiny bit awkward and flushed. The effects of my most recent double endorphin rush are still lingering and I wonder if it's obvious to them that Alexander and I spent the weekend having very hot sex. "It's nice to meet you both."

"How was the wedding?" Noah is clearly trying not to stare, but he's riveted and mildly entertained by the way Alexander is touching me.

"It was good," Alexander replies, not elaborating.

"Everything went…well?" Noah's digging for details.

"Yes," Alexander confirms. "*So* well that you two can feel free to leave anytime you want."

Colton finishes his beer, smiling widely. "Wow. Now, that's a first."

"I'm sure it's not. I've definitely kicked you out of my apartment before," Alexander's voice is deep and graveled, like his comment is a veiled warning.

Which Colton completely ignores. He obviously enjoys getting a rise out of his oldest brother. "Ivy, you should know that Alexander has *never* brought a woman home to his fancy penthouse before, not in all the time he's lived here."

I glance up at Alexander. "Really?"

"Not once," Colton says. "We were starting to wonder if our boy here is allergic to—"

"No one asked for your opinion, little brother," Alexander cuts him off. "And I'd hate to have to rearrange that pretty-boy face, so my advice to you is to shut the fuck up."

Noah laughs, shaking his head as he flips the burgers he's grilling. "Sorry about them, Ivy. They're like this all the time. And you can't kick us out yet, Alex, because we're just about to eat. Do you guys want a burger? There are plenty here. And we just opened a bottle of Moët because it was in your fridge and we figured you'd either be celebrating or you'd need to drown your sorrows."

"Definitely celebrating," drawls Colton, grinning at me. "Big time."

So we end up eating a late lunch together, as Alexander keeps me close to him. His brothers watch his protective way with me with low-key fascination, like his behavior is unrecognizable to them.

But they're easy to be with and their crude banter is funny and full of affection.

All three of them are gorgeous, successful, built (I can't help but notice) men. At any other time of my life, I'd be intimidated to be surrounded by three of the four coveted-by-every-woman-in-Manhattan-with-a-heartbeat Maddox brothers. But they're welcoming and so comfortable in their own skin and their close-knit family dynamic, I end up just relaxing into it. I find myself enjoying their company.

Their extreme comfort around each other reminds me

that I've sort of…missed out on a family. I have Josh, of course, and the two of us have always had an us-against-the-world outlook, but I'm still responsible for him. I'm always pushing him to work hard and make the most of his talents, and I'm sure I sound like a broken record most of the time. I know he gets annoyed by it and I would too. But if *I* don't do it, who will? I know for a fact he wouldn't have achieved half the things he has if he hadn't been encouraged (okay, and lectured) on practically a daily basis.

It would be nice to have the kind of support these brothers clearly give each other, on a more even level.

It felt so good to *lean on* Alexander for the weekend. To feel protected by him. To not be alone for a change.

Don't get used to it, girl. You're going home tomorrow.

For now, I let Alexander hold me against his big, warm body, his hands casually stroking my hair and my skin.

It's amazing to me that he already feels so familiar. Being with him is so *easy*, in a way that very few things in my life have been. It takes me a second to put a name on the way Alexander Maddox makes me feel and I'm almost unnerved by the realization.

He feels like home.

As they talk and laugh, I let that thought settle, holding onto it. For tonight and tonight only, I'll let myself savor it.

Listening to their conversation, I learn that Colton is the youngest, at 26, and all four brothers are only a year apart. "Our parents were very busy for four years," Noah explains. "Then they barely spoke to each other ever again."

Alexander told me that his father was stern and business-minded and the two of them had a difficult relationship before his death a few years ago. Colton and Noah add more details to the story.

Their father was a tyrant, according to Colton, and a genius, according to Noah. Their father wasn't interested in earning their love but did earn a certain amount of their respect, mainly because he taught all four of them how to make a shitload of money.

It's easy to see that Colton is the wild child youngest son who enjoys winding his brothers up. He's got a rebellious streak and spends a lot of his time "sowing his wild oats," as Noah puts it.

Colton is gorgeous but in a more college-boy way than Alexander, whose masculinity is seasoned and swarthy and baked in. I have no doubt Colton Maddox could have any woman he wanted. Alexander knows this about his brother only too well, it seems. He keeps me very close to him, shielding me and shutting down Colton's naturally flirtatious jokes.

Noah is more relaxed. He's built like a football player, slightly stockier than his brothers, but still tall and lean. He's almost romantically good-looking, with hair just a fraction longer and lighter than the other two. The blue of his eyes is more of an aquamarine than sapphire. His sense of humor is wry and genuine, and his low laugh is infectious. It's easy to see that he's the diplomat of his family, keeping the peace between the other two, whose personalities rub up against each other like flint and steel. He's smart, and his brothers clearly respect him and rely on his advice.

They talk about their other brother Cash, who recently fell for a woman he met in Hawaii. "They had a one night stand," Noah tells me, "but they never told each other their first names. And when he woke up the next morning, she was gone."

Colton shakes his head. "We were all wondering what his problem was when he got back because he was *so* distracted, searching for clues about who she was on the internet all hours of the day and night. But he couldn't find her."

"How did he find her?" I'm already deeply invested in this story.

"She turned up a month or two later as his new junior analyst." Colton tops up our glasses, laughing about it. "I swear Cash would have given her the keys to his office if she'd only said the word. The cynic of our family—or one of them, anyway—was *slayed*."

Noah grins. "He really was. And still is. I think it's getting worse."

Colton tips back his drink. "That ring on her finger is ridiculous. We're talking two mil, easy. Cash said he knew the minute he saw her that he'd marry her. I asked him if he got abducted by aliens in Hawaii and they swapped his brain for some sappy romantic's, but he only smiled and told me it'll happen to me one day. Personally, I can't think of anything worse."

Alexander's arm wraps more securely around me. "I think it'll happen to all of us. In fact, I'd bet money on it." Alexander presses an open-mouthed kiss to my neck.

It's incredibly intimate.

And both his brothers are watching.

Noah takes the hint. "Yeah, we should think about hitting the trail, Cole. I've got to stop by the office and pick up some paperwork Cleo was working on for Cash, about a legacy company he wants to buy. It's floundering and the price is right."

We've finished eating and two people dressed in wait-staff uniforms are discreetly cleaning up. They collect our dishes before disappearing. I guess I shouldn't be surprised that Alexander has *staff*.

Alexander is holding me so close I'm practically sitting on his lap on the large couch. "I'm going to show Ivy inside," he says. "You two can let yourselves out."

Colton nudges Noah. "I guess that's our cue."

"It was a pleasure to meet you, Ivy," Noah stands, reaching to shake Alexander's hand. "Cash and I will be at your office at eleven-thirty tomorrow morning."

"Right," Alexander says, like he'd forgotten about whatever meeting they'd scheduled.

"We're having an office party out at my Hamptons

place a week from Saturday," Noah says, to us both. "You two should come."

"We might be away that weekend," Alexander tells him.

Away?

That weekend?

We?

Colton follows Noah's lead, putting his shirt on. "Ivy, I'd kiss your hand like the gentleman I am, but I know from experience that Alex's right hook is a doozy and *extremely* painful. I do have to tell you though that this is a brand new look for our esteemed and very lone wolf oldest brother and I'm digging it. I'm sure we'll see you again. And you should also know that, despite the billionaire grump shtick, he's without a doubt the most trustworthy person I know. I've never in my life heard him say something he didn't completely mean."

I smile. It's somehow exactly the right thing to say. "It was nice to meet you, Colton. Bye, Noah."

Noah grabs Colton by the scruff of his shirt and pretends to drag him away.

"Bye, Ivy!" Colton yells.

The elevator to the street level closes behind them and Alexander pulls me by the hand toward the open glass and steel sliding doors leading into his apartment. "Sorry about them."

"They're nice."

He leads me inside and I'm speechless for a few seconds.

His apartment is unreal.

The room is open plan and so spacious I wonder if this room takes up the entire floor. Three walls are steel-framed glass, so clean it looks like there's no glass at all. The twinkling lights of the city at dusk spread out like a textured, glittery carpet all around us.

All the furnishings are chunky and masculine, but comfortable-looking and very clearly the best that money can buy. A few tropical plants continue the theme from the outdoor area. Low lights illuminate a wall of built-in shelves, where spotlit compartments contain single pieces of glass, stone and metal sculptures.

It's sort of minimalist but there's a plush comfort to it too. The whole place sort of hums with safety and luxury.

"Wow."

"I'll give you a tour tomorrow. But right now there's only one room we need to see."

Alexander leads us down a swanky hallway with art on the walls. I pass by one of them and it looks vaguely familiar. I think it might be a freaking Picasso. The carpet's so cushiony I feel like I'm walking on clouds.

He opens another door that leads into yet another gigantic area.

So I was wrong about the other room taking up the entire floor. This is the other half of it.

His bedroom.

Again, three of the walls are glass. His bed looks like it might be…is there such a thing as a double king?

I don't know.

All I know is that the colors are muted, shades of gray and black, lit by the early evening setting sun over the city, down below and far away.

They can't touch us here. Nothing can.

We're in a realm that might as well be heaven itself.

It's almost daunting, how good it all feels. How unreal and how lucky.

Slowly, Alexander pulls me against him and his hand slides under my hair. He gives the nape of my neck a squeeze, sending a current of electric warmth through my entire body, centering in the light pulse that's already taking hold.

His voice is low and his eyes burn like blue embers. He leans close, his stubble scraping lightly against the shell of my ear. "Stop charming everyone, Jones, including my over-attentive brothers. It makes me want to fucking throttle them. It also makes me want to fill you up with my hot cum again so everyone—and especially you—knows you're *mine*."

I look up into his midnight blue eyes and I don't care anymore, about what I should or shouldn't be doing or worrying about. Alexander has a way of soothing every-thing. All normal considerations are no match for his power over my body, which comes alive whenever he touches me.

"Then do it," I whisper.

His grip is hard and lust-heavy as he pushes me onto the bed. "Bend over. I want you on your knees."

I crawl onto the bed and he's already there, pushing my dress over my ass.

He goes still. "Are you telling me this whole fucking time, in this short little white dress that barely covers you, you weren't wearing panties?"

"Cleo packed my bag for me. She seems to have forgotten that detail."

Alexander unzips my dress, pulling it completely off. Then he pushes my head down to the soft duvet and shoves my knees wider. "Give me everything," he commands, his voice low.

And I will. I *want* to. I feel different today than I ever have. Like I hold the key to the universe.

I arch for him, offering myself. I'll give him whatever he wants.

Some buried feminine instinct *loves* that he's pinning me down and taking control. I can't stop him. And even though I don't *want* to stop him, the thought gives me a quiet, primal thrill. Which is strange, when you think about it. The simple biology of it. The deep, voracious cravings of my body for *him* and his aggression and the liquid gush of his pleasure. I want it inside me. I want to inspire it and make it overflow.

I know I can. Very easily. Just by inviting him and leaning in to how damn hot I am for him. He, too, is sort of rough and crazed with his lust. It's a heady twist, to fully realize your own sensual power over someone so much bigger and stronger.

He licks me *everywhere*, eating me slowly at first. Opening me for his own pleasure.

"Fuck, you get me hot, baby girl," he growls, and I can feel the heavy bulk of him, sliding against me as he mounts. "Are you *trying* to fuck with me, Jones? Strutting around in this dress like you're doing it just to push me over the edge? I'm going to have to teach you a lesson."

The head of his huge cock is there, pushing into the tight, wet constriction of my body. He teases me with his heavy thickness, dipping inside, then retreating.

I arch back and he slides a little deeper and I moan because he feels too good. I want to come. *I need it.*

"Beg me for it, baby girl. You're so fucking gorgeous. So wet for my big cock."

I don't care about anything except tempting him so much he loses control and gives me what I need. "*Please*," I breathe. "I *need* you. *Please give it to me.*"

"That's my good little girl." He grips my hips and drives slow but so, so deep, until he's all the way inside me. Thrusting, in, then out, then *deeply* in. He's kissing and biting my skin as he fucks me hard.

The sweet, pain-edged ache begins to spread and build deep inside me.

He pulls out a little, but not all the way, pushing back in, stoking the fire. With each plunge, he retreats a little less, until the cyclical glide isn't a withdrawal at all, but one rolling thrust that stays with me, never leaving the stroking contact of that deep, perfect trigger.

The pleasure compounds, riding a silky wave, coasting then breaking with a force that sends clenching stars through my body that I can feel in zapping surges all the way to my fingers and toes. My inner muscles draw lusciously around his massive, pulsing cock until he groans and lays his body heavily over mine, gripping me as his climax racks through him.

29

ALEXANDER

I watch her as she puts her dress on. Just the sight of it, covering her perfection and shielding her from me, has me pining for her nakedness and her complete submission.

I can't decide what details of her I'm most obsessed with: the sassy attitude mixed with her angelic sweetness, her crazy talent or her ethereal, otherworldly beauty. One thing I *do* know is that the writhing little nymph side of her personality, the one that pleads and begs for my raging cock is the one that has me on my fucking knees.

But now, she's all business. It's Monday morning.

"I should get going," she says, sitting on the edge of the bed where I'm still sprawled out, my arm propped behind my head. The sheet's not covering me and I love that she's suddenly all demure at the sight of me. My cock is draped across my stomach, only half hard, still spilling from our most recent fuck.

We both came extremely hard. Again.

She let me kiss her for a while, which I can't seem to get enough of. She closed her eyes and listened quietly, a half disbelieving smile on her lips as I murmured promises.

But then her phone pinged with an incoming message and she wriggled out from under me to check it. As soon as she read it, she switched gears from sexy little kitten mode to fucking flight mode.

And now I'm in a mood. "I meant what I said."

"About what?"

"Move in with me."

She blinks at me, keeping her eyes closed for a fraction too long, like she's exasperated with these outlandish suggestions I keep making. "We agreed—"

"I didn't agree to anything." I climb out of bed, walking over to my closet, if you could even call it that. It's a room with its own climate control and racks of bespoke suits, shirts, ties, shoes, and some casual clothes, although I have less of a need for those since I basically live and breathe work. I grab a blue shirt and start putting it on. "Who was the text from?"

"What text?"

"The one you just got."

"Oh." Like she doesn't want to tell me. "It was just

my brother. He's getting ready to board his flight back to New York."

"Then we have some time before he gets back." I pull on some pants, stuffing myself into them. We had a shower at some point during the night so I could taste her, unsullied by my own lust.

And now I don't want to wash her off. I want to spend the day marked by her until I can be inside her again.

I'll get what I want. Because I'm fucking addicted. I'm also in love—which is irrational and intense and doesn't comfortably fit with my usual MO at all because I can't control her.

I control everything in my life. And now she's holding her own cards.

"I'm heading back to my apartment now."

I love this. Her sternness. She's telling me how it's going to be. But I have a couple of aces up my sleeve. "I'll drive you."

"You don't need to drive me, Alexander. I can grab a cab."

"Absolutely not." It's unbearable, the thought of her wandering out onto the streets alone, unprotected, where any random fucker could see her or watch her or fucking touch her. "That's not happening."

She rolls her eyes at me.

"Do that again and I'll stuff my cock into that sassy little mouth."

Ivy exhales a huff of laughter. "I *am* going home now, Maddox, whether you like it or not." She stands up, slinging her bag over her shoulder.

"Sure you are. But first, I have some things I need to show you. I meant to give them to you last night, but I was preoccupied." We both know what I was preoccupied *with*—pumping my cum into her as many times as my new superpowers would allow.

"What things?" Petulantly. Like I'm holding her up.

I don't know why her coy, pouty sulk would make me fall even more cataclysmically in love with her, but it does. I do my best to get a grip.

I walk toward the bedroom door, opening it and striding into the living room, and she slides her high-heeled sandals on, following me.

On the table, where I requested they be put, are the things I had my lawyers and assistants organize for me. There are two wrapped boxes, one large and one small, and a large manila envelope.

"Open the big one first."

Another light eye roll.

"What *is* all this?" she asks.

"I guess you'll have to open them to find out." I shove my fists into my pockets and lean my shoulder against a wall as I watch her. My shirt is still unbuttoned and I'm barefoot. I feel more reckless than I've ever felt. More unhinged. I literally can't deal with the thought of her leaving. Or of not knowing how many hours it'll be until I can see her again.

She sighs, as though opening gifts is a chore. But I've learned enough about Ivy Laine over the course of the weekend to know that at least part of this act, of disengaging and wanting to run, is for her own emotional protection. The only men she's had in her life have either abandoned her completely or relied on her for everything. This is new territory.

She doesn't know how to handle the next step we take any more than I do.

"Just open them, sweetheart, without all the drama."

"You don't need to buy me gifts, Alexander. You already…" She stops herself.

You already paid me.

It's hardly an elephant in the room. But it does need to be placed firmly in the past. "That was for an agreement that ended yesterday. What's in these packages is something else."

She carefully tears the wrapping paper off the larger box.

Opening the box, she gasps, carefully taking out the acoustic guitar I bought for her.

"It's a custom-built Taylor PSGA Koa guitar," I tell her. "With mother-of-pearl on the fingerboard. Played by Taylor Swift on one of her earlier tours, I've been told. We bought it from the Country Music Hall of Fame in

Nashville." They didn't want to let it go, but everything has its price.

"What?" She holds it, fingering the inlaid pearl. "Are you serious?"

"Of course. I'm always serious. Open the smaller one next."

But she takes her time, playing a few chords on the guitar. It's got a nice tone. "Alexander." She says my name sort of dreamily but with a scolding edge, totally stunned by the gift.

"Go on. There's more."

She very gently places the guitar back in its box. "I can't *believe* this." Then she picks up the smaller box and unwraps it, holding up the glinting tennis bracelet I bought her.

"Those are yellow diamonds. They're rare because the color is so intense. They reminded me of your eyes."

"Alexander," she says again.

I go over to her and take the bracelet from her fingers, looping it around her wrist, clasping it. "Now open the envelope."

Her golden eyes are soulful. "You don't need to buy me gifts."

"I don't *need* to, Jones, I *want* to. Because you're so fucking gorgeous. And because you've just given me the best weekend of my life and I wanted to say thank you. Open it."

She picks up the envelope and slides out the paperwork.

"There are a few things in here." I take the first contract off the top of the pile. "This is the deed for your apartment building, as promised."

"What?"

"You thought I was kidding, didn't you, sweetheart?" I grin at her. "I wasn't. You own it now, but the contract names me as your co-owner at one percent. That way, if you need help with anything or have any legal issues at all anywhere down the line, I can take care of them for you without any hassles."

"But…how?"

"How?"

"*Why?*"

"Why did I buy your building for you?"

"Yes."

"Because. You live in it."

"That's not a reason to—"

"Actually it *is* a reason to buy a building. It's a done deal. Too late to protest." I take the next piece of paper from the small stack she's still holding. "This is an offer of management for your singing career, for one year, which you'll then have the choice to continue with or not. My lawyers have looked through it and it's a very good, very legit offer. The manager's name is Roxie Tucker. She's young but one of the best in the business, according to my sources, who are trustworthy. She manages her brothers' band. You might have heard of them. They're called the Tucker Brothers."

"Of course I've heard of them. They're huge."

"She also manages a few solo acts, like Ruby Hayes and Sky Rose. All the artists she manages are hitting the stratosphere. Or are getting close to it. I had my people send her the links to your platforms. Apparently she's excited about the prospect of taking you on board. She sent this offer through yesterday, only an hour or two after we contacted her."

It takes her a few seconds to process all this, and I give her time to do that. It's a lot. "But…how did you *do* all this? You had…a busy weekend."

"I have a lot of people on speed-dial who know how to get shit done." And I pay them a lot of money to do it.

I take the next two pieces of paper. And I hesitate for a few seconds because the next two things I'm going to show her need to be handled carefully.

"There are two new accounts here that are in your name," I tell her. "This first one is, at least. The second one has all our names on it."

"What do you mean?"

"They're bank accounts. With some money in them. This one's for you, to help with the bills you're going to be paying for your brother, for the upkeep of your new property and just…to give you a buffer."

"A buffer." Like she's not sure she likes the sound of that.

"Against worrying about anything. At all. Ever again."

She takes the piece of paper out of my hands and stares at it. Reading it. She shakes her head a little and hands it back to me. "Alexander. This is insane. I can't accept this. Of course I can't. You need to calm down."

This makes me smile. "I actually feel calmer than usual."

She eyes me. "I can't accept this."

"Except that you *have* to accept it because it's in your name, which means I can't touch it. It's yours."

An uneven laugh escapes her. "Twenty million *dollars*? Are you crazy?"

"To answer the second part of that question, yes and no. To answer the first: to tide you over. For now."

At this she really does laugh. "Okay. Very funny, Maddox. You got me."

It's fine. I was expecting it to take a while to sink in. I hand her the next piece of paper. "This one has the same amount in it, with both our names on it. And a blank space."

She looks up at me and goes very still. "What…blank space?"

"You know what blank space." I say it gently. "We've talked about this. We spent the weekend having all kinds of incredible—and incredib*ly*—raw dog sex. Ultimately it's your call. But I'm also a part of this. Half, to be exact. So I'm going to do everything in my power to stop you from making any decisions out of fear, one way or the other. I want us to make the decision together, and this is me telling you that I've *made* my decision. I'm all in. Colton was right about me. I don't say things I don't fucking mean, and I mean this: I'll take care of you. I'll take care of you both. I *want* you, Jones." I don't know if I realized how true it is until I say it and the words come out sounding raw. "I want you both."

I'm tired of being lonely. I'm sick to death of living my life as a robot and an empty shell. I never knew how empty I *was* until this little supernova of a girl jump-started my heart and set wildfires along my bloodstream. I feel alive and so fucking *happy* she's here and that I spent the weekend fucking *breeding* her like a goddamn caveman and now she might be knocked up with my baby, I don't even recognize myself.

Her amber eyes are shiny and I keep talking because there's so much I want to say to her. Which isn't like me at all but there it is. So I keep going.

"It's crazy and I know it's fast. But that's how it happened for us and I think that means something." I take her hand, twirling her new bracelet slowly, playing her fingers. "I'm in love with you, Ivy Laine. And I know this because I've spent my whole life lonely as fuck. Really, *really* fucking lonely. Miserable in anyone's company that has anything to do with relationships or romance or any of that bullshit. And that's what it felt like. Just all wrong. Until *you* stepped through that door. I *knew*. I knew right that second that I wanted you. I wanted *you*. And it's okay if it takes some time for us to get to know each other. We *have* time. We have all the time in the world. Give me a month, Jones. Move in with me and let me *show* you how much I want you, angel girl. Because I do. I want you."

There are tears in her eyes as she blinks up at me. "You're crazy, Maddox," she whispers.

"Your fault." I touch my finger to her chin and a tear paints a shiny line down her face. "There's one more thing."

"There's *more*? I can't handle more."

I give her the last small envelope. She opens it. Inside are two first-class e-tickets and a brochure of the resort. "We found some of those huts in Tahiti. I wasn't joking about that either."

She gasps. "*The huts*?"

"Yeah. Over the water. So you can dive straight in. They have glass floors so you can see the fish. Do they look okay?"

She puts her face in her hands and she starts sobbing. Really sobbing. Like she's letting out years' worth of angst that's been bottled up all this time.

Of all the gifts I've given her, the huts are the one that's hit some nerve of deep-rooted sorrow—the kind that doesn't have to be sorrowful anymore and the relief is almost too much to bear.

"Hey." I take the tickets and set them on the table with the other papers. Then I lift her into my arms and take her to the couch and just hold her on my lap, wiping her tears and kissing her face. "You're okay now. I've got you."

Her sobs are starting to ease now. "You know," she says softly, "you said those exact words to me on that very first night."

"And I meant them."

"Alex?"

"Yeah?"

"I'm scared."

"Scared of what?"

"You. Me. All of it."

I tuck a strand of her hair behind one small, perfect ear. "That's fair. I'm scared too."

"What are you scared of?" she whispers.

"That you'll leave. That you don't believe that I'm just not a guy who runs. I'm the guy who stays. Being rock solid has been branded into me alongside my earliest memories. I can't operate any other way, even when I don't want to. And when I *do*, watch out, Jones."

"But it's so *much*. These gifts…"

"You haven't seen anything yet, baby. Just wait until I pull out the big guns."

"One big gun is more than enough. I'm having trouble walking as it is."

I kiss her lips, smiling because I can't help myself. "There she is. There's my feisty girl. I'm going to take you back to your apartment. We're going to deal with the other issue that's going on when your brother gets home.

Then you're going to come back here with me tonight and we'll take it from there."

I can still feel her hesitations, but she gives a little nod, her eyes still shiny with tears.

"One month and you'll be putty in my hands, Jones. You'll see."

I finally get a hint of a smile out of her, and a weak, *what-the-hell* laugh. "You better make it good."

30

ALEXANDER

M y driver takes us to Soho and we pull up to the curb, next to a pale yellow building with those fire escapes that have been turned into a zig zag of small balconies. But the building has charm. It's somehow very...*Ivy*. Artsy and romantic, with a decorative flair.

I help her out and take her bag from my driver. "I'll be back in a few minutes," I tell him.

We go inside and I can tell it's strange for her having me here. She's been quiet since we left my place, still adjusting to the warp speed of whatever we're calling this. "I can't believe you own the building now." She pushes the elevator button for the fourth floor.

"I don't own it. You do."

The elevator doors seal us in. The thing feels rickety and ancient as it starts taking us up and I make a mental note to have it upgraded.

"Want to do it in the elevator?" I joke, nudging her gently.

"Stop," she scolds me, her cheeks getting pink. She's suddenly self-conscious on her home turf.

But I know by now how turned on she gets when she blushes like that. How wet she probably is for me right now. "That's cool. We'll have other opportunities."

She gives me a look, biting back a smile, but she doesn't reply.

I get it. It's overwhelming. I basically steam-rolled over her entire life with too much too soon, probably, but it's something she's going to have to get used to. Even if she hates me by the end of the month, one detail might tie her to me for life. Either way, she's getting every single one of her dreams answered and then some, in spades. It's my new mission in life.

She asked for it when she sat on my lap that first night and kissed me with those soft, pink, perfect lips, squirming and wet, then singing to me with her angel's voice. It's not my fault I'm fucking whipped.

We get to her apartment and she unlocks the door.

The place is tiny but nice. There's a small living room with tall windows that let in a lot of light. Outside is a minuscule balcony that has enough space for two chairs, a small table and some plants. I can see a yoga mat out there, where she must have left it on Friday afternoon.

Imagine if Cleo hadn't called her. Imagine if she hadn't needed the money for her brother's tuition and refused to do it. I'd never have met her. I'd have lived my whole life not knowing that the most beautiful girl in the world was out there, swanning around just waiting for me to discover her. What if I never had? I would have been doomed to be a lonely, miserable grump for the rest of time.

I make another mental note to send Cleo flowers and give her a huge bonus.

It's clear to me now that Cleo did this on purpose. She knew Ivy was drop-dead gorgeous but couldn't see that about herself and had shut down all relationships because she was snowed under by the life she was busy carving out, a little desperately. Cleo also knew my brothers were worried about me and my dumpster fire of a love life. She hoped the two of us might click. *And* she packed Ivy's bag but conveniently forgot to pack panties.

Well done, Miss Cleo. You're getting a raise.

She set us up.

I can admit Cleo irritates me to no end, but I owe her one and it's a doozy.

"So, this is it," Ivy says. "It's small but I love it."

She walks into the postage-stamp-sized kitchen and I follow. There's a kitchen table that barely fits and two chairs. Everything is neat and tidy except for the odd football jersey or baseball hat or empty orange juice carton left on the six inches of counter space. Signs that a seventeen-year-old boy lives here.

The dynamic is easy to read. All the girlish stuff is organized and thoughtfully placed. All the oversized little brother stuff is messy and haphazard. It reminds me again that she's done this the hard way because she had no other choice. She's been a parent to him as well as a provider.

The kid and I need to talk. He's a genius but a punk—as all three of my brothers were when they were seventeen. Josh got into Columbia and he also somehow managed to reappropriate funds from a Bahamas bank account into his own—which is basically the digital equivalent of breaking into Fort Knox. I could use someone like him and so could Cash. I'm sure the two of us can come to an agreement that works for both of us.

Ivy's leaning a hip against the kitchen counter, arms folded across her chest. "I should probably clean up a little before Josh gets home and I have a million emails to answer."

"Are you kicking me out?"

"You can sit there and watch me answer emails if you want to."

I walk over to her, towering over her. She's so small. So perfect. I touch a finger to her chin and tip her face up to me. "Look at you. You're so beautiful."

Softly, I kiss her, touching my tongue to hers, dizzy with lust that has sharp, heart-piercing claws that dig and slice all the way down to my soul.

Fuck. How am I so in love with her?

Both our phones are buzzing.

She glances at hers. "I should probably take this. I'll see you later, okay?"

"You sure you don't want me to stay?"

Her smile is heartbreaking. Because I'm not going to see it for at least three hours. "I'll be fine."

"I'll either come get you or I'll send a car for you," I tell her, and my voice sounds husky. "You've got my number. Don't go anywhere. Make sure your doors are locked."

She places her palm on my chest, pushing gently, walking me to the front door. "Goodbye, Alexander."

It's fucking unbearable. "Not goodbye, Jones. Later."

She stands on her toes and kisses me. "Alex?"

"Yeah?"

"Thank you."

"For what?"

"For everything. I mean it. I can't…I don't know what to say."

"Say you'll move in with me." I lean in to kiss her again and she lets me, but then she smiles and gently pushes me out the open door.

I feel like someone is ripping out my heart, beating and bloody, and now expects me to go out there and leave it behind and somehow still function. "Later, baby girl. Be ready for me."

Fuck.

31

ALEXANDER

"Grumpy" takes on a whole new meaning once I'm back at work. I'm like a shark in the water, feeding on anyone who happens to rub me the wrong way as I swim through the next few hours.

Cash and Noah are already in my office.

"Why do I give you people so many keys?" I grumble.

"Good morning to you too, sunshine." Noah hands me a mug of coffee, patting me on the back sympathetically. "You'll be okay."

Cash has helped himself to my desk chair and has his feet propped up on the corner of my—and my father's and grandfather's before me—mahogany desk. He's got the relaxed air of a man who's getting laid whenever he wants with a woman he's in love with. I'm happy for him, I really am, but I'm too mired in my own agony right now. "Make yourself comfortable," I tell him.

"I hear the weekend went well." Cheerfully. The other two have obviously told him all about Ivy.

I glare at him. *I* should have the air of a man who's getting laid whenever he wants with a woman he's in love with. But it's too fucking raw. Too new. And I'm here, instead of where I should be, in bed with her…*licking that sweet pussy until she's coming in my mouth.*

"Oh, shit," Cash laughs. "It's worse than I thought."

Noah isn't helpful. "Told you."

Cash is enjoying this. "Dude, I get it, believe me."

"I'm in love with her." I don't even mean to tell them. But the magnitude of it feels like it's consuming me. It wants out. Besides, they already know. Noah's met her. He *saw* how fucking gorgeous and perfect she is. "I met her three days ago and I've already asked her to move in with me."

Cash's eyebrows go up, and he can't suppress another impish smile. "What did she say?"

"She's thinking about it. She agreed to come home with me tonight." I think. Did she?

"It's rough to begin with," Cash says philosophically, like he's the expert in this scenario. "Once you get a ring on her finger it gets easier."

"Thank you, Wise Leader."

Noah laughs.

Someone knocks on the door.

"I'm expecting Bruce." Bruce Drake is the lawyer who leads the Maddox Enterprises team. I open my office door for him and he comes in, taking a seat at the table.

"I've got all the info you wanted on Roy Laine," Bruce tells me.

"Let's hear it. I want this matter settled today."

Bruce leafs through some of the paperwork he's brought with him. "He's embezzled over twenty-five million dollars from the law firm he works for, Finlay & Hobbs of Stamford, where his title is Senior Divorce Lawyer."

Cash lets out a low whistle, looking at me, then Noah, then Bruce. "Who's Roy Laine?"

"Ivy's father, I'm guessing," Noah says, and I don't correct him.

"Ah. The plot thickens."

"Three years ago," Bruce continues, "his bid to become partner—his fourth—was denied. Soon after that, he began slowly siphoning the firm's money into three separate Bahamas accounts. He's covered his tracks very well. Incredibly well, in fact. But one of those accounts had ten million dollars withdrawn last week. It was deposited into a new Bahamas account with the name GnarlyDoomRiderX15."

I stare at Bruce for a few seconds. "GnarlyDoom-RiderX15?"

"Yes, sir."

Josh, you need to be smarter than that. Way too obvious.

"Who the fuck is GnarlyDoomRiderX15?" asks Cash,

amused.

"The kid we're about to hire," I tell him, "once I make sure we can curb his felony tendencies."

"Mr. Laine is waiting in the lobby to meet with you, Alexander," Bruce tells me.

"Does he have any idea why he's here?"

"I told him you needed some advice about a prenup. It's one of his areas of expertise. Along with custody arrangements."

Which is how he was able to pay so little in child support and make sure two of his kids lived lives of quiet desperation. I buzz Esther. "Show Mr. Laine to my office, please, Esther." To the others, I say, "I'm going to need a minute alone with Mr. Laine."

The three of them get up and head toward the door. Cash pats me on the back as he walks out. "We're here if you need us, bro."

"Thanks."

While I'm waiting, I pace in front of the wall of windows, staring out at the Empire State Building. Maybe for the very first time in my life, I feel like I can almost relate to the stone-cold grit my father approached everything in his life with. Maybe that's what having kids will do to a man. Drive you to focus so hard on success and the illusion of safety at all costs, you're willing to kill all joy as you bulldoze your way toward it.

Actually, no. Fuck that.

I plan on showering my girl with so much joy she'll be rolling in it.

Naked. Wet. So happy she'll give me anything and everything I want.

There's a knock on the door.

I open it, bracing myself against the fury I already feel for this man.

He's dark-haired, younger than I was expecting. Maybe around forty-five. I'm almost relieved to see he looks almost nothing like Ivy. His eyes are green, not gold.

This observation hits me.

What color eyes will our baby have?

Ivy and I didn't actually get to the point in that conversation where she told me what she's intending to do. I made it clear how *I* felt but it suddenly feels like a glaring omission that I don't *know* one way or the other what she's thinking. And right now she's alone and I have no idea how she feels or if she's okay.

I should fucking be there. I'm her rock now. I need to make sure she knows we're in this together, so there's not a shadow of a doubt in her mind that I'm all in. Did I do enough?

With a desperation I don't even recognize, I want her safe. And I want that *baby* safe. And if there isn't a baby, then we'll make one. I'll take her to fucking Tahiti and keep her in my bed until she's round with our baby and suntanned and so happy she feels like she's dreaming me.

I don't have time for this shit. I need to go.

I don't bother shaking his hand. "Take a seat, Mr. Laine."

"I was honored you chose me to work with you, Mr. Maddox. Your reputation precedes you."

"So does yours," I tell him, cuttingly. "I'm afraid I've called you here under false pretenses, Mr. Laine. And I'm going to make this really fucking quick."

"Oh?" He's suddenly uneasy.

"It has to do with your embezzlement of more than twenty-five million dollars from the law firm you work for."

He stands up.

"*Sit down*, Mr. Laine." Fuck, I sound like my father. And I use that. Right now, I need it. "This is what's going to happen. You're going to stop stealing money, immediately, before you end up behind bars. Your other two kids might need you at some point."

I've already decided I'm not going to force him to return the money. He *would* end up in jail. And so would Josh. I've also decided I don't want another cent of this fucker's money anywhere near either Ivy or Josh. They don't need it anymore.

"Mr.—"

"You'll call off Jack Dempsey. Today. As soon as we finish this conversation. And if either one of your two oldest children ever sees or hears from him again, I'll instruct my lawyers to anonymously present your crimes —in excruciating detail—to the authorities. We have enough to put you away for a very long time, Mr. Laine. Possibly for life."

He's speechless, the coward.

"You'll allow the individual who withdrew ten million last week from one particular offshore account to keep it, uncontested. The matter is closed. And you'll put fourteen million into trust funds for your two youngest children, divided equally, with their names solely on the trusts —not yours—to be given to them when they turn eighteen. My lawyers will be discreetly contacting you in the coming weeks to make sure you can prove that this has been done."

He's given up protesting. He understands that I'm not fucking around.

"That leaves you with just under one million dollars of your own. And you'll still have a job, if you can keep it. My final stipulation is that you'll never contact Ivy or Josh again unless they contact you first. Do you understand these terms, Mr. Laine?"

"Y-yes. You know them?"

Do I know them? I resist the urge to punch the asshole. "That's irrelevant to you. Any other questions?"

"No."

"Good. I won't take up any more of your time, then." I stride over to the door and open it, practically running for the stairs because the elevator's too slow. To Esther, I say, "Show him out."

32

ALEXANDER

I REACH Soho around twenty minutes later. The car is stuck in traffic so I end up getting out and running down the street like a fucking lunatic. I'm almost to the building when I realize I have no way to get in. I'm about to call Ivy's number when I see a kid getting out of a cab. He's tall and slim, that gangly teenage phase when you've grown a foot in six months and haven't had a chance to beef up yet. I know who he is instantly. The dark hair and the golden eyes are dead giveaways.

I follow him to the door, which he opens by punching a code into the keypad. "Hold that, would you?"

He does, taking in the suit, the crazy look in my eyes, maybe, and the couple of inches and thirty or more pounds I have on him. He's suntanned from his weekend away.

We wait for the elevator together. "Do I know you

from somewhere?" he asks. It happens. I get written up a lot in the Economist, the Wall Street Journal and so on.

"Alexander Maddox." I hold out my hand and he shakes it.

"*The* Alexander Maddox? Investment guru and CEO of Maddox Enterprises?"

"Guru might be overstating it."

"I'm Josh. Josh Laine." He's got a decent handshake, which is always a good sign. He walks into the elevator, punching the button for the fourth floor as the doors slide closed. "What floor do you want?"

"Four. Thanks."

He eyes me curiously. There are only two apartments on the fourth floor. Which means odds are pretty good I'm going to the same place he is.

"We'll wait until Ivy's with us, then I'll tell you everything you want to know," I tell him. "You and I need to talk."

33

ONCE ALEXANDER LEAVES to go to his office, I take a deep breath.

I pace a little, feeling like I just re-entered reality after taking an impromptu trip to an alternate universe for the weekend.

I change into some yoga clothes because I've been wearing this outfit for two days.

Then I vaguely check my messages. I've missed five calls from Cleo, but she's going to have to wait. And so are the seven thousand DMs I have on Instagram because I haven't posted since that picture by the pool in the Hamptons. That must have been Saturday morning and now it's Monday.

Usually I post at least ten times a day.

I glance at a few of them.

Did something happen to you? R u
alive??

Where u at?

We miss you!! Your content is my favorite
thing on IG

Girl, ur gonna lose followers if u dont post
more. This is bullsh!t

Give us deets! Where in the Hamptons r
u? I'm in the Hamptons! Tag ur location?
Msg me? I'm such a huuuuge fan!!!!!
Ilysm

U should post more

Ur hot will u go out with me

And so on.

I don't know any of these people. And suddenly having my life on display to millions of strangers feels weirdly invasive in a way it hasn't before. Maybe because I haven't had the luxury to worry about that until now.

I toss my phone onto the table and go out onto the balcony, staring down at my view of the street.

Holy fuck. I own this building.

Did I dream him?

What the hell just happened?

I miss him so much. I feel like I'm missing not just my right arm but…my haven.

With the sudden absence of his huge presence, the craziness of how much has changed fully hits me.

I'm not a virgin anymore. I had sex *a lot* with a guy I just met. I fucked a total stranger and it was the most beautiful thing that's ever happened to me. I have a bank account with an insane amount of money in it. There's a very real possibility I could be pregnant.

It's that last one that wakes me up.

I promised myself I would do something about it. Today. When I googled it a few days ago, I remember reading that the morning after pill is most effective up to 72 hours after the fact.

The first fact happened on Friday night.

Which means it's been 72 hours almost exactly.

You don't want to take it. You never did. You've put it off and if you don't take it now it'll be too late.

There's another bank account. With a blank space.

Tears pool in my eyes.

I'll take care of you. I'll take care of you both. I want you, Jones. I'm all in. I'm in love with you, Ivy Laine.

Is it even possible to fall in love this fast?

I go get my phone and I google it again.

I start reading: "It's really quite simple. No morning-after pill works during or after ovulation since they're designed to delay it. If you've already ovulated, the emergency contraceptive pills will have no effect."

To be honest, I've never really spent a lot of time thinking about ovulation before. When you've never had sex it's not something that tends to show up on your radar very often. But my period is due any day. Any minute.

Which means I ovulated a few weeks ago.

A pill wouldn't work anyway.

I let the tears stream down my face.

They're not tears of sadness. Or even of fear.

I'm crying because I'm happy.

I want it. And I want him. Of course I do. He's gorgeous and rough and rock-hard and loyal to the people in his life. He's grumpy and gruff. And his baby won't ever have to feel like I've felt my whole life.

He's already proven it.

I'm the guy who stays.

I sit there on my—*my*—balcony for a while, just crying like an unhinged crazy person. Like a girl who's fallen in love so hard it hurts, with a guy she's known for a total of one weekend. Like a hopeful dreamer who *wants* to move in with him because being with him feels like being wrapped up in a love bubble of orgasms and laughter and sweaty, throbbing, dirty-talking alpha man connective bliss.

Who cares if my family was dysfunctional as fuck. *We* can do better. We already are.

Come on, Ive. It's not rocket science. This is a no-brainer. You're in love with him. Take a chance.

I'm surprised when the door of the apartment opens, banging loudly.

Josh walks in. Followed by a stormy-looking Alexander.

For some reason, it's jarring seeing the two of them together. My fantasy and my reality, side by side.

I swipe at my tears, trying to look normal and steady, my default mode for whenever my brother is around. "Hi, Josh. How was Florida?"

"It was good, Ive. How was *your* weekend? Seems like it might have been even more eventful than mine." He kisses my cheek. "You've got a visitor."

I can't help it. I'm crying again because my life has just taken a pretty fucking gargantuan shift and all of it makes me happier than I've ever, ever been.

It's scary, the leap I'm about to take. But I want what's on the other side of it so badly I feel like I'd kill or die for it.

Alexander's expression is layered. It's stern, with a lot of crazy volatility going on behind his eyes. It's concerned because I'm crying. But most of all, it's relieved.

He's really, really happy to see me. As happy as I am to see him.

I run and jump into his arms and he envelops me in a bear hug, holding me like I'm the most precious cargo. He wipes my tears. "Why are you crying, Jones?" Then: "Made any major decisions this afternoon without me?"

"Yes."

The yearning in his eyes and the devastation at the thought of losing something we might not even have is…I don't know. It's enough to make me love him in a way that three days shouldn't really allow. I'm as sure as a person can be sure of anything that this man might just be the love of my life.

Which is a probably a good thing, considering what we might be about to do. "I decided that we're going to be filling in the blank space if we need to."

Alexander's eyes get very blue. His smile is hot and connective and heartbreakingly genuine. He kisses me.

My arms and legs are wrapped around him and we get a little carried away.

Until Josh exhales a laugh. "Um. *Excuse* me? Could someone please tell me what the hell is going on here?"

Shit. I forgot about Josh.

We break the kiss, both staring over at my brother.

"Ivy's moving in with me," Alexander tells him.

"What?" Josh squawks. "When did this—"

"Next time you steal money, I won't be bailing you out," Alexander says, and I'm almost surprised at the way Josh quiets and stands up straight. Alexander is clearly very used to dealing with younger brothers.

"I was going to give half of it to Ivy, obviously." Josh is defiant. "We deserve that money."

"I agree." Alexander says, in his CEO's voice. "Which is why you're keeping it. Ivy doesn't need any of it. She has her own money. You should both know I met with your father earlier this afternoon."

"What?" Josh and I gasp in unison.

"I told him you're keeping the ten million. On several conditions. One, you won't do it again. Ever. Two, you'll learn how to invest it properly, which I'll teach you how to do. And three, you'll come work for me. Anyone who can syphon that much money out of the Bahamas needs to learn how to use their skills to make money, not commit further felonies. My brother will try to poach you, but we can deal with that later. You might be able to work for both our companies eventually. We'll work around your Columbia schedule and typically, when we hire students, we pay the tuition bills. You'll be responsible for your own room and board. Where are you planning on living?"

Alexander is so no-nonsense Josh is stunned into silence for a few seconds. No huffing. No attitude. Just a measuring glare that almost looks like respect. "Uh, one of the guys I went to Florida with has an extra bedroom in his apartment and they want me to move in. It's right across from campus. I was going to head over there now to take a look at it."

"Good," Alexander says. "You can pay for it. I'll pay for everything else. We can talk about the contractual details when you come in to the office tomorrow. Actually, make it Wednesday. I'm going to be busy with Ivy tomorrow. Do we have a deal?"

Josh doesn't even hesitate. He shakes Alexander's

hand—somehow, as Alexander is still holding me like I weigh nothing. "We have a deal."

"Good. It's settled, then."

Josh looks at me with real feeling in his golden eyes, so similar to mine. "You okay, Ive?" I think it might be the first time he's ever asked me that question.

I nod. "Love you, Josh."

"Love you too." To Alexander, he says, "I'd say treat her right but it looks like you're already doing that."

"You have my word."

Josh nods. "Okay, then." His grin lights up his whole face. "Holy shit." He crooks a thumb toward the door. "I guess I'm going to go check out my new digs now and leave you guys to it."

"Okay. Bye, Josh."

"Later, kids. Don't do anything I wouldn't do." Then he slams the door behind him.

"Wow," I comment, about the existential curveball that's made my life almost unrecognizable over a single weekend. It's going to take a while to adjust.

Alexander is carrying me into my bedroom, kicking the door closed behind us. "You won't need this apartment anymore, but I want you to keep it just like it is. So you have your own space if you need it. You can come here and relax and do yoga and whatever you need to do to get inspired and write your next record. *Fuck*, this little yoga outfit should be illegal, Jones. From now on, these are for me and me only, not fucking Instagram. Are we agreed?"

I guess that's fair. And a weird relief in some ways. "Okay."

"I'll be installing a doorman and security. You'll have your own driver, of course. And I'll help you invest the income you'll be making from the other apartments."

I kiss his perfect mouth. "Okay."

"I missed you today," he murmurs, laying me on the bed and peeling off my clothes, kissing his way down my stomach. "I know it's fast. We'll figure it out. We'll just go with it and see where it takes us. Don't leave me."

"You're too well-hung to walk away from," I smile, repeating the words he said to me at some point during our whirlwind love affair.

"Damn straight."

My laughter turns to moans because I'm already coming.

EPILOGUE

"SHE SHOULDN'T MARRY the guy from New York. She's obviously supposed to be with the guy from Alabama," Alexander comments grumpily, like he's pissed off Reese Witherspoon isn't going to end up with the man she's destined for.

"Just keep watching. The best part is coming up."

"How can I concentrate on them when the most beautiful woman in the world is riding my cock, Jones? I can't multi-task like this." He spans my waist with his hands, sliding them higher to hold my breasts, pinching my nipples until they're taut and rosy. "How are you so fucking perfect?"

I moan a little. It's true my breasts feel full and sore and extra sensitive. I think I know why. I hope I know why. I felt crampy a few days ago and thought I might be wrong. My body has never run like clockwork and I thought maybe the stress of recent events might have affected my cycle. But my period is definitely late.

I brought a test with us. I don't know why I haven't taken it yet. I'm pretty sure I am pregnant. I think we're just *happy*, either way. *Trying* to make it happen, if it hasn't already.

"Pause the movie. I need to fucking breed this little goddess who can't get enough of my giant, bursting cock."

"Because it feels so damn good." My laughter is more of a gasp.

"You're insatiable, Jones."

I giggle, pressing pause on the remote so we don't miss the wedding scene. I need to concentrate on making sure my man is getting all the attention he deserves. I want him coming hard, filling me up with his lustrous, life-giving heat. "You're worse."

"Because you get me so fucking hot." Another groan. "That's it, baby girl, take all of me."

I'm deeply, deeply in love with him. I never even thought about having babies before Alexander. But I want his. I want to spend every minute with him for the rest of time. I want to do everything in my power to make him as happy, turned on and blissed out as he can be. I give him everything he wants and it's working. He only gets grumpy at movie plot lines and the occasional phone call from New York.

We're in Tahiti, in bed in our spacious hut, where

we've been living for a whole week. Alexander has just extended our trip by another two weeks. His brothers are covering for him while he's away and they all thought he needed the break—his first vacation ever.

Josh and I talk every couple of days. He's moved in to his new apartment and is having the time of his life. He signed contracts to work part-time for both Maddox Enterprises and Invested Enterprises and met with Alexander and his brothers before we left. He already idolizes all four of them. The signing bonuses were… crazily generous. And all four Maddox brothers have sort of taken Josh under their wing. They see huge potential in him, Alexander said. Josh even went to a party at the Sky Bar last weekend. I've never seen my brother so happy and excited about his future.

Cleo was, of course, overjoyed at the news. She called me in tears because Alexander, as a board member of Invested Enterprises, made sure she got not only a huge bonus but also a raise. Some of the money will go toward the wedding she and Sam are planning in the fall, but her bonus was so substantial, she and Sam are looking at buying a two-bedroom loft…in my building. Two floors down. We're *so* excited. Not that I'm going to be living there, but Alexander is going to have Josh's old bedroom converted into a recording studio, so I'll be spending time there to work and to write. Alexander told Cleo we'd give her a good deal.

I've fantasized about seeing a place like Tahiti my whole life, but the fantasy was never as good as the reality.

The turquoise water is completely transparent, all the way down to the white sand, as warm as bathwater. The floor of our hut is made of glass, so we can see the tropical fish swimming around underneath us.

When I pictured these huts in my imagination, they were cute and rustic. *Our* hut doesn't happen to be rustic at all. It's incredibly luxurious, with a king-sized bed, its own kitchen—which we haven't used because Alexander insists on ordering room service, which is delivered by boat and is the freshest, most delicious food I've ever eaten—a large, beautifully-decorated living area, a fancy European-style bathroom, and a deck that's the same size as the interior.

The hut sits on stilts and has its own private boardwalk that takes us all the way back to shore. We also have a Jet-ski we use to ride over to one of the restaurants or the spa at the exclusive resort our hut is a part of. We're in our own little cove, so we have complete privacy.

Which is a good thing, because we've spent the entire week mostly naked, swimming, making love and occasionally watching rom-coms. I'm educating Alexander on the classics.

We spend very little time *not* connected. I'm sitting on top of him, his thick length deep inside me, taking my time. By now I know exactly how to tease him and drive him wild with lust. I squeeze myself around him, rising up a little before bouncing gently back down. I do it again, squeezing more strongly, taking him deeper.

"Good girl," he growls, gripping my hips, driving so deep I feel like he's as much a part of me as *I* am. His possession is complete and total, forcing the deep, skewering pleasure into me with each thick thrust.

His thumb skates over my clit and the pleasure peaks and shatters into a cascade of clenching bliss so extreme, I cry out. My inner muscles work him lusciously, over and over, until he groans and comes, pumping his gushing cum deep inside me, overflowing and spilling down my thighs.

I lay myself over him, keeping him inside, kissing his perfect lips as his brawny arms pull me close. His voice is rasped and deep when he says the words. "I love you, Ivy Laine. You're my dream."

It's not the first time he's said it. He told me he loved me the day we arrived in Tahiti and he's said it at least ten times a day since then.

I haven't said it back yet, even though I *do* love him. *So much.*

I don't know what's holding me back. Everything about our relationship has been fast and uncontrollable. You hear about people falling in love at first sight and it sounds so unrealistic from afar. But I know for a fact that I fell in love with Alexander Maddox the minute I saw him.

And I fall deeper in love with him every minute we spend together, exponentially. My body and my heart are so full of him, and the combination of our mingling essence so euphoric and life-affirming, I don't know what to do with all the overload.

It feels like Rocky's advice, but different. The glowing fire in my heart isn't about touching an audience, but about loving him with everything I have. So I let one of my fireflies touch him with my words. "I love you, Alexander."

All I can say is that my grump has turned into a very sexy romantic because his eyes turn that shade of blue that's as brilliant as the night sky and he rolls us over so he's holding his weight over me, caging me with his comfort and his warmth. "I'm going to take such good care of you, angel girl. We're going to have lots of babies and grow old together and I'm going to make sure every single one of your dreams comes true."

I think he already has.

We make love again and doze for a while. I let him sleep, being careful not to wake him.

I put on a beach wrap that was a gift from a client I haven't worked with yet, but I like their company. They build schools in developing countries and source their fabrics from women artisans, paying them well and helping them create better lives for themselves. I can relate to at least some of that. So I sit outside and take a selfie against the backdrop of the blue water.

I tag them and post it, linking the product. *Absolutely in love with this stunning piece!*

That one's on me.

Since I arrived in Tahiti, I've only posted a couple of times. Just random, off-hand photos that aren't really staged at all. I look sort of ridiculously happy and relaxed in them. Suntanned with beachy hair.

They've had more likes by far than any of my other posts. And the news is out. A few photos of me sitting on Alexander's lap while kissing him at the Hamptons wedding surfaced on the internet. And one of me singing. Crazily, my follower numbers have almost doubled in the last month.

Alexander talked me into taking some time off from social media, only supporting the clients I actually want to support and taking a step back from the rest.

And so I have.

It's amazingly freeing, to not feel chained to it.

We video called Roxie Tucker the day before we left for Tahiti. She seems like the nicest person in the world and definitely has an impressive track record. She said she already has interest from the same record label that her brothers' band is signed with.

The offer she mentioned was…insanely generous.

Alexander had already had his lawyers check all the details of the contract and I ended up signing that same day. She's going to come to New York once we get back from our trip and we'll start to make a plan to record my next album, which I'm putting the finishing touches on with the guitar Alexander bought me—which he made sure was on his private jet that we took to Tahiti.

A warm hand wraps around my hair, pulling it gently but firmly until my face is lifted to his. He kisses me. "You didn't watch the end without me, did you?"

I smile at his concern about it. "Of course not."

He's not wearing a stitch of clothing, his cock half hard again and still slick from our lovemaking.

He's very close to the edge of the deck, the blue of the shimmery, sunlit water reflecting across his big, buff body.

And I can't resist. I use my foot to gently push him off-balance.

He falls in.

It's the funniest thing I've ever seen and I laugh like I haven't laughed in a long, long time.

He climbs up the ladder, not looking grumpy at all but so hot and playfully stern I fall even more in love with him. I get up out of my chair, ready to run. "Don't throw me in."

"As if I would touch the mother of my child with anything other than worship, Jones. I have no intention of doing anything to you except showering you with lust, love and gifts.”

At that very moment, a wave a nausea rolls through my stomach and I groan a little, bending over.

“Ivy?” Alexander's there, his arm steadying me. “What's wrong?”

“I think it's probably time to take the test I brought with me.” He knows I have it. We just haven't been in a rush because we both sort of already know what the outcome will be. We're too content in our bubble of *hoping* that we don't want to rush through it.

“Let me help you. Sit here for a minute.”

He helps me back to the chair.

The concern in his blue eyes as he smooths my hair is…heartbreaking—in a way that not only breaks my heart but repairs it, fixing all the broken pieces of me with its magnitude and its realness. No one has ever looked at me the way Alexander looks at me. Like he'd die if anything ever happened to me. “I'm okay,” I tell him.

“I'll get you some water.” He wraps a towel around his waist and goes inside.

“It's going away.”

He comes back and sets the glass of water on the table next to me. In his hand he's holding a small box. But it's not a pregnancy test. It's light blue.

Alexander gets down on one knee.

Oh my god.

His hair is still wet and his deeply-tanned skin glistens with little water diamonds. He's quite simply the most beautiful thing I've ever seen.

"Before you take the test, there's something I need to ask you."

"There is?" I whisper.

He opens the box and, inside, there's a yellow diamond that matches my bracelet, golden and glinting. The diamond is…very big. It's set beautifully into a solid gold nest with a thick gold band. It's absolutely stunning.

"My beautiful Ivy, I can say with all honesty that you light up my life. You're my dream girl, my soulmate and my true love all wrapped up into one sexy, sweet, perfect little package. I fell cataclysmically in love with you that very first time I saw you on the rooftop, slaying me with your beauty and ruining me for anyone else before you even said a word. Every second we spend together only compounds my obsession for you, sweetheart. I'm addicted to everything about you. I love you more than I thought I was capable of loving anything or anyone. I can't imagine spending a single minute apart from you and all I want to do is give you everything I have. I know it's fast but I've been waiting for you for a long time and I don't want to wait anymore. I'm yours and you're mine. Please say yes, baby girl. I love you. Ivy Laine, will you marry me?"

He's blurry now, through my tears. But I can still see

the blue of his eyes and the hope in them. And also the edge of vulnerability, like he's not sure if I'll say yes.

I crawl into his arms. "Of course I'll marry you."

Alexander takes the ring out of its box and slides it onto my finger. It fits perfectly, like it belongs there.

"I love you," he whispers, kissing me. He laughs lightly, like he's wildly relieved. "Thank God. I thought you might think we were rushing it."

"We are rushing it. But who cares."

He laughs, lifting me into his arms and carrying me to our bed.

He's already set the pregnancy test on the bedside table. "Take all the time you need. I'll wait for you outside."

I stare at the small, wrapped test for a few seconds. Then I take it into the bathroom and unwrap the stick. I pee onto it, then set it on a tissue. I wash my hands. Then I carry the stick out to where Alexander is pacing on the deck.

"It takes three minutes," I tell him. I set it on a towel that's laid out on the deck. I sit cross-legged on the towel, watching it.

Alexander sits next to me, holding me in his arms. "If it doesn't happen this time, it'll happen next time," he says, consoling us both, just in case. We both *want* this baby. It already feels like a part of us. I definitely didn't set out to get pregnant that first night. Or the second. After that, maybe I was. I already *knew* he was the one, and that all of this felt like it was somehow meant to be.

I wasn't expecting it. And I can't explain it, but I can barely breathe I'm *hoping* so much.

"We're going to have the best life together, angel girl," he's saying, kissing my face. And we watch those two blue lines forming and shining up at us so clearly there's really no doubt. "You and me and all our babies are going to live happily ever after."

And that's exactly what we do.

Thank you so much for reading **Billionaire Grump**. If you enjoyed this book, please consider leaving a quick review or rating on Amazon.

Want to see what happens with Alexander and Ivy two years down the road? Get the free bonus epilogue here: https://BookHip.com/VSWDGFB

Below I've included the first chapter of **Billionaire Devil,** Colton and Lila's story, the next standalone book in the **New York Billionaires** series. Cash and Noah's books are also now available!

xoxo,

Julie

Please come join my Facebook reader group, Julie Capulet's Romantics, where I share cover reveals, insider info and we discuss all things romance!

Sign up for my newsletter to receive my free bonus content and get access to sneak peeks and exclusive giveaways!

Visit my website @ www.juliecapulet.com

Hot playboy billionaires? Definitely not my type. Until one offers me a ride to California—with some dangerously irresistible "lessons" thrown in … and he somehow starts to change my mind about what dreams are actually made of.

Making it as a fashion designer in New York City feels a lot like trying to fly to the moon with homemade wings. My Instagram is slowly gaining traction, but the grind is exhausting. So when my best friend asks me to be the maid of honor at her shotgun wedding in Malibu, I'm tempted to head back to L.A. for good. Especially since my unrequited crush is also on the guest list.

The night before my road trip, my friend Sloane drags me along to a swanky Hamptons party where I happen to meet her drop-dead gorgeous billionaire boss, Colton Maddox—also known as the King of Heartbreak. Definitely one to steer well and truly clear of.

But the next morning, I open the door to find Colton standing there with coffee in one hand and the keys to a luxury tour bus in the other. In my tequila haze, I must have told him about my road trip—*and* my unrequited crush. Now he's insisting we had a deal.

Did I really agree to travel across the country with a hot, cocky devil? Even worse, did I also agree to let him give me "lessons" on how to seduce a man, after I admitted I have zero experience? How mortifying.

Turns out, Colton Maddox is maddeningly persuasive. He's also an *exceptionally* good teacher. He showers me with luxurious gifts and takes me to all the hot spots on my wish list. Including Vegas.

As we get closer to L.A., the insufferably sexy billionaire is starting to convince me that maybe, all along, I've been holding out for the wrong man…especially since the cocky devil is now my husband.

Sometimes what happens in Vegas doesn't end up staying in Vegas after all…

Billionaire Devil is a steamy billionaire romance in the New York Billionaires series, starring the four Maddox brothers. Each book in the series is a complete standalone with a sexy fairy tale HEA.

New York Billionaires

Chapter One

Lila

Wednesday
Southampton, New York

"I wish I could help you, Miss Bailey, I really do," says the woman on the phone. "But I can't forward your information to my boss for the simple reason that she doesn't take unsolicited phone calls. At all. You'll have to go through the usual application process just like everyone else."

"I have," I tell her. "I never heard back."

"That means you weren't selected. They only get in touch with people they're interested in meeting with."

"But if she could take a quick look at my Insta—"

"There's nothing else I can do," the woman interrupts sharply. "You'll just have to wait until another position is advertised and try again. Have a nice afternoon." She hangs up on me.

Damn it.

I sigh, putting my phone face down on the tiny kitchen table in my postage-stamp-sized studio apartment, gazing out the window at my neighbor's rusty air conditioning unit in the back alley of what most people would consider a very beautiful town. Southampton *is* beautiful, of course. Once you get out of the back alleys and away from the air conditioning units that happen to whir very loudly at all hours of the day and night.

Not that I'm complaining. I chose to be here and I'm doing my best to make the most of it. I moved to the east coast from L.A. almost a year ago, leaving the only home I've ever known, because I desperately needed a change. The place never felt the same after my mom passed away suddenly, two and a half years ago. Once I graduated from UCLA with a degree in fashion, I figured the best thing to do was to dream big and try my luck in the fashion mecca of New York City.

I also wanted to get away from the love of my life, who—and yes, I'm aware of how pathetic this sounds— I've only actually spoken to a handful of times. Usually when he was being drooled over by other women. Even so, I hold onto those rare moments of charged eye contact—which are etched into my memories like they've been lasered there with a sadistically red-hot blowtorch— like little gems.

Troy Beckett. Star hockey player. Center for the Bruins and record-holder for the most goals scored in one season. Playboy of the highest order. Gorgeous, in a tousled, just-rolled-out-of-bed kind of way that was basi- cally the equivalent of crack to every woman with a heartbeat during all four years of my college experience.

I never really even got close to him.

Of course I regret that the only man I've ever loved—

from afar—might not even know my last name. It was another reason I needed to leave L.A.

You'd think in a city of almost four million people, a girl could have figured out how to avoid one ego-inflated jock.

But luck was never on my side in that regard. I ran into him everywhere. On campus, at the beach, during my part-time job at a trendy café. The one right around the corner from the Bruins' practice rink, as it turned out.

He was always being fawned over by beautiful, scantily-clad puck bunnies. He'd catch me staring. He'd smile. He'd say things like, *Hey, Lila,* which caused my heart to erupt with joy because he actually *did* know my name. Or, with a grin, *You're not stalking me, are you, babe?*

As I said: etched into my brain on a repeating loop that I had to move clear across the country to try to escape from.

It's worked, mostly.

I've been too busy holding down two jobs while also trying to make inroads for myself as a designer to think much about my unrequited love. I'm grateful for that, as exhausted as I might be. At least I don't run into him during my waitressing shifts or through the long hours at my job as a stylist in the boutique on Main Street. Both of which are slowly but surely destroying my soul.

The job in the boutique, Threads on Main, was offered to me before I left L.A. The owner was a contact of one of my design collaborators on the last of my senior projects. A girl named Solange whose mom had a couple of rich friends in Southampton.

The boutique looked amazing on paper. I accepted the job offer, rented out my old apartment in Venice, packed my bags, thanked my lucky stars I was finally getting a change of scene, and drove my mostly-trusty Toyota Corolla three thousand miles to start work the following week. It's an exclusive store in the Hamptons with direct links to several of the major fashion houses and it sounded like a dream come true.

I fantasized it might be a launchpad to New York Fashion Week. *Bryant Park, here I come*, I'd thought. I pictured myself sipping coffee in one of the park's little cafes, then rushing off—in some impossibly cute outfit of my own design—to get my very first solo show ready for the catwalk, where the front row would be full of Kardashians and Beckhams.

For a whole year now, after my other jobs' shifts are over, I work late into the night, painstakingly sketching and sewing pieces that might catch the eye of my boss and, with her contacts, maybe even the design houses themselves.

Things haven't worked out quite like my fantasies, to say the least. My boss, Veronica Wade, fits every stereotype of the steely, ball-breaking fashion dragon a la Miranda Priestley. She thinks of herself as the go-to know-all of Southampton. She attends parties with the likes of Christian Siriano and—once—Ralph Lauren and his wife Ricky, who, for reasons known only to herself, she considers not only equals but close friends.

Veronica won't even look at my designs. Which means that asking her to show them to people in the industry is out of the question. She also pays me so little, I had to get a second job as a waitress four nights a week just to make ends meet. The tips from the old school billionaires—who are misogynistic dinosaurs but throw money around like it grows on trees—help pay the bills, but they're not getting me any closer to my dream of making it as a designer.

I scour the internet looking for opportunities. I work on my Instagram profile, which is slowly gaining some traction. I spend my nights sewing my garments. But none it seems to get me any closer to making my goals a reality.

The non-stop grind is starting to make dents in my stamina. Maybe because I haven't had a solid night's sleep in months.

My phone vibrates. Hoping it might be one of the jobs I've applied for calling me back, I pick it up.

Jess's name pops up on the screen. My bestie from home, who grew up a few houses down from mine. We also went to UCLA together. I majored in fashion and she majored in film.

"Hey, Jess."

"Hi, honey. How's life? You haven't called me in over a week, just saying."

"Sorry. I've been so busy." Just hearing her voice

makes me pine for familiarity. I'm surprised to feel the slightest sting behind my eyes. God, I really must be strung out.

Jessie is like a sister to me. We were both only children, both raised by single moms. The difference is, hers is alive and well and thriving as a Hollywood casting director. Mine got sprinkled into the ocean, which she made me promise I would do, months before she had any idea she would drop dead of a sudden brain aneurism in the middle of a regular Tuesday afternoon.

Reading my voice like only Jess can, she comments, "You sound tired."

"I am, a little," I admit.

"Well, the good news is, you're about to get a vacation."

"Yeah, right." I exhale a light laugh. "I can't take a vacation."

"You have to. I'm getting married."

"What?" I splutter. "To who?"

"Remember the guy I was telling you about a few months ago?"

"The hot tech guy you met at that beach party?"

"Yes. His name is Jacob."

"But…you're *marrying* him?"

"We've seen a lot of each other over the past three months and, well, the thing is…"

Her pause goes on just a little too long. "The thing is what, Jess?"

"I'm pregnant."

I'm speechless for a couple of seconds. "Holy shit, Jess." Jessie has always wanted kids. It's been a dream of hers for as long as I've known her.

"I know. It's a lot. But I'm happy. It feels like it's meant to be."

"It's a little *sudden.*" I'm about to say, *you barely even know the guy*, but it's hardly going to be helpful right now to point that out.

"Yeah. It is sudden. It just kind of happened. It was a shock. We used condoms and everything, but one of them must have broken. I like him so much and he's been so incredibly *nice* about the whole thing. He's sweet and caring—and hot and also loaded—and we both know those attributes don't converge in one human being very often. He's basically perfect. And then the look on his face when I told him my period was late…he was *excited*, Lila. Not scared or spooked or trying to worm his way out of anything. His reaction really made me want to…I don't know, just go with it. His parents are still married and they still live in their family home in Mendocino. We went up there last month and he introduced me to his whole family. He's got two older brothers and his parents were so welcoming and they're all so *normal*, Lila. He's stable and…*real.* Not like every loser I've ever dated—and God knows there have been plenty of them. He has a house in Malibu. An *amazing* house. With a view of the ocean. And then two nights ago he got down on one knee out of the blue and he asked me to marry him. With a big-ass diamond ring. So I said yes. We want to do it soon. We want to do it before I start to show and we can't see any reason to wait."

Maybe so you can get to know each other? I want to say. But the truth is, I've barely talked to Jessie for months. I've been too busy to make the time to chat for hours, which is what we always end up doing.

I mean, maybe it *is* possible to make decisions like this on the fly if it feels right. How would *I* know? The only man I've ever connected with was too busy connecting with every other female within a three-mile radius to even notice me. I'm hardly the best judge of these things. "Wow, Jess. I'm so happy for you. If you're really sure."

"I'm sure I want to have this baby. And so is he. We just…clicked. Before this even happened. I don't know if I've ever felt this excited in my entire life, Lila. For all of it. So I figure that's a good sign."

"Yeah. It must be a good sign. This is amazing."

I can tell she's crying. "I know, right? Who would have thought I'd be married and knocked up before I even turn twenty-four? Will you come? Will you be my maid of honor, Lila? I can't do this without you."

"Next Saturday? Way to give a girl some advanced warning, honey."

"I know. It's quick. Please please please come, Lila. I need you there."

"Of course I'll come." I actually do have some time

off accumulated at the boutique since I haven't taken a single day off for the whole year. I'm owed two weeks, in fact. My boss at my waitressing job is laid back enough to also give me time off, at least I hope he is. Even if he isn't, it hardly matters. I can't exactly say things have worked out for me here in New York. I haven't even come close to achieving a single one of my goals. I'm still stuck in this overpriced limbo that involves styling billionaires' wives whose faces are pumped so full of Botox they look like they're made of plastic, and whose only fashion consideration is flaunting price tags to their equally-obscenely-loaded friends.

"I can send you a plane ticket if you want," Jess offers. "If that's helpful."

"You know me." I laugh off my fear of flying. "I prefer to remain on solid ground, rather than suspend myself thirty thousand feet in the air inside a flimsy metal tube."

"I thought you were going to go to therapy about your phobia," she chides me.

"I haven't had time. It's on the list."

"It's a long drive, Lila."

In some ways I feel like this might be a sign. Maybe it's time for me to cut my losses and accept defeat. I *tried* to make it in New York, I really did. I gave it a year. I've worked my ass off with nothing to show for it. I've made progress, but I still have such a long way to go. Plenty of designers base themselves in L.A., after all. It's not like I can't build up a following from the West Coast. "I was actually thinking of coming home." I hate that, as I say it, a piece of me feels like I'm a failure who's giving up too soon.

"For good?" She can't disguise her hopefulness.

"I don't know. I've made one friend and I can't get an interview for a job I actually *want* to save my life."

"Would you move back into your apartment?"

"The tenant just signed another six-month lease, so no, not right away." I inherited the one-bedroom apartment I grew up in (and its mortgage) when my mom died. My mom was a working actor and single mother and she did the best she could. I admire her for so many reasons, but most of all because no matter how hard things got, she always stayed true to her art. It was her passion. The one lucrative role she ever got allowed us to buy a tiny apartment only one block from one of the more scenic canals, in a quaint but run-down house that was converted in the seventies into two apartments. Ours is on the top floor, with its own rickety exterior staircase and a closed-in balcony with a peek-a-boo view of the water.

My apartment is cozy and cute and still my favorite place on earth, with all its memories and its quirky little Californian personality. It needs a lot of work and there's still a substantial mortgage to pay off, as well as the forever-ongoing expenses of taxes and insurance. The rent barely covers its costs, and even though property values have skyrocketed over the past few years, I could never sell it. That would feel like selling off a big chunk of my soul.

"Move in with *us!*" Jess gushes. "Jacob's house in Malibu has five bedrooms."

"Wow, Jess. That's incredible. But I'm not moving in with you and your new husband—and baby, soon enough. Thanks for the offer though."

"You could stay with us until you find somewhere else. Just think about it, at least. You'll have plenty of time to mull it over on the 40-hour drive."

"True."

"So you'll come?"

"Yes. I'll be there by noon on Saturday. Does that work?"

"You can't get here by Friday night?"

"I'm going to say Saturday just to be on the safe side. It's going to take me all week to get there."

"Okay. The ceremony starts at three. If you could get here by noon so we could get ready together, that would be perfect."

"It's a date."

"Lila, I'm *so* excited to see you. L.A. isn't the same without you in it."

"I've missed you too, bestie."

"Listen, my mom's here to take me to try on wedding dresses. I would've asked you to make me one if it wasn't so rushed. Call me tomorrow though. We need to talk through details."

"Okay. I'm working two shifts but I'll call you in between."

"You work way too much. There's seriously a free room for you to call your own here if you want it. You could sew all day and put your own show together."

As tempting as that might be, it would never work. I'm far too independent to rely on other people. Just like my mother was. The mere thought of mooching off Jess's new fiancé makes me feel uneasy. I guess it's one of my quirks. I always need to feel like I'm fully in control of my own destiny. "I'm really happy for you, Jess. I'll call you tomorrow."

"Thanks, honey. It means the world to me that you're coming. Oh, and Lila?"

"Yeah?"

"Remember Brittany Wells?"

"Yeah." She lived down the street from us when we were teenagers. We used to go to the Santa Monica pier together sometimes.

"You know how she was always baking cupcakes and started that cupcake business a while ago?"

"I think I remember you mentioning it."

"Well, she's offered to make our wedding cake."

"Great."

"And since she offered to make the cake, I invited her to the wedding. She asked if she could bring...a plus one."

"Is that a problem?"

"She said…" Jessie pauses. "I'm just going to blurt this out because I don't know how else to say it, but her plus one is Troy Beckett. She's been dating him off and on and…he's coming to the wedding. They're not exclusive. She said they're 'friends with benefits'. That's how she put it."

I feel myself pale. "Oh."

"I just wanted to tell you, so you weren't caught off-guard or anything. But you're over him now, right? That was a long time ago."

"Of course," I laugh breezily. "Are you kidding? As if I'd still be pining for that loser."

"Thank God." She sounds relieved. "I knew that. I just wanted to make sure."

"Don't give it another thought."

"Okay. Good. I better go. I'll talk to you tomorrow."

"Bye, Jess."

We end the call.

Fuck.

I *am* over that loser. Totally. It's ridiculous that I ever loved him in the first place. He hardly even gave me the time of day and I hate that I wasted so much of my life on him. I *saved* myself for him, all through college. Hoping maybe he'd notice me. Fantasizing that maybe once he got to know me, he'd fall in love with me and leave all the others behind.

Which means I'm a huge sucker and a complete idiot.

And I'm basically *still* saving myself for him—not

intentionally, but it's not like I'm out on the town every weekend picking up men. I'm too busy working.

I also hate that my heart is beating faster at the thought of seeing him again. *They're not exclusive? Does that mean…maybe, just maybe, there's a chance that he might finally…*

Stop it.

I force myself to snap out of it. I've given way too much of my energy to that black hole of a not-even-close relationship. I can't allow myself to spend another second of angst or longing on a guy who's never treated me like anything more than a piece of furniture.

Snap out of it, girl! You're better than that.

Of course I am. I've moved on. I'm a strong, independent woman, taking the world by storm.

Who's also thinking of giving up on her dream of making it in New York because it's lonely and nearly impossible to get ahead. And who still hasn't met anyone else because she spends all her time striving like a madwoman but basically getting nowhere.

Anyway, I'm *trying* to take the world by storm, that's got to count for something.

ALSO BY JULIE CAPULET

I Love You Series

The Obsession Begins (free)

XOXO I Love You

XOXX I Love You More

Love You the Most (free)

Sexy Standalones

Max

Cowboy

McCabe Brothers Series

Hopeless Romantic

My Hero

Arrogant Player

Music City Lovers Series

Nashville Days

Nashville Nights

Nashville Dreams

Nashville Lights

Hawthorne U Series

Lovestruck

Paradise Series

Devil's Angel

Wild Hearts

New York Billionaires Series

Billionaire Boss

Billionaire Grump

Billionaire Devil

Billionaire Romantic

Standalone Rom-com

Beautiful Savages

ABOUT THE AUTHOR

Julie Capulet is an Amazon top 20 bestselling author of contemporary romance. She writes steamy he-falls-first romance with heart, heat and fairy tale HEAs. Her stories are inspired by true love and she's married to her own real life hero. When she's not writing, she's reading, traveling, walking on the beach and watching rom-coms.

www.juliecapulet.com